THE ABDUCTEE CHRONICLES

THE HEROES OF FEBRUARY 22ND
VOLUME I

D. B. GIBB

World Castle Publishing, LLC
Pensacola, Florida
Copyright © 2024 D. B. Gibb
Hardback ISBN: 9798891261945
Paperback ISBN: 9798891261952
eBook ISBN: 9798891261969
First Edition World Castle Publishing, LLC, August 27, 2024
http://www.worldcastlepublishing.com
Licensing Notes
Cover: Cover Designs by Karen
Cover-designs-by-karen.com
Editor: Karen Fuller

Dedication

To my college sweetheart and the mother of my children. You are my rock, and the glue of our family.

Acknowledgements

Many thanks to Wally P., Logan G., Simone Q., and my fellow Scribophiles. Your honest insights, opinions, and advice have greatly improved my story.

Thank you, Steve S. and Aaron G. for your efforts with crowdfunding and marketing my novel, and for those that supported the crowdfunding project.

IMPORTANT NOTE: The Faux Author's Foreword is written from a future perspective and provides insights into the structure and purpose of this document.

Author's Foreword

07 JULY 2114

When my publisher released *The Complete History of the Heroes of February 22nd and the End of the Dumal Federation* in March 2103, its limited printing sold out within twenty-four hours. With my intended audience being academia, I couldn't believe the broad appeal for the nineteen-volume reference library documenting events from nearly one hundred years ago.

For eight years, my publisher pestered me to write Heroes of February 22nd (commonly known as HOF22) historic nonfiction for mass-market consumption, which I repeatedly turned down. Creating an equitable historic representation of eighty-five individuals from nine countries in a single volume seemed an impossible task.

My colleague, Ellery Talbot, suggested I narrow my focus to a select group of participants involved with a specific segment of HOF22 history and take a journalistic or possibly a docudrama-like approach in telling their stories.

Dr. Talbot reminded me that as the only known *temporal-ethereal historian*, I have the unique ability for being an embedded observer of past events and to interview participants, both living and dead, and together with historic documentation, could tell their stories with some level of thoroughness.

In my twenty-seven years as a researcher, the evidence shows many of the key human players in human-extraterrestrial history were unwilling participants in Dumal Federation, or Intergalactic Council sanctioned abduction and manipulation.

In telling abductee stories, we can learn much about the history, intentions, and actions of their extraterrestrial counterparts from different eras.

Seven of the sixteen American heroes had their initial abduction experiences originate near Blue Lake, Utah. The historic gathering of these sixteen people would later become known as *The Blue Lake Event,* a major precursor for the Proxy Wars.

The two-volume set focuses on the stories of the players involved with *The Blue Lake Event and the Noble Four,* and not the remaining sixty-nine Heroes of February 22nd.

I wrote the original manuscript for HOF22 in English. Much of the original dialogue was translated from different human and extraterrestrial languages for the convenience of the reader. The speech used by certain actors and writing styles may reflect the language usage of their day and not post-war social mores.

Any errors or misinterpretations of events are unintentional and are the sole responsibility of the author. Please accept my apologies in advance.

I hope you enjoy reading the *Heroes of February 22nd* as much as I enjoyed writing it.

JWW Hernandez, PhD

Chief Historian Emeritus
Société Universelle de L'humanité et des Amis

PROLOGUE - THE BLUE LAKE GENESIS

"If aliens ever visit us, I think the outcome would be much as when Christopher Columbus first landed in America, which didn't turn out very well for the Native Americans."
-Stephen Hawking

SEVENTY-ONE YEARS, EIGHT MONTHS, TWENTY-SEVEN DAYS UNTIL THE BLUE LAKE EVENT

Blue Lake
South of Wendover Army Airfield
Tooele County, Utah, USA
Saturday, May 26, 1945

The Jeep screamed across the Bonneville Salt Flats, the remnant of an ancient seabed. Arrival at the hills and bluffs brought it to a crawl. It descended on a treeless high-desert range and navigated over a rolling sea of sagebrush, prairie grasses, and Russian thistle mired by sections of bone-jarring, washboard road. It took the four airmen over an hour to arrive at their destination—a barren alkaline mudflat, where over a dozen Jeeps waited.

Sergeant Eric Anders and Private Jardine Wolstenholme slid out of the driver and passenger seats. Corporal Frank Murphy and Private David Hosek bounded from the back of the topless vehicle. Unprepared for the condition of the ground, Hosek and

Murphy skated on the slick surface. Hosek's stout backside took the brunt of the fall. The gangly Murphy glided on one foot, arms gyrated to maintain balance before his toe found a rock, and he flew headlong into a belly slide. Murphy cursed and wiped the wet concrete-like muck from the front of his trousers, coat, and gloves.

Wolstenholme and Anders roared.

"Don't laugh, Wolsty!" Murphy said

"Ignore him, Private. That was hilarious!" Anders guffawed.

Hosek wiped the brackish gunk off his trousers and the back of a standard-issue olive-drab wool coat. "It was funny, Murph."

"Shut up, Hose!"

∞

They arrived at Blue Lake's southwest bank to find steam rising from the warm-springs-fed body. Although it was a chilly evening, a couple of dozen soldiers frolicked in the tepid water: thrashing, yelling, cannon-balling, belly-flopping.

An armed MP pointed. "Fishing's up that way."

Not in the mood for a crowd, they passed the long row of airmen fishing from the bank. They leaped over the narrow outlet brook and attempted to pass an MP patrolling on the other side.

"That's far enough, boys," the MP said.

"Come on, Private," Murphy said. "The fishing's all FUBAR with all those goons making a fuss in the water — scaring all the fish."

The MP pointed with the rifle barrel. "Two packs of smokes, and don't go past that sagebrush clump."

"One pack and to that bare patch."

"And I get to keep the biggest fish."

"Private, you drive a hard bargain," Murphy said. "Deal!"

"Remember, anyone or anything outside the boundaries, I

have orders to shoot to kill."

∞

Side-by-side on the chalky banks, the four airmen dangled bare feet in the warm water, extended cane poles, and drowned worms.

"Wolsty, will that girl of yours still be around after the war?" Anders asked.

"Sarge, my Eileen is the truest girl you'll ever meet. She told me not to get killed, or she'll die an old maid."

"I hope you're right, Wolsty. Colleen's giving birth any day now, and I won't be able to see my firstborn until old Tojo's head's on a pike," Anders said.

Hosek stared at his feet swirling in the water. "At least you got to see her on last leave. My cousin spent two years fighting Krauts in Africa and Italy before he got to go home to meet his son."

"I know. You've told me before, Hose. Those damn Japs need to surrender now!" Anders said.

"You know, once the atom bomb is dropped, there won't be many Japs left," Murphy said. "The poor slant-eyed Nip bastards won't know what hit 'um."

Anders backhanded Murphy's shoulder, followed by a stony stare and a finger to lips, and whispered, "Loose lips sink ships, Corporal. Didn't you learn anything at Los Alamos? Most of the personnel present lack full Silverplate clearance."

"Sorry, Sarge. I didn't think anyone could hear."

Wolstenholme whispered. "Good thing that MP's out of hearing range — or you'd have OSS and G-men crawling up your backside for the duration of the war."

"I hear Alaska's kind of nice this time of year," Hosek murmured. "Soon to be Buck Private Murphy."

"Shut up, Hose!"

∞

From a distance, the sound of a canid bark rolled across the desert. Another replied from the opposite direction. The barks soon turned to howls.

"You think the coyotes will join our little soiree?" Wolstenholme asked.

"The mangy mutts are wondering if red-blooded American fighting men taste better than Jack Rabbit." Hosek chuckled.

Those frolicking in the water and those on the banks became still as the chorus of howls echoed across the desert. The origins were hard to trace as the vocalists, volume, and intensity of the chorus grew. The ruckus continued for several minutes, then abruptly ended.

A bellow broke the silence. *"What the hell's that?"*

"Coyotes, moron!"

"No! Over ground zero, moron!"

A collective murmur grew along the shoreline. The four airmen saw other airmen staring across the lake to the bombing range to the north. They put down their fishing poles and stood up.

Above the horizon, three cigar-shaped objects, bathed in a cream-colored glow, silently rotated and weaved in a uniform pattern.

"What the heck?" Wolstenholme said.

"The flyboys testing something we don't know about?" Anders asked.

The desert was quiet—not a peep from coyotes or men. All were mesmerized by the silent, fluid waltz of the three luminous objects over the salt flats. There was a general sense they were witnessing history in the making, even if they weren't sure what they were seeing.

From fifteen miles away, the faint, unmistakable sound of air raid sirens reached the lake, signaling that these objects weren't experimental army aircraft. The craft ignored the alarm and kept weaving in the same elliptical motion.

The air raid sirens were the call for the men to return to base, but being spellbound by the sight, they forgot their duty. The military police should have rounded up the men, but the same distraction afflicted them.

The distant rumble of four P-47 Thunderbolt fighters sounded. As the fighter aircraft neared, the three unidentified objects froze in mid-air. The two lower ones levitated parallel to the highest. Two craft remained still as the third inched forward. It shot across the sky faster than any aircraft the men had ever seen. Experience taught them that the faster fighters and bombers flew, the louder the roar from the exhaust manifolds. Yet, this object remained silent as it curved upward at a forty-degree angle and out of sight.

As the fighters shot past the remaining two objects, the full-throttle rumble from the Pratt and Whitney engines gave chills to the men on the ground. The fighters banked hard after passing over Blue Lake and engaged the targets.

With eight .50-caliber Browning M2 heavy machine guns mounted on each Thunderbolt, the fighters lit up all thirty-two guns with a combined firing capacity of over 26,000 rounds per minute. One enemy craft rocketed upward and out of sight. The remaining one moved straightaway to the east. The Thunderbolts matched course but couldn't keep up.

The craft stopped at the edge of the bombing range, out of view for the men on the ground, and rotated in an elliptical motion as if winding up for the pursuing aircraft. As the fighters neared, the enemy craft froze a couple hundred feet above the desert floor.

In firing range, the lead Thunderbolt lined up with the object, let loose two bursts of machine-gun fire, and banked left. The second plane took the center position, fired another blast, and passed to the left. The third repeated the action, and the fourth, too.

The pilots were confident to have hit the target. Near the maximum speed of three-hundred-sixty air knots, the pilots took half a nautical air mile to turn around to continue their engagement.

As the Thunderbolts neared, the alien craft shot across the bombing range and returned unscathed to its original position at Blue Lake.

The men on the ground released a communal sigh.

A few moments later, the P47s returned with guns blazing. Those at the lake hooped and hollered and had a perfect profile view of the skirmish. From their perspective, the phosphorescent tracer rounds disappeared into an invisible wall shielding the craft. The lead Thunderbolt made a kamikaze course for the unidentified object. A moment before the fighter made contact, the enemy craft rocketed upward and out of sight.

The Thunderbolts circled back for another pass but found nothing.

∞

West Desert Bombing and Artillery Range
Wendover Airfield
Tooele County, Utah
Saturday, May 26, 1945

A tumbleweed rolled past as the last Jeep arrived at the bombing range's southwest auxiliary gate.

An MP jumped from the vehicle and saluted. "All men accounted for and returning to base, Major Fishburn."

"Very good, Sergeant. Keep your eyes open. We don't want to leave anyone stranded."

The lead Jeep had two MPs seated up front and one in the back. The second Jeep contained a driver and Fishburn up front, and another MP in the back.

The Jeeps reached the hills and bluffs. They bounced and sputtered up a sandy incline among sagebrush and cacti. As the lead Jeep started its downward descent and the second crested the hill, the electrical systems of both vehicles failed, and the engines stalled. Both drivers turned the ignition switches, but the Jeeps were void of power.

Fishburn looked at his wristwatch. The radioactive pigments on its dial didn't illuminate. "Radio ahead and let them know of our predicament."

An MP cranked the dynamo on the two-way radio. "The radio's dead, sir."

"What the *hell's* going on?" Fishburn said.

Fishburn had scarcely spoken when a beige light appeared 150 yards ahead. It took him a moment to recognize an alien craft thirty feet above the next promontory. An intense green-blue beam radiated to the ground. The men shielded their eyes, and across the valley, coyotes wailed.

"Gunners, lock-and-load! Fire-at-will! Take down the sonofabitch!" Fishburn yelled.

The rear-seated gunners stood. With both hands, they gripped .50-caliber machine guns mounted on tripods secured to the floor. They pulled back on the actions, aimed, and squeezed the triggers—but nothing happened.

After a few minutes, the hum and blue beam terminated. Coyotes hushed as the alien object crept silently from the promontory, cleared the cliff's edge, and shot out of sight. The men were startled out of a stupor when a single round fired from each machine gun, and the Jeeps' electrical systems came back on as if nothing had happened.

"Get Colonel Tibbets on the SCR," Fishburn said.

The MP cranked the dynamo. The radio worked fine.

∞

The Jeeps arrived at the promontory, where the enemy craft

previously hovered.

"Halt, I hear something," Fishburn said and gave hand signals.

A soldier rolled out of the back of the Jeep and crept toward the hill's edge before dropping to a crawl. He reached the rim and scanned the moonlit scene below. He stood, signaled the others, and crept downhill with M1 Carbine ready.

The others arrived to find an empty Jeep. Its front bumper was wedged against a rock outcropping. Still in gear, the engine idled roughly as tires spun out the fine white sand. Fishburn turned off the ignition. He recorded the Jeep's motor pool number on the back bumper and had the radio operator call back to base. Sergeant Anders, head ordinance crew chief, requisitioned the Jeep.

In the moonlight, soldiers searched and called out names. "Private Hosek!" "Corporal Murphy!" "Private Wolstenholme!" "Sergeant Anders!"

∞

Skull Valley Band of Goshute Indians Reservation
Tooele County, Utah
Sunday, May 27, 1945

Sheriff Bob Hendricks arrived at Gabriel Bear's two-room home a little past midnight. The Sheriff remitted a U.S. Army request for an Indian tracker. The Goshute, or Desert People, were the only trackers for the West Desert. A millennium before Hendricks' rancher-grandfather helped settle Grantsville, the Goshute survived off this godforsaken land. Among Goshute trackers, Bear topped the list. Over the years, Bear rescued several missing tourists, hunters, and fugitives wandering the deserts and mountains of Tooele County.

The Sheriff didn't know if Bear would help with this case. Bear's ancestors had a long, sordid history with the U.S. Army.

∞

Wendover Army Airfield
Wendover, Utah
Sunday, May 27, 1945

A guard at the front gate shone his flashlight in the driver's side window. He turned to his colleague. "Great. Another drunken Injun."

Bear rolled down his window. "Hello, I'm..."

"Sir, you need to turn around. When you reach the highway, make a left turn back to your reservation."

"Not my reservation." He shrugged. "The name's Gabriel Bear. I'm here at Major Fishburn's request."

"Just a minute, sir." The guard scanned a clipboard with a flashlight. "You can park at that hangar first on the right."

Escorted inside the hangar by a junior officer, Bear contained his surprise at over two hundred men gathered. Most gawked at the Goshute scout in their mist—surprised that he wore cowboy attire instead of a feathered headdress, buckskins, and moccasins.

Bear realized that for many of the men, this was the first encounter with a real, live Indian. He was well-acquainted with the stereotypes created by Radio City, pulp fiction, and Hollywood. He envisioned white families huddled around the radio rapt to the Lone Ranger and Death Valley Days, or how these boys had highly idealized imagines of noble cowboys and savage Indians populated from Zane Grey and dime novels, or when these young men had an extra two bits, they'd purchase a soda pop, popcorn, and admission for two to see the Saturday matinee with a young gal. Hollywood created a vision of the natives: Caucasian faces painted with rust-colored make-up, black war paint stripes, and black wigs with braided ponytails held in place by a headband. The bloodthirsty savages were ready for war at the slightest provocation. Bear hoped to educate these men otherwise.

His head waggled at the whispers of Tonto, Geronimo, and Cochise as he followed the officer up the wooden platform.

"Major Fishburn, Mr. Bear, to see you, sir."

"Thank you, Lieutenant." Fishburn extended a hand and winced at Bear's unexpectedly firm grip. "Mr. Bear, thank you for coming on such short notice. These men are at your disposal. What do you need from me?"

"I need actual boots from your missing soldiers, or at least the same size and type they were wearing. Also, I need a topographical map of the area."

"Right this way."

Fishburn led Bear to a table of maps.

"Where were they last seen?" Bear asked.

Fishburn provided location details, physical descriptions, and activities of the men. He omitted any mention of the unidentified craft.

Bear pointed to the map. "I only need four soldiers with me. Here, here, here, and here."

"What about the other men? We can cover more ground with them."

"Too many soldiers trampling the vegetation will make identifying the missing soldier's tracks impossible."

He realized Fishburn was worried about losing face with the men—so eager to find their missing comrades. The Major also kept something close to the chest.

Bear ran a finger across the map. "The rest of the soldiers can search at the base of the escarpment here."

He understood the men may have wandered over the cliff in the darkness. More soldiers at the bottom of the promontories might speed up the process—assuming the men plummeted to their deaths. This allowed Fishburn and the soldiers to feel as if they were making a Herculean effort to find their missing comrades, yet kept them from getting in Bear's way.

Bear almost got his wish. Four soldiers in one Jeep, while Fishburn drove in another with a driver and radio operator. As long as they stayed put, Bear figured they'd be no harm.

Before leaving the hangar, Bear explained each of the four soldiers' roles in the search. A Lieutenant led the larger portion of soldiers away in six-by-six troop carriers across the salt flats to the base of the cliffs.

About a hundred yards north of the missing airman's Jeep, Bear left a soldier with a wooden staff — a head taller than the man and with a red bandanna tied to the top. The convoy continued until reaching the abandoned Jeep. While Fishburn set up a field command center (a Jeep with maps on the hood and a two-way radio), Bear took four single boots, shoestrings tied together, and hung them around his neck. He led a soldier with a wooden staff and bandanna about a hundred paces to the south. He cautiously checked for signs of human passage. Bear retraced his steps precisely for the return to the command center. Bear took a man to the west. He guided the last man east to the top of the promontory.

He looked for signs of the missing men at the precipice until he was certain no one had taken a step into the abyss. Below, dozens of soldiers searching. Bear turned in the opposite direction to see his other three soldiers holding their staffs with red bandannas and waved. The other three waved back in acknowledgment.

Bear carried a full quiver of sticks with pieces of red yarn tied to the ends to mark any signs of passage. He moved from the top of the promontory toward the red bandana to the south. The Indian scout reached the man on the south and made a beeline toward the red bandana to the west. From west to north and north back to the top of the promontory, he still had a full quiver of markers on the first perimeter sweep.

His raised arms overhead with hands pointed inward to signal to move the search grid inward ten paces. Had Bear found signs of human activity near the original perimeter, he'd point hands outward to expand the search perimeter ten paces — except for the one soldier at the cliff's edge. Bear repeated the process and moved the perimeter inward four more times. He worked back to the start but found no trace of human traffic past sixty paces from the field command center.

The mystery made Bear chuckle at the thought of childhood stories about Isapia-ppeh, the legendary mischievous coyote. Given Isapia-ppeh's character, he might have something to do with the missing men. Maybe Isapia-ppeh's mortal enemy, Kinniih-Pia, or Mother Hawk, spirited the soldiers away to safety. He knew these were just tales, but Goshute children learned morals, life lessons, and useful principles through story. He felt the white man's story of Hansel and Gretel might be relevant, except no breadcrumbs were left behind by the missing men — or any footprints or trampled vegetation. He couldn't tell either fairytale explanation to the Major.

"They found nothing below the cliff. What did you find?" Fishburn asked.

"Major, your soldiers did not walk out of the area."

The seasoned Goshute scout pointed to a map. "The only tracks on the outer perimeters are from coyotes and deer. Many human tracks from this point inward. It could be your missing soldiers, or your men looking for them last night — or both. There are no man-made tracks outside of the third perimeter."

"Are you sure? How in the world did they leave the area unseen?" Fishburn asked.

"Maybe I missed something. Does this map show any subterranean cavities?"

Fishburn and Bear scoured the map and found an

abandoned tin mine and a couple of caves — but no place for the men to hide underground within five miles from where they were last seen.

"Either your soldiers drove away in another automobile." Bear looked skyward. " — or flew away."

Fishburn turned toward Bear with a dismayed expression that quickly turned to closed body language.

"What are you not telling me, Major?" Bear asked.

"You wouldn't believe me if I did," Fishburn said.

"Why not? My grandfather told stories of Goshute disappearing in the sky."

∞

West Desert Bombing and Artillery Range
Wendover Army Airfield, Utah

Eric Anders felt gratitude for the lack of a breeze. He wished the humidity level was lower, too. Moist air penetrated through the layers of clothing and deposited a layer of frost on the surface. He sat cross-legged on the crusty salt flats, huddled with his three comrades for warmth. The two army-issue wool blankets they shared provided little additional warmth.

They considered trudging across the bombing range back to base to keep warm, but one false step in the dark and *kablooey*! Setting off an unexploded ordnance was too big a risk. They'd stay put until dawn's first light.

"How the hell did we end up here? The last thing I remember was us fishing," Murphy said.

A thought entered Anders's mind: *some are carpenters, and others are sledgehammers*.

"Me, too. I remember coyotes howling," Hosek said.

Heads nodded.

Some are eagles, and others are pidgins.

"I'm so cold — but this throbbing in my temples is much

worse," Wolstenholme said. "And the big toe in my left foot hurts like heck."

Heads nodded again.

Some are wanderers, and some are travelers.

The audio hallucinations convinced Anders that hypothermia was setting in.

∞

They planned to leave at dawn, but overcast skies delayed the journey until sunrise. Walking for miles, the sky brooded and darkened with every step. Oversized raindrops splattered on the hard pan-salt surface from time to time.

Anders spotted an unidentified airborne object heading toward them.

"What the hell's that?" Anders said.

His heart raced as a gray craft flew silently and rapidly from the north. As the object arrived, it engulfed Anders in a beam of light. The intense brightness and a rhythmic thumping shot a déjà vu-like terror through his heart.

"Run!" Anders yelled.

He turned to see his colleagues already sprinting across the flat, barren, and vast surface with no place to hide. Anders tried to catch up as instinct took over choice and reason. Under a massive surge of adrenaline, Anders' legs felt as if they were churning through deep sand. His heart pounded, and breath couldn't come fast enough to his burning lungs.

Alkaline dust swirled from the ground, causing a searing pain to the eyes and lungs. Anders fell to his knees, ribs hurt from coughing, and gritty, viscous tears flooded his eyes. As his vision cleared, Anders realized a craft hovered directly ahead. An out-of-nowhere second craft hovered to their flank. He'd seen multiple records broken for airspeed, payload, and distance by America's latest experimental aircraft, but had never seen a machine that maneuvered like these—and it scared the hell out of him.

A portal in the lead craft's midsection opened. Anders shuddered with the recognition that running wasn't an option. A command emanated from the aircraft confirmed his observation. Out of the dust cloud, a figure sprinted toward Anders. He instantly recognized the slim build and unusual gait of the runner.

"Murphy, halt!" Anders yelled.

Murphy maintained course and speed. Anders rose from his knees to a four-point stance. The former high school defensive end drove a shoulder into Murphy's thighs and wrapped arms around him. The two crashed to the ground as the heavens released a deluge that seemed to blow in all directions.

∞

Anders' heart raced. Strapped in a jump seat, blindfolded, with wrists and feet restrained, only heightened his anxiety. The craft's swooshing thumps were confusing. He sensed terror in others around him. He flinched at a shoulder brush.

"Who are you?" Anders shouted over the din.

"Murphy, Jack. Corporal. United States Army Air Forces, Serial Number: 19837622!"

"Murph, it's me. Anders!"

"*Sergeant Anders*? Why the hell did you tackle me?" Murphy shouted.

"To keep you from being shot!"

"How did you know they would shoot me?"

"By the sniper taking aim at you and the order over the loudspeaker to halt or be shot!"

"Huh? Who has us? *The Japs?*" Murphy shouted.

"No way! It's not the Japs!"

"Where are they taking us?"

"Don't know, but definitely not to Wendover!"

∞

TWO YEARS, FIVE MONTHS LATER

The Pentagon
Arlington, Virginia
Tuesday, October 21, 1947

After the fateful night in the Utah desert two years ago, Sheldon Fishburn remained sorely amazed at what he'd witnessed since. He headed the Roswell investigation in July of this year. The event revealed more than he could imagine. The biological and technological evidence collected would provide decades of research and development.

It still felt unreal that President Harry S. Truman hand-picked him to lead the special group with countless men and hundreds of millions of dollars — under the auspices of twelve men.

Fishburn inserted his key in the Pentagon's executive elevator on the main floor. Another officer tried to join him. "Sorry, single access only."

The door closed. He turned his key again, and the elevator lurched downward before stopping at Sub-basement 12. Until three weeks ago, he believed the Pentagon only had three basement levels.

∞

Fishburn felt like a fraud among a quorum of the most powerful government and military leaders and the greatest scientific minds of the twentieth century. He scanned each face seated around the conference table.

Physicist and engineer Lloyd Berkner, one of the lead developers of radar and modern naval navigation systems. The world's leading biophysicist, Professor Detlev Bronk. Dr. Vannevar Bush, head of the Office of Scientific Research and Development and co-founder of the Manhattan Project. Secretary of Defense James Forrestal. Assistant Secretary of the Army,

Gordon Grey. Rear Admiral Roscoe H. Hillenkoetter recently appointed as director of the newly created Central Intelligence Agency. Jerome Clarke Hunsaker, M.I.T. professor and chairman of the National Advisory Committee for Aeronautics. Theoretical astronomer and astrophysicist, Dr. Donald Menzel. Former intelligence director, Rear Admiral Sydney Souers. General Nathan Twining, author of the Air Force memo: *AMC Opinion Concerning "Flying Discs."* And last, former U.S. Chief of Military Intelligence, General Hoyt Vandenberg.

Fishburn nodded at the senior aides hovering around the conference table, dispensing coffee, data, and reports.

Armed with a rubber-tipped maple pointer stick, he stood by the projection screen.

"For the next three years, we'll be evaluating the three proposed sites in Nevada, California, and Utah as the lead R&D facility," Fishburn said. "Next slide."

A salt-crusted dry lakebed appeared on the screen.

"The area around Groom Lake is ideal, given its natural runway and isolation. However, we must acquire significant acreage to keep prying eyes away. Also, the site is too remote for movement of personnel by ground transportation. Next slide."

Another infinite dry lakebed filled the screen.

"As of today, I believe Dugway Proving Grounds is the ideal site," he said. "Next slide."

On screen, a few hangars and a paved tarmac.

"As you can see, Dugway has plenty of land, including a large section of the Bonneville Salt Flats, existing infrastructure, isolated from the populace, and the Lincoln Highway is within reasonable driving distance to the facility."

"As of today, you say, Colonel," Hillenkoetter said. "We need to think more long term. You know my concerns about Dugway. The Lincoln Highway is too close for my tastes, and Salt Lake City will encroach on the site within the next hundred years. Secrecy is more important than the cost and logistics of air transportation, Colonel Fishburn."

"Duly noted, Director Hillenkoetter," Fishburn said. "We have leading futurologists and a Nobel Laureate mathematician forecasting multiple scenarios for each site."

"We can build a base in less than three years," Forrestal said. "Let's go with Dugway and move forward."

"Given that we want a facility that lasts a minimum of two centuries, spending three years to analyze our decision is a drop in the bucket," Souers said. "Besides, Wright Field is more than adequate for the next ten years."

"Colonel Fishburn, is the plan to still transfer the Extraterrestrial Biological Entity from Wright to the new site once it's up and running?" Forrestal asked.

"Yes, Mr. Secretary. Nothing has changed."

"Excuse me, but why are we still keeping *It* alive?" Vandenberg asked. "Hasn't *It* already provided all the information we need? *The Thing's* a security risk."

"General, the E.B.E. has given much useful information about the IGC and Dumal factions and is still providing vital technological data," Twining said.

"Nathan, I'm uncomfortable with *It* reading our minds. *It* could be a spy," Vandenberg said. "I'm uncomfortable with the whole IGC alliance, too."

"It isn't an alliance, per se. It's an advisory relationship," Grey said. "As you know, the Soviets and Dumal entered a secret alliance at the end of the war. We need the IGC on our side during this so-called *Cold War*."

"Call the alliance what you will, Mr. Grey," Vandenberg said. "We're still in bed with a superior military force that shouldn't be trusted."

"The Dumal alliance with the Nazis didn't work out too well for Hitler," Twining said. "The IGC-Allied cooperation is partially responsible for that outcome."

"The Dumal, the flying saucer friends of fascists. Now they should be called *the flying saucer friends of Stalin*." Grey laughed.

"I didn't trust Von Braun and Oberth before they introduced the President to the Dumal bastards — and even less since," Forrestal said. "I guess the President choosing the IGC over the Dumal is the lesser of two evils. Similar to crawling in bed with former Nazi rocket scientists to defeat the Russians."

"We should drop H-bombs on the lot of them. Stalin, the Dumal, and the IGC — before they get us," Vandenberg said.

"Hear, hear, General," Forrestal said. "Let me reiterate that the American people must be made aware of the danger that lurks in our midst. The Nazis and the Soviets are nothing compared to them. It's the right thing to do."

Fishburn locked eyes on Forrestal. "Mr. Secretary, might I remind everyone present that our mission is to protect the American people and avoid panic in the streets. The President's directive is crystal clear. Keep industry moving, and keep citizens working, shopping, and procreating in ignorant bliss at all costs — and leave the little green men up to Majestic Twelve."

PART 1-THE BLUE LAKE INCIDENT

"Older men declare war. But it is youth that must fight and die."
-Herbert Hoover

FOUR YEARS, ONE MONTH, ELEVEN DAYS
UNTIL THE BLUE LAKE EVENT

Blue Lake
Tooele County, Utah
Friday, January 11, 2013

Wilkie wanted to go on a moonlight adventure. Zach cared little for fishing and held no desire to keep company with Jeff DeBoer. It was nearly impossible for Zach and Jeff to say no to Wilkie.

With every step, Zach questioned why he left the warmth of the campfire and the safety of the scout troop to traipse across the god-forsaken landscape of the lowest precipitation county of the second driest state. Yet, he wanted to see the hot springs lake he'd heard so much about.

The smell of sulfur hung in the air as they neared a slick mudflat that doubled as Blue Lake's makeshift parking lot. They crossed the lifeless field, which left a gray, sticky mud that added a few pounds to each shoe before reaching the surer footing of the boardwalk.

They ascended the railroad tie and treated-pine plank

pathway in order of height.

Wilkie, the athletic blond with broad shoulders and a narrow waist that exemplified his Nordic ancestry, took large strides down the path.

Jeff, the olive-skinned and sinewy competitive swimmer, struggled to keep up.

Zach's pre-growth spurt physique and ginormous feet made him feel like an Irish Wolfhound trapped in a lapdog's body. He resented Mother Nature for delaying his accent to the rarified air of his older brother Seth, the former high school star center, his absentee and retired NBA forward father, and even his mother. Being the only mix-race curly-haired ginger with pale, freckled skin in high school made him feel out of place and often inadequate and frustrated.

Zach longed to be near Wilkie, so he stepped off the boardwalk to pass Jeff. His flashlight skimmed over the washtub-sized puddle, but his size-sixteen Nike Air Force 1 Retros didn't. He sank ankle-deep with a splash and slurp.

Jeff glanced back and laughed without breaking stride. "Don't get those clown shoes muddy, *Sideshow Bob*."

Zach tried to step out, but the wet sediment held a tight grip. Now mid-calf and a stone's throw behind the others, he yelled, *"Help! Wilkie, help!"*

Wilkie returned, removed his backpack, and drew a collapsible army shovel hanging from a loop.

"What the hell am I stuck in? It smells like crap."

"Quicksand," Wilkie said.

Zach attempted to churn his feet and sank more.

"Don't move. The silt shifts and creates a vacuum," Wilkie said. "Jeff, I saw a piece of plywood about twenty feet back. Please, get it."

Zach tried to pull out again and sunk knee deep.

"Dang it. Stop moving." Wilkie put a hand on Zach's

shoulder. "It will be alright, bud. We'll do this together. Just don't move, or it will make it harder."

Jeff returned with the board. "Have those clown shoes reached China yet?"

Zach grimaced. "Not funny, DeBoer."

Wilkie positioned the plywood under Zach's backside. "Sit back. It will stop you from sinking."

Zach felt his weight supported and released a sigh.

Wilkie knelt at the puddle's edge and thrust the shovel along the side of a leg. He drew the handle away to allow air to enter and relieve the suction that surrounded Zach's leg.

"Jeff, pull that leg side-to-side," Wilkie said.

He sat on the edge of the boardwalk and wrapped two hands around Zach's leg.

Wilkie worked the shovel deeper and moved back and forth to form an air pocket.

"Sideshow Bob. Sideshow Bob…" Jeff waggled the leg as he chanted.

"Just shut up and pull, dipwad," Zach said.

Jeff laughed and pulled the leg toward himself, and the limb freed with a slurp.

No sooner had Wilkie removed the shovel, Zach leaned sideways to the firmer ground and pulled. The slurping of air entering the cavity released Zach's other leg.

"I'm free!" Zach said. "Oh, crap. I've lost my shoe."

Wilkie dug quickly, but his shovel failed to match speed with the ever-collapsing slurry or land a hit on Zach's pre-growth spurt size sixteens.

"It's all good. Stop looking," Zach said. "I'm just glad to be out. Thanks, dude."

"I'm not giving up. You need your shoe," Wilkie said.

"Just stop. Those were my crap shoes. I have another pair in my pack."

"You sure?"

"Dang it! Just stop."

Zach climbed back on the boardwalk. "I bet you've never got stuck in quicksand before."

Wilkie laughed. "I've been trapped in it a couple times."

∞

They reached the southwest bank of Blue Lake and assessed the T-shaped aluminum dive dock for seaworthiness before boarding. The gangway extended thirty feet from shore to the pontoon-supported main platform atop steamy water.

Zach rushed down the gangway. Wilkie reached the main dock, dropped his backpack, and removed a winter jacket. Last on board, Jeff put down a tackle box, and spinner combo, and removed a parka, followed by a beach towel hanging from his neck.

"Keep your pants on, DeBoer," Zach said. "We don't want to see your man-thong."

Jeff glared at Zach and raised his pinkie finger. "I'm only giving you the wing because you don't deserve the whole bird."

Zach laughed. "Your Speedo's still gay, and only fags wear Speedos."

"Watch your mouth!" Wilkie scowled at Zach. "Those are hurtful words. You know my cousin Bryan's gay."

Zach hung his head. "Sorry, Wilkie. It's just a saying. You know I have nothing but love for Bryan."

"I know," Wilkie said and put his arm around Zach's shoulder. "Just watch it from now on, okay. We're not twelve anymore."

The use of homophobic slurs didn't trouble Zach nearly as much as the secret he kept from his best friend — or the feelings he still held for his cousin.

Wilkie glanced at Jeff and back at Zach. "In your defense, Jeff shouldn't bait you with birds and wings." Wilkie faced Jeff.

"And for future reference, Jeff's Speedo is Euro-chic and totally inappropriate for an American dude to wear outside a swim meet."

"DeBoer's a Euro-chick?" Zach crowed.

"Shut your pie hole, jerk," Jeff said.

"Hey, you're a jerk for wanting to go swimming in twenty-degree weather—in a speedo," Wilkie said.

"Your dad said the lake is like eighty degrees, and we could go swimming."

"It's a huge difference coming out of the water during the day when the outside temperature's above freezing and the sun's shining."

∞

Jeff and Wilkie set up their fishing tackle.

First to finish, Jeff cast out to the middle of the lake. He let the lure sink before starting a slow retrieve, hopeful to cross the path of an angry largemouth bass.

Wilkie, LED flashlight in mouth, searched through the tackle box.

"There you are," he mumbled and shook the lure to hear the BB rattle inside.

"That top-water lure won't catch any bass. You should use spinnerbaits," Jeff said.

"Hasn't seemed to help your luck," Wilkie said, while tying a six-pound rated monofilament into a Rapala knot. "What is that your tenth... uh... eleventh cast without a bite?"

"You won't catch anything either... *Bruce*," Jeff said.

Wilkie withheld a rejoinder. He hated being called by his given name, and Jeff knew it.

∞

TWO YEARS, EIGHT MONTHS EARLIER

Abundance Jr. High School

Abundance, Utah
Monday, May 18, 2009

Lester Cline, the biggest bully from the ninth grade, tormented Wilkie and the other seventh graders incessantly. Although large for a seventh grader, Wilkie didn't fight back. He kept cool, knowing that *Lester, the Molester,* would move to high school next year.

The last month of the school year, Wilkie's grandparents died in a head-on automobile accident. The funeral was on Saturday. On Monday morning, he wanted to crawl into a hole to grieve, but couldn't miss school.

Wilkie had wonderful memories of Grandma and Grandpa. They put countless miles on their car to attend the grandkids' ball games, plays, and recitals—and always took the family out for dinner or ice cream afterward. Wilkie enjoyed spending summers on their farm and at their Bear Lake cabin. The realization that there were no new memories to make with two extra special people ripped a jagged piece from his heart.

On the walk to school, Wilkie hid behind a neighbor's garage to avoid friends. Intentionally ten minutes late for homeroom, he hoped to reach his locker unseen.

"Hey, Bruce Banner!" echoed down the hall.

Bruce Banner. Bruce Lee. Bruce Wayne. Wilke hated the same insipid movie-hero nicknames since elementary school.

He turned red-faced and with fists clenched. "Shut the hell up!"

Lester's eyebrow raised. "What did you say? You shouldn't talk like that if you know what's good for you, *Bruce.*"

"You heard me. Don't call me that again."

With Mr. Green still making copies in the office, his classroom door opened, and a head poked out the door. "Lester's going to beat up Wilkie!"

Several students, mostly boys, rushed from the classroom.

"What's gotten into you, Wilkerson? Walk away while you're still in one piece."

Wilkie shook, teeth and fists clenched. As tears welled up, he turned to walk away.

"What's wrong, crybaby? Whittle baby Bwuce is going to turn into Hulk? Make Hulk mad? I won't like it when you're mad?"

Wilkie kept walking.

"Hey, Bruce Lee. I heard granny and gramps bit it — just like you."

Wilkie turned toward Lester with a homicidal glare. He charged, leaped off one leg, and twisted in mid-air. The bully was unable to react before a Bruce Lee-like roundhouse kick landed on the side of his head. He flew askew against the lockers with a clank.

The spectators' collective ooh-and-awe reverberated down the hall.

Lester crumpled to the floor and lay motionless before slowly rising on wobbly legs.

No less enraged, Wilkie got in Lester's face. "Don't dis my grandparents! *Next time, I'll kill you!*"

"I won't. I won't."

"Also, my name's Wilkie. Got it, butthead?"

Lester nodded.

"*Got it?*"

"Yes. Yes."

Had Lester known that since pre-school, Wilkie studied Kenpō and later Kung Fu, the bully would have eschewed bullying the underclassman. Until this moment, Lester and all the other school bullies had Wilkie's teacher, Master Ng, to thank for teaching emotional discipline, a core value of Kung Fu; avoid fighting at all costs — run away if necessary. Only fight when exhausting all options.

The following week, Wilkie apologized to Ng Sifu for using sorrow as an excuse to use his training for violence.

The school district suspended Wilkie for the final three weeks of the school year and required him to complete anger management counseling before returning in the Fall.

The schoolyard gossip surrounding Wilkie cleaning Lester's clock spread quickly and grew wilder with each retelling.

In one version, Lester's jaw was shattered in two places. A further embellishment included a broken nose and missing teeth.

One popular yarn told of Wilkie hitting a pressure point and stopping Lester's heart. According to legend, if not for Mr. Green's timely return and swift action, Wilkie would have faced manslaughter charges. The science teacher saved Lester's life by giving mouth to mouth resuscitation. Additional falsehoods included Wilkie spending the summer locked up in Juvie and the scandalous innuendo that Mr. Green may have slipped his tongue in Lester's mouth.

Regardless if students knew the truth or believed in fables, the result was the same. No classmates, except his closest friends in jest, ever called him *Bruce* again.

∞

TWO YEARS, EIGHT MONTHS LATER

Blue Lake
Tooele County, Utah
Friday, January 11, 2013

The fishing was fast for a couple of hours, then slowed to a stop. Wilkie, Zach, and Jeff laid on the dock using jackets for pillows while having typical late-night campfire conversations. Music, sports, girls, friends, jokes.

"Who knows a scary story?" Zach asked.

"I know the scariest story of all because it's true and happened right here at Blue Lake," Wilkie said. "The story of the Blue Lake Monster."

"Stop it. Stop it." Zach laughed while waving his arm. "No Loch Ness Monster lives in this puddle. You're just making it up."

"Who said anything about a sea monster? Two divers told me their story right here on this very dock a couple years ago," Wilkie said. "They were night diving and shined their lights on something moving on the bottom of the lake and swam toward a half-man half-lizard holding a ten-pound bass with both hands and eating it like corn on the cob. They said the beast was yellow and scaly with long legs and short arms and webbed fingers and toes with razor-sharp, retractable claws. It had a long tail and large frog eyes on the corner of the head.

"The lizard-man opened its mouth to show razor-sharp teeth, then it let out an ultrasonic scream. The divers said it felt like being kicked in the chest. When they recovered, they watched the monster descend into one of the hot spring vents at the lake's bottom. When they returned right here." Wilkie pointed at the dock. "They found their duffle bags with wetsuits and flippers all shredded—and their lunches eaten. Apparently, the creature has a taste for PB and J."

"That's just made up to scare DeBoer," Zach said.

"I ain't scared 'cause it ain't true," Jeff said.

"I heard it from the horse's mouth with my dad," Wilkie said. "You can ask him when we get back to camp."

"Swear it's true and not something you made up," Zach said.

Wilkie held up his right hand with index, middle, and ring fingers extended and thumb crossed to pinky. "Scouts honor. That's what the two divers told me. I can't attest if they were telling the truth, but I stick by what I heard."

∞

Stars filled the horizon. Zach still fretted about the Blue Lake Monster. Wilkie and Jeff silently waited for passing satellites and falling stars.

Wilkie's acute olfactory senses detected a nearby interloper and raised a hand. "Shh! Somebody's smoking over there."

Footfalls on creaky boards caused Zach to jump up. "What the heck was that?"

"It's the Lizardman," Jeff said. "No, someone's on the path, dumbass."

"I wish you two would play nice with each other," Wilkie said.

"Okay, mother, but we've heard you drop a few atomic f-bombs — and call people much worse things than we ever say," Jeff said.

Wilkie smirked.

"Sorry, bro. I haven't heard you cuss in over... not since your mother. Sorry, I didn't mean it that way."

"It's okay, bro. I still find it hard sometimes to keep my promise to my mom when I hear profanity around me," Wilkie said. "It makes it easy to slip."

"Sorry, Wilkie," Zach said.

Their attention returned to spy a petite girl with mid-shoulder-length wavy red hair emerging from behind the cattails and reeds that blocked the view of the path. She kept pace until arriving at the gangplank.

"Only one ginger is allowed on the dock," Jeff whispered. "So, you'll have to leave, Sideshow."

"Permission to come aboard," she said, then took a drag from her cigarette.

Being so petite, the boys couldn't tell if she was a child or an adult — but a smoker had to be at least their age.

Smoke exited her nostrils. "Can I take a look?"

In a single motion, Jeff rose and moved toward the girl.

"Welcome aboard. My name's Jeff, and you are?"

"Eliza, but everyone calls me Liza."

Jeff extended his hand down the gangplank. "After you."

Her porcelain skin, which seemed to glow in the moonlight, immediately captivated Wilkie.

She peered over the dock. "Is it deep enough to dive off this end?"

"About ten feet deep," Wilkie said.

"I'm going for a swim," Liza said.

"Mind if I join you?" Jeff asked.

"The more the merrier," Liza said.

"Oh, goodie," Zach said. "We get to see the Speedo."

Jeff extended a pinkie toward Zach.

∞

"Where do you think they went?" Zach asked. "They're awfully quiet."

"I think they swam over to the east end, where it's shallow enough to sit," Wilkie said.

"I still wouldn't believe it unless I saw it," Zach said. "She stripped buck-naked right in front of us. She didn't even hesitate — and neither did DeBoer in joining her. Thank goodness he kept his Speedo on."

"Jeff's self-conscious about the zits on his butt," Wilkie said.

Zach laughed hysterically and struggled to speak between breaths.

"I'd forgotten about good old Pizza Butt;

"Pizza the Butt;

"Hey, DeBoer! Baboon called. He wants his ass back."

Wilkie chuckled as he shook his head. "I'd forgotten how cruel we were back in junior high."

Zach groaned. "If you haven't noticed, DeBoer's mean to

me all the time."

Wilkie shrugged. "Fair enough. What I can't believe is Jeff was making out with her. He's always saying French kissing a smoker is like licking an ashtray."

"You know what the Bastard always said," Zach murmured.

"I wish you wouldn't call your father that. You never know what the future holds. He might change."

"You don't know how lucky you are, Wilkie," Zach said. "Your dad is the most awesome man I've ever known. He'd never abandon you."

"Okay, what did your poor excuse for a father always say?"

"The pot-smoking druggie used to say, *if she smokes, she pokes*."

Wilkie chortled. "That's horrible!"

"I didn't say it. My no-good father did. Don't shoot the messenger."

Wilkie snickered again. "Fair enough."

"So, in relation to why, Jeff went swimming with a naked girl that smokes. I think you get the point—and even naked, she still looks like a ten-year-old boy."

Wilkie shook his head. "You never cease to amaze me, Zack—and by the way, I've seen ten-year-old boys with more curves and bigger boobs than hers."

Zach roared. "I can't believe you said that—or that you looked at her. I expect that from me and DeBoer, but not you. You're usually a bit of a prude."

"Shut up, dude! How couldn't I look? I'm still a man."

In reality, Wilkie couldn't keep his eyes off Liza from the moment she arrived. It's too bad she smoked. He couldn't date a girl who stripped in front of complete strangers, either. Smoking and nonchalant stripping were both deal breakers. Yet, Wilkie had a gnawing pang at the thought of Jeff being with Liza—and not him.

∞

Liza and Jeff frolicked in a small cove formed by the bank and the dive dock gangway.

"They've gotten awfully quiet. Look at them," Liza said.

Wilkie and Zach stood motionless near the dock's center.

"They're in full fishing fever mode," Jeff said.

"It's time to get out. I'm getting all pruney. I'll get their attention."

Liza hoisted herself onto the gangway. She walked behind the two young men and observed they weren't fishing.

"Ahem."

"Shh!" Zach and Wilkie said without looking back.

"Excuse me." She forced her way in front of them, but her swagger failed to garner a glance. She grabbed a towel, dried her hair, then looked up to something that gave her pause. Her towel dropped back onto the dock.

"Zach, throw me my towel," Jeff said.

"Shh," came in unison from Zach, Wilkie, and the stark-naked girl, standing side-by-side.

"*What the hell*? Throw me my damn towel, Sideshow!" Jeff said.

Without turning his gaze, Zach reached down and threw the towel backhanded. The towel shot over Jeff's head and into the water.

"You fuckin' clown!" Jeff yelled, then muttered. "I should kick your scrawny black ass.

He nearly jumped from the water onto the gangway. Scarcely standing, he saw the reason for everyone's purposeful inattention toward him.

"What is it?" Jeff asked.

"UFOs, dumbass!" Zach said.

∞

THE FOLLOWING DAY

Near Blue Lake
Tooele County, Utah
Saturday, January 12, 2013

Dark clouds hindered the dawn as Bruce Wilkerson, Sr. crossed the mud flat toward a uniformed law enforcement officer leaning against the Winnebago motorhome with block letters overhead: *Mobile Incident Command Unit.*

"Harold, I beg you. Please issue an Amber Alert," Bruce said.

"Give it a rest, Bruce," Sherriff Hendricks said. "Who'd randomly abduct four kids out in the middle of nowhere?"

"How would four strong swimmers all drown in the ponds or get lost on an alkali plain without a tree or mountain for miles?"

"Get real, Bruce. It was dark. They probably got disoriented."

"Please, Harold. Issue the Amber Alert... just in case."

"I don't want to divert limited law enforcement and search-and-rescue resources away from where those kids are most likely at."

∞

The clouds thinned, and the morning sun broke forth across the high desert.

Sherriff Harold Hendricks panned the gathering with great satisfaction. Dozens of volunteers sporting yellow vests were antsy to get moving. Drivers of over sixty off-road vehicles, both official and personal, would cover more ground. The sound of the public safety helicopter searching nearby. Salt Lake and Reno television stations were ready to go live. In the backdrop, parents desperate for good news with miles of sagebrush and Russian thistle behind them.

Hendricks resisted smiling on camera but maintained a somber, official bearing as he approached the cluster of microphones. He couldn't ask for a better portrait during an election year.

"For those that don't know, I am Harold R Hendricks, Sheriff of Tooele County. My department will coordinate this operation from our state-of-the-art Mobile Incident Command Center.

"Last night, four youths went missing from this area. Three young men, Bruce Wilkerson, Jr. and Jeff DeBoer, both fifteen-years-old and fourteen-year-old Zach Davidson, were on an overnight camp with their Varsity Scout troop approximately a mile from our present location."

The chief deputy placed headshot enlargements on display easels as the names were read.

"They were last seen leaving their campsite around eight pm last evening to fish at Blue Lake."

The deputy placed the girl's photo on the fourth easel.

"Also missing is Liza O'Reilly, a twenty-year-old sophomore at the University of Utah. She was last seen leaving her camping trailer to investigate the lake around ten pm last night.

"We are uncertain if the scouts and Ms. O'Reilly are together or not. We assume the possibility that they are.

"The Tooele County Sheriff's Department has already searched Blue Lake and the surrounding ponds three times by its recovery dive teams, so we are certain that none of the four children have drowned. After this press conference, we will focus our efforts across to the east and south, and north up to the bombing range. The western search parameter will continue to US Route 93. Today's search will cover about a ten-mile radius.

"I'd like to thank the eighty-three civilian volunteers that have arrived this morning. I want to thank the civilian Jeep Posses and volunteer search-and-rescue teams from Elko, Tooele, Salt Lake, Davis, and Utah Counties. We also want to thank the cooperation of law enforcement agencies from along the Wasatch Front and Elko County for joining our efforts."

The Sheriff glanced back at the parents. "We have four families worried sick about their kids. I promise the Tooele County Sheriff's Department will not rest until we bring their children home. Questions?"

Hands raised. Voices shouted. Bodies jockeyed for position. Hendricks singled out one.

"The bombing range is only a short distance from Blue Lake, so why does the search end there?" the reporter asked.

"Because of unexploded military ordnance and the sheer size of the testing grounds, Hill Air Force Base will coordinate with the Sheriff's Department and search the area by air."

"Follow up question about the bombing range. Why are there no searchers on the ground? Can you really spot everything from the air?"

"Yes. Absolutely. You passed through the salt flats on I-80. You could see everything on the salt flats, right?"

"I guess."

"The entire bombing range is flat, barren of vegetation, and shiny white. Anyone or anything on the salt flats would be completely visible from the air. That should answer your question. Next question?"

"How certain are you that the youth haven't drowned?" a reporter shouted.

"A hundred percent. The conditions of the lake and ponds are crystal clear. If bodies had been in the water, our divers would have found them. We stand by our theory that the youth couldn't have walked farther than ten miles in any direction. No more questions. We have work to do."

Hendricks pivoted, nodded at the parents, and turned back. "Volunteers meet up with your team leaders. Law enforcement personnel, you already know your assignments. Move out!"

Hendrick left the podium as an unexpected blur moved past.

"Damn it, Bruce," he murmured.

"Excuse me, ladies and gentlemen," Bruce said. "The other parents have asked me to be the spokesperson for our families."

Cameras flashed. Video transmitted. The Sheriff's internal smile vanished.

"First, we want to express our gratitude to the Sheriff's Department, extended law enforcement, and especially the scores of volunteers sacrificing their time to search for our children. We are grateful for the efforts of the dive teams to determine that our children did not drown. However, all the parents agree—with Jeff DeBoer being a member of the high school swim team and a lifeguard, and Liza O'Reilly being a member of the university varsity dive team, and Zach and Wilkie also being strong swimmers—they couldn't possibly all have drowned.

"We agree with Sheriff Hendricks' theory that our children might be somewhere out in the desert. We need your efforts to search for them to continue. However, as parents, we are unified that abduction of our children is also a possibility. Our pleas with the Sheriff to issue an Amber Alert have fallen on deaf ears. Let me lay out our case for their possible abduction."

Bruce turned back to acknowledge the parents, then noticed the scorn in Hendrick's eyes.

"Foremost, this area has sparse vegetation, and you can easily get your bearings from the mountains to the east and west of this valley. My son, Bruce Jr, who goes by Wilkie, is a nationally certified outdoor guide and wilderness advanced first aid technician, and expert in wilderness survival. He's an extremely responsible and mature young man who helps run our family's wilderness adventure and outfitting company. Wilkie also knows this area like the back of his hand and can find his way back to camp, or this parking area with his eyes closed. We can safely assume my son has been either injured, incapacitated, or abducted.

"All three of the young men are Eagle Scouts. Jeff and Zach have extensive outdoor experience, including orienteering, first aid, and wilderness survival. Assuming Ms. O'Reilly joined up with them, she'd be guided by experienced outdoorsmen who could find their way back to this very spot."

Hendrick's eyebrows raised, and he whispered in a deputy's ear. The deputy nodded and crept toward the command center.

"Our unified plea with the public is..." Bruce extended his hand toward the photos of the youth. "If you see our children or anything suspicious, please immediately call your local police or 911. Thank you.

Reporter's hands and voices shot up.

"Sorry, no questions." Bruce turned to the disdain in Hendricks' eyes as they passed.

Hendricks reached a side of the podium, turned slightly toward the parents, and leaned into the microphones. "I thought my deputy told you that an Amber Alert had already been issued. My apologies that you weren't told."

∞

A sudden downpour forced Wilkerson and Hendricks to move their discussion under the command center's awning.

A deputy poked his head out of the RV. "Sheriff, you better come hear this. I think the Air Force found them."

Hendricks and Wilkerson hurried inside.

"I recorded this radio transmission," the deputy said, before hitting the play button.

The background static of helicopter rotors made the transmission difficult to hear.

"I've listened to it five or six times. I'm certain this is what they said." He handed a notepad to the sheriff and replayed the transmission.

Hendricks' smirk told it all. He handed the notepad to Wilkerson with sadistic pleasure: *Confirmed, four contacts in custody. Returning to base.*

Hendricks struggled to show restraint. He wanted to say; *I told you so, Bruce* — but others were present. The grin of self-satisfaction told more than words. "We found them."

∞

Wilkerson and Hendricks stood alone near the command center.

"Harold, I'm begging you. Please don't stop the search until we have confirmation from the Air Force."

"Give it a rest, Bruce. Who else would the Air Force pick up? No one else is out there."

"I hope you're right, Harold."

Three black Chevrolet SUVs with US government license plates arrived at the mobile command center.

"What the hell are the Feds doing here?" Hendricks answered his own question. "Damn it, Bruce. Why do you always have to one-up me?"

"This has nothing to do with you or me, Harold. This is about finding those kids, and I don't care who stands in our way."

"You prick."

The front passenger, who wore a dark suit and aviator sunglasses, exited the lead SUV. He opened the rear door. Another agent, wearing an Italian suit and designer sunglasses, headed straight away to the Sheriff.

"Sheriff Hendricks?"

"Yes. And who the hell are you?"

"Special Agent in Charge Adams. Federal Bureau of

Investigation."

"We didn't ask for the Bureau's help, and you have no jurisdiction here," Hendricks said. "I'm afraid you've wasted your time. We found the missing children."

"When? We've received no reports of the youth being found," SAIC Adams said.

"The Air Force discovered them on the bombing range moments ago. We expect them back any minute now."

"You've received direct confirmation from the Air Force?" Adams asked.

"Well, no, but we've overheard an Air Force radio transmission."

"We've been in regular contact with the Air Force and have not received confirmation," Adams said. "Let me make things perfectly clear. The Salt Lake City Field Office has jurisdiction in this case and is taking over the investigation into the missing youth."

"Like hell, you have jurisdiction! My department is in charge, and we didn't invite you."

"I don't want to get in a pissing contest with you, sheriff, but these are our orders."

Adams handed tri-folded papers to Hendricks.

On the first page, the office of the U.S. attorney general, Utah's attorney general, and the county attorney gave full authority to the FBI to investigate a possible kidnapping on federal lands involving possible interstate flight. The orders also committed federal, state, and county law enforcement under the command of the special agent in charge.

Also attached was a scathing letter from the U.S. House Intelligence Committee Chair into the lapse by local law enforcement for failing to treat the situation as an abduction from the beginning. Last, a letter from the Secretary of the Interior addressed to the Attorney General that requested the FBI to lead the investigation into a possible kidnapping on BLM lands.

Hendricks felt the burn of razor cuts along old, thick scars. He felt satisfaction that all of Wilkerson's back-channeling served no purpose. He wasted political capital for nothing. The kids were found.

∞

An Air Force helicopter hovered over a flat, dry area north of the command trailer. Like a flock of Canada Geese landing on a golf course, the aircraft made a few circles before descending.

"You certainly have all your ducks in a row, Special Agent In-charge Adams, but the point is moot. The children are being delivered by the Air Force as we speak."

As it touched down, Bruce Wilkerson ran to meet the aircraft, hoping Hendricks was correct. The alkaline dust burned his eyes and lungs, but he hardly noticed with anticipation of Wilkie hopping out of the UH-72 Lakota. Bruce's heart sank seeing a man exit the helicopter, followed by an aide. Typically, the sight of his former platoon leader brought joy—but seeing Jim Callahan today didn't provide the comfort Wilkerson sought. Yet, he still had gratitude that Jim moved mountains and dropped everything to support his former platoon sergeant.

Bruce had plenty of other Washington connections at the Pentagon and within the intelligence community. However, he trusted U.S. Congressman James R. Callahan (R), New Mexico, to get things done fastest, hardest, and until completion like no other. Bruce still couldn't believe that Jim left Washington and his busy position as chairman of the House Intelligence Committee to help find Wilkie and the others.

Bruce and Callahan embraced as brothers before fleeing the helicopter's downdraft toward law enforcement huddled near the command center.

"Chairman Callahan, welcome to Blue Lake," SAIC Adams said. "This is Sheriff Hendricks, and apparently, you already know, Mr. Wilkerson."

"Thank you for your cooperation," Callahan said. "Any new developments, Sheriff?"

"We've heard the Air Force found the children on the bombing range and should return them anytime now."

"Unfortunately, the Air Force doesn't have young Mister Wilkerson and his three friends in custody," Callahan said. "The search teams arrested four anti-war activists seeking to infiltrate Dugway Proving Grounds. They picked a bad day to be on the gunnery range."

PART 2-GO TO THE LIGHT

"Walking with a friend in the dark is better than walking alone in the light."
-Helen Keller

Unspecified Location & Date

A chill and a migraine woke Jeff. *Why am I on top of my sleeping bag? Man, I got to piss.*

Jeff really despised getting out of his warm mummy bag in the dead of winter to fulfill a simple bodily function. Pre-adolescence, he sometimes wet the bed rather than get out from under his toasty quilts before morning. With others in the tent, he'd never live it down if he did the same.

He decided sleep would be wanting until exiting the tent to water a bush. Reaching behind for a flashlight, Jeff felt silty earth and not a tent floor. He pawed at his sides to discover a warm body on each.

Jeff quickly stood and slammed his head into a low rock ceiling. *"Ouch! What the hell?"* He rubbed to ease the pain and check for the formation of a goose egg. "Where the hell am I?"

"In a cave."

"Who's that?" Jeff asked.

"Zach."

"Why are we in a cave?"

"Don't know."

"Who else is in here?"

"I think Wilkie and that redhead. What's her name?"

"Liza. Do you have a flashlight or cellphone?"

"My phone's dead," Zach said.

"How do I get out of here?"

"I could point, but obviously, you can't see."

"Lead me out."

"I'm too terrified to move. You know how claustrophobic I am."

"I don't get it. Don't you want to get out of an enclosed space?"

"I'm doing some relaxation exercises my therapist taught me." Zach paused. "You can ride it out with me until morning or just head out opposite my voice."

"You're completely *useless*, Sideshow," Jeff said.

∞

Muted voices and a faint whiff of campfire stirred Wilkie.

It felt reminiscent of the morning two months earlier, after completing his first Ironman triathlon race, when pain surged throughout his body in an unfamiliar, dark environment. His father's voice, accompanied by drapes opening to mid-morning sun, brought almost instant orientation. Burrito-wrapped in bedding on an extra-firm hotel mattress was not ideal for recovery from the world's greatest endurance race.

Today, Wilkie also felt restrained, and his pain was far more intense. Even in the darkness, the earthy scent assured him this wasn't the Honolulu Hilton.

"How did I get here?" he muttered.

With his strength restored, he shuffled toward muted voices and a tiny circle of light. One hand gliding along the sandstone ceiling, the other protecting his head. Forced onto hands and knees stirred a choking dust. He had to belly crawl until reaching the narrow outlet and emerged out of a hole protected by a rock overhang and indentation in a sandstone wall. The forward view revealed sparse vegetation and forty-odd-feet of reddish sand that abutted a striated, four-story-tall Cretaceous sandstone wall. The drab sky's flurry moistened the ground but didn't accumulate.

At this moment, Wilkie was more disoriented than when he woke in Hawaii. When the curtains opened to a view of Waikiki Beach, he awoke in the same place he went to bed. The current landscape, although still desert, was entirely dissimilar from the surroundings at Blue Lake. He felt relief to see his friends at the edge of the alcove, huddled around a modest fire.

"Good morning," Wilkie said.

An impression entered Liza's mind. *Some are the leaders of men. Some are leaders of nations.*

"It's almost evening, dude," Jeff said. "You slept all day."

Some are soldiers, others are mercenaries, others tyrants.

"Where are we?" Wilkie asked.

"The Book Cliffs," Zach said.

Some are chronometers, others sextants, others watchtowers.

"It certainly looks like the Book Cliffs," Wilkie said, understanding that outside of the Boy Scouts, Zach never engaged in outdoor activities. The Davidson family considered a day at an amusement park a wilderness experience. "Are you sure? Have you ever been to the Book Cliffs?"

"Yes and no."

"Then how in the world do you know where we are?" Wilkie asked.

"I can't explain it. I just know. We're eleven miles as the crow flies east of State Highway 6. By foot, we have to go the long way. About thirty-one miles."

"You've finally gone bonkers, Sideshow," Jeff said.

Zach ignored Jeff. "Check out the petroglyphs behind you,

Wilkie."

Wilkie turned and moved closer. "It's Fremont."

The sandstone canvas showed a pre-Columbian hunter's bow aimed at a Bighorn Sheep next to a Prong-horn Antelope. In the middle, three giant beings hovered. The largest was a man with a square head, no neck, and an inverted triangle body. The two females appeared to be wearing buckskin dresses. A smaller one didn't have legs. The medium-sized one appeared to have Daddy Long Leg spider legs.

"That looks like a helmet?" Zack pointed at the largest being. "You can see his face through the face shield."

"Could be," Wilkie said.

"Are those antennas coming from his helmet? The other ones look like they have antennas or cow horns," Liza said.

"The fat woman looks like she has a bullwhip," Jeff said. "You think those big ones are gods?"

"Maybe," Wilkie said. "Is that a boat floating over them?"

"Who knows?" Jeff pointed. "I like the scorpion. I think the other thing's a turkey."

"Definitely a turkey," Zach said.

"Who asked *you*, Sideshow?" Jeff said.

∞

The fire's kindling dwindled, and darkness filled the sky. Frigid gusts sent the youth crawling back into the cave where they slept last night.

"We shouldn't go any further," Liza said. "Something's back there."

Zach's chest tightened. "Did you hear something?"

"No, I can feel it—and it's scared," she said.

"Who's scared?" Wilkie asked.

"I don't know, but something is back there."

"What kinds of animals live in these caves?" Zach asked.

"Bats and bears. Lots of black bears and bats live in these

caves," Jeff said, goading Zach's phobias.

Zach felt an icy shiver.

They froze at the thud of falling rock. The low, throaty growl that followed sent a tsunami of terror across the cave.

Jeff fled first. Wilkie last. Normally, the sight of a hunched-over youth stampeding in single file, changing to all fours, followed by a rushed belly crawl, would be comical. When faced with being eaten by a hungry bear brought out of hibernation by meaty humans, any pretense of bravado disappeared.

In near-blizzard conditions, Jeff ran straight away behind a fan of tamarisk as the others followed. Crouched on knees, they peeked through the shrub, trying to anticipate the size of the bear.

Liza released a nervous chuckle upon seeing a young man with braided black hair, donning buckskin and moccasins, around thirteen- or fourteen-years-old, exit the cave. He surveyed the area.

"He's confused and still worried we'll hurt him," Liza whispered.

Wilkie sidestepped from behind. "mykWH! Att nu-ba."

The boy's face dropped.

"Katz suhdteeh-ayh," Wilkie said.

"Tu-tu-wish-er-re kadz-att moo-or," the boy yelled and sprinted up the canyon.

"Woon-e. Katz ar-tawk. Katz pwap-ter-eb-e," Wilkie yelled.

Wilkie turned to three bewildered expressions. "What?"

"*What?* I think the question is, *who*? Who was that?" Zach said. "My second question is, what language were you speaking?"

"You and that Indian kid weren't speaking English," Jeff said.

"Are you crazy? I only speak English — and a little Spanish and Japanese."

"Trust me, you weren't speaking any of those. What did

you say to him?" Zach asked.

"Don't be afraid. We won't hurt you. Don't run."

∞

THE FOLLOWING MORNING

Book Cliffs
Emery County, Utah
Day 2

Zach leaned against the canyon wall, his eyes closed, enjoying the morning sun's warmth.

Wilkie approached. "Are you sure you want to stay?"

As the sun reflected off Zach's face, he pursed his lips and nodded.

"Come with us," Liza said.

"No, thanks. I'll see you soon enough."

"We're not coming back for you," Jeff said.

Zach opened his eyes and turned toward Jeff. "Oh, I'll be here when you come back."

"You know you're crazy, Sideshow," Jeff said. "You can't know what's down the canyon."

Zach waved goodbye. "Adios, amigos."

∞

Liza, Wilkie, and Jeff followed a brooklet of reddish melt that meandered down the narrow canyon. They navigated around snowy patches, thorny vegetation, and the occasional boulder that dislodged from the cliff tops.

The journey felt endless. It seemed they kept passing the same rocks, rabbitbrush, and tamarisk over and over.

The group finally reached the top of a slight rise on the canyon floor. Ahead, a hard-right turn. A slit between the canyon wall gave a glimpse of a dirt road leading to a highway. Their hearts faltered as they reached the opening. A two-thousand-foot cliff lay between them and civilization.

Zach had forewarned. "You'll need climbing gear."

Before leaving, Jeff had relentlessly mocked Zach about ingesting peyote and suffering from altitude sickness and dehydration. Jeff dreaded the thought of Zach saying, *I told you so.*

∞

Unspecified Slot Canyon
Book Cliffs
Emery County, Utah
Day 2

Discouragement lingered with each step of the return journey. Wilkie dipped a finger in a clear trickle of water coming from the diminutive slot canyon jutting from the main canyon. He put his finger in his mouth. "It's probably from a spring."

A thin laminate of ice lined the edges of the boot-width flow as Liza stepped straightaway into the narrow red sandstone passage. She held both walls for balance and disappeared. Jeff and Wilkie entered the opening sideways for their shoulders to fit, crab-walked with backs to the wall, and made pantomime-like hand gestures on the other. The dimly lit, narrow cavity twisted and curved before opening to twenty-odd-feet-wide with the mid-day sun directly overhead.

"Someone lost their pants!" Liza shouted, and kept moving.

Wilkie stopped to examine the weathered denim. It lay near a small fissure at the nexus of the sandstone wall and sandy floor. With fresh adult and juvenile bear tracks littering the area, he initially thought the opening might be a den. He examined the telltale flash flood watermark stains on the canyon walls. Some marks were higher than he could reach, and the lowest was only a foot above the canyon floor. He determined this den wasn't a suitable habitat for bears or humans.

"Hey, you guys. Look what I found." She held a nylon pack in each hand.

When they arrived, she handed a hydration pack to Jeff and the day pack to Wilkie. He unzipped the largest compartment and dumped the contents on the ground; a pair of wool socks, moleskin, an aluminum cup, and a travel-size first-aid kit. Wilkie unzipped a small pocket and discovered a bundle of paracord. Another pocket contained a survivalist knife. He removed the ten-inch blade from its leather sheath, which revealed a double-edged blade on the bottom and a serrated saw on top. Wilkie unscrewed the compass cap from the hollow handle; a small whetstone, waterproof matches, and a wire saw inside.

∞

A head-tall wall of boulders blocked the path. A fountain discharged from the elbow where boulders and the canyon wall met. Water collected into a sandstone basin carved by millennia of erosion.

"Give me that cup," Liza said.

Wilkie retrieved the cup from the day pack and handed it to her.

She quickly drew the cup into the basin and its contents quicker down her gullet. She refilled the cup again. Wilkie refused Liza's offer to allow Jeff to go first. After Jeff drank, the basin needed a minute to refill before Wilkie could quench his thirst.

Liza emptied the hydration pack's stale contents on the sand and refilled the bladder with the cup.

Jeff gave Wilkie a boost to the top of the boulders. He traversed the narrowing path, hoping that civilization lay ahead. It didn't take long for Wilkie to return.

"Any luck?" Jeff asked.

"It's a dead end. It's time to go back," Wilkie said, leaping from the edge. He landed on the balls of his feet and grunted as the momentum sent him to all fours. His impact was cushioned by deep sand.

"Are you okay?" Liza asked.

Wilkie nodded.

She hefted the hydration pack and left the boys behind. They watched Liza walk with a delicate sashay.

"Nice butt, don't you think?" Jeff whispered.

"I think her face is much nicer," Wilkie said.

"I'm glad to know you're still attracted to girls, but just remember that one's mine. Stay away from her."

Wilkie's face contorted. "You don't need to worry. She isn't my type."

"I saw you looking at her. Don't you think she's attractive?"

"What's going on?"

"We don't want another Kaitlyn Morris situation," Jeff said.

Wilkie scowled. "*Why* would you bring that up? That was all on you." *I could never do that to a friend,* Wilkie felt tempted to say. He would not let Jeff pick a fight today.

After walking a while in silence, Wilkie bent over to tie a shoe. He noticed a straight, weathered stick laying near a canyon wall. He bent down, wrapped his fingers around one end of a straight staff, and lifted it upright. With one end in the sand, the other reached Wilkie's nose.

A rock pile on the other sandstone wall caught his attention. "What the heck?"

He was uncertain if his eyes were playing tricks on an oddly familiar object wedged inside. Wilkie removed rocks and matted grasses from the pile. "Holy crap! It's a freaking skull!"

Jeff leaned over. "You aren't kidding. I wonder who it belongs to."

"Could be the owner of the packs or some Native American remains," Wilkie said. "When we get back to civilization, we'll notify the police."

The skull made Jeff think about teen horror films. Young people stranded in the desert discovering human remains. Zach would be the first to die. In scary movies, the minority male always dies first. Jeff would be next — being the heroine's boyfriend. Wilkie would sacrifice his life and save his best friend's girl. She'd be the lone survivor. Ultimately, Liza would defeat or escape the monster alone. The character missing from this movie would be Liza's sorority sister — a self-absorbed, bleach-blond bimbo with big fake boobs and a father richer than God. Her name would be Muffy, Ashley, Buffy, or some name ending with Y.

The boys turned a corner and froze, seeing Liza kneeling with her hand extended. "Come here, cutie. I won't hurt you," she said.

Wilkie and Jeff observed a potential real-life horror movie scene as Liza coaxed an animated ball of fur.

Jeff stayed put as Wilkie moved judiciously between Liza and a two-to-three-month-old black bear cub.

"Liza, stand up and back away slowly," Wilkie said.

"He can't find his mama and his twin," Liza said.

"It's his momma I'm worried about."

"The little guy's hungry."

Wilkie used the staff to keep some distance between the cub as they backed up. The creature sniffed, growled, pawed, and bit at the stick. Encouraged by the game, he followed them.

∞

Around a bend, they sat with their backs against the canyon wall. From time to time, Wilkie peeked around the corner to watch for mama bear's return.

Liza stretched out her hand. "Come here, little one. Come here."

"Careful, it's still a wild animal," Jeff said.

"I know what he's feeling. He's unsure, but he wants to

trust me. With his mom gone, he needs physical contact. He's just a baby, for goodness' sake."

"Just don't think about taking him home." Jeff snorted.

The cub sniffed a couple times, then licked Liza's hand. She scratched his chin and worked toward its cheek. The cub pressed against Liza's palm. The cub eventually crawled on Liza's lap and fell fast asleep. She leaned back against the canyon wall and stroked his fur.

Wilkie and Jeff, the veteran outdoorsmen, still couldn't believe what they were witnessing.

"I think I'll call him *Jacob*," Liza said.

"Why Jacob?" Wilkie asked.

"After the character from Twilight," Liza said.

"How can you like that crap?" Jeff asked. "Those were the stupidest movies ever made."

"Have you read the books?" Liza asked.

"No, but I've heard the endless yapping from my mom and her book club—and tons of girls from school." Jeff paused. "Did you know Wilkie has read all the books? He's a Twilight expert."

Liza grinned. "Wilkie? Really? Isn't he the rugged, outdoorsy type?"

"Under that rough exterior lurks a soft feminine side." Jeff laughed.

"In my defense, I read them to my mom and sister," Wilkie said.

"Uh huh, tough guy. Admit it. You're a closeted Twihard," Liza said with a grin.

"It kept mom distracted during her chemo," Wilkie said. "She was too sick to read."

"Sorry, I didn't know," Liza said. "Did she have cancer? Was that too insensitive?"

"It's cool, and yes. She's passed a couple years,"

Liza gave a knowing nod. "I know what it's like to lose a mom."

"I'm sorry about *your* mom," Wilkie said. "What happened?"

"Well, she didn't die. She abandoned us when I was eleven. We haven't heard from her since."

Wilkie's heart broke for Liza. The agony he felt when cancer took his mother, who did all in her power to stay with her family, was still unbearable at times. He couldn't imagine the pain of having your mother choosing to leave you. He continued. "So, now, back to my original question. Why Jacob?"

"They're both orphans. He's a black bear, and Jacob's last name's Black. Both are cute, warm, cuddly, and a little wild."

"So, how do you know *this* Jacob's an orphan?" Wilkie asked.

"His mother's dying. I can't explain how I know. I just know it."

Jeff snickered.

"What's so funny?" Liza asked.

"The stupid things you say."

Liza groaned and glared at Jeff. "So, I guess I'm stupid."

"I didn't mean it. I..." Jeff said.

"Just shut up. Haven't you said enough already? You're such a jerk." Liza closed her eyes and held the sleeping cub closer.

"I'm sorry. I didn't..."

Liza extended an open palm toward Jeff's face.

What a bitch! Jeff raised a middle finger toward the *talk-to-the-hand* sign. He was relieved Liza's eyes stayed closed as he retracted the bird as fast as he presented it.

Except for the trickling spring water and whistling snot from the sleeping cub's nose, the canyon remained unusually quiet. Yet Jeff could feel Liza's scorn from a mile away. It didn't take long for Jeff to sulk away—before doing or saying something else he'd later regret.

Liza felt the ugliness in Jeff's heart. She nearly succumbed to his advances at Blue Lake.

She had tried to get a read on Jeff ever since. Unlike Wilkie and Zach, her new abilities only revealed hate, lust, and resentment in Jeff. Certainly not love.

She felt gratitude for dodging a bullet at Blue Lake. Jeff claimed to be a college student. His dark facial stubble made the claim seem legitimate. However, after spending time with the boys, she realized Jeff had a couple of years left in high school. Liza hated liars who risked her personal freedom. Even if Jeff had been of the age of consent, this user certainly wasn't a keeper.

∞

Wilkie found the absence of birds unsettling. Yet, the quiet gave him the ability to question the possibility of lost time.

The natural evidence didn't lie. The sun's later setting and more northerly position. Black bear cubs born in late December or early January don't toddle out of the den until two or three months old. He couldn't tell anyone. Because losing two months with no recollection is crazy. Liza and Zach's claims seemed crazy, too.

Yet Wilkie had witnessed Zach's dead end canyon prophecy fulfilled. Liza knew they weren't alone in the cave last night.

Wilkie spoke in an unfamiliar tongue. Still haunted by the native boy's reply. *"Be quiet, evil spirit!"*

Wilkie kept an open mind about Liza and Zach's claims. He wouldn't ignore their warnings but wouldn't take what they said on blind faith, either. He hoped for definitive evidence that Liza's mama bear prophecy was true.

∞

Wilkie lashed the survivalist knife to an end of the staff and led the way back into the main canyon. He followed bear tracks about fifty yards and stopped at blood droplets in the snow. "Something's wounded."

"What is it?" Jeff asked.

"I hope it's not the sow," Wilkie said. "Nothing more dangerous than a mama bear protecting its cub—except for a wounded mama bear protecting its cub.

A few hundred yards further, he halted at a bloody platter-sized dent in a snow patch, speckled with black fur bits and pinkish offal scraps left on the Ursidae dinner table. Blood droplets revealed the diner fled up the canyon with the leftovers. Jacob jumped from Liza's arms and greedily sniffed around the crime scene.

∞

Wilkie continued tracking paw prints about a quarter mile to discover evidence of an epic battle. With a finger to the lips, he waved the others back. He crept closer, finding the signs of a death stroke. A patch of snow corrupted by a wide bloody smear and stretched intestines led to a large black creature laying prone against the slot canyon's south wall.

Jacob leaped from Liza's arm and cut across unraveled intestines to his mother's head, where she greeted him with a nuzzle. Jacob whined and grunted as he tried to root for a teat from under mama's tender underbelly. She moaned, but didn't budge.

Liza rushed past the boys. The sow roared, lifted its head, and teeth snapped at Liza's arrival.

"Be at peace. I won't harm Jacob or you," Liza said. The sow's head lowered. Liza kneeled beside and rubbed the top of the creature's head.

"It's alright. Everything's going to be alright." Liza embraced both mother and cub and whispered something in the sow's ear. She released her final breath. Liza sobbed and held the cub and its mom until regaining her composure.

"We need to be careful. The male took the other cub up the canyon," Liza said.

Wilkie's skepticism about Liza's abilities finally abated, having witnessed the fulfillment of *The Dead Mama Bear Prophecy*.

∞

Wilkie deconstructed the makeshift spear. He fashioned a paracord harness for Jacob with a leash for Liza to hold him back. He wanted to build a harness for Liza and a leash for Jeff to hold her back from running on impulse to greet the male. Afterward, he used the whetstone to sharpen the blade.

"Take Jacob a bit that way." Wilkie pointed down the canyon. "You won't want to see what I'm going to do."

"Do what?" Liza said, and her eyes went wide. "Oh, shit! You're not! No, you can't!"

"We need sustenance to survive," Wilkie said. "It could be the difference between life and death."

"She's Jacob's mother and not an *it*. I won't eat her. We can go days without food."

"You don't have to eat any," Jeff said. "When you're hungry enough, you'll change your mind."

"Go to hell!" Liza stormed away with Jacob.

PART 3-DISCOVERY TRAIL

"If you do not expect the unexpected, you will not find it,
for it is not to be reached by search or trail."
-Heraclitus

Near Unspecified Cave
Book Cliffs
Emery County, Utah
Day 2

Zach awoke from a dream of being mounted on a spit, roasting over a fire. Wilkie hand-cranked one end of the rotisserie with Jeff on the other. Zach felt awkward only having grape leaves covering his genitals and butt crack. His bare flesh was becoming richly brown as Joy Wirthland hand-basted him with melted butter. He suddenly went tense, fearful Joy might discover his hard-on under the grape leaf.

Someone yelled. "He's done!"

He saw red plastic sticks released from pop-up turkey timers covering his chest. Jeff ripped off an arm at the shoulder and bit a sizable chunk of biceps. A simultaneous pain woke Zach. He vigorously rubbed where an ember penetrated a shirt sleeve.

Zach kept his front warm by facing the fire. He was ready to turn over, thaw his frozen posterior, and go back to sleep.

Zach had earned an extended nap for his labors. He had only a few juniper berries for sustenance and limited the amount of snow for hydration while avoiding hypothermia, but not enough for replenishment.

He'd tried to convince the others of the two-day trek back to civilization. Instead, they wasted a day ignoring Zach's advice. With the others gone on a wild goose chase, he figured he could do something useful. He could do things for their survival.

∞

Zach hiked over a mile before exiting the main slot canyon. He reached a crossroads at the base of the foothills. In his mind's eye, a deer trail led to salvation. The potential of a meal, a hot shower, and a warm bed were tempting, but personal desires were to be sacrificed for the needs of his friends.

As fast as the elevation changed, the vegetation grew in both frequency and size, from small to large desert shrubs and scrub trees.

Zach reached a hilltop, and his knees buckled. His natural eyes confirmed his mission in the dell below. Although he'd visualized what to expect, he still shuddered at the damage in front of him. A half-acre of lifeless Pinion Pine and Rocky Mountain Juniper toppled in one direction. In the middle, a bus-wide earthen scar was void of rocks and vegetation.

He hiked down to the destruction's edge. A thin layer of brown coniferous needles varnished the ground. The ground lacked grasses and new growth trees, exactly as envisioned back at camp. Yet, he still doubted.

Zach traversed the fallen trees to reach another hillside for further verification. On arrival, he shuddered at the Fremont petroglyphs that surrounded this cave, too. "I was right!"

He envisioned miles of interconnected tunnels and caverns, and now had a theory about how they ended up in the Book Cliffs. Finding the fallen timber and other cave entrance was proof enough.

In his mind's eye, he saw how the subterranean system could get them home. However, he expected to have a total claustrophobic meltdown long before completing the spelunking expedition back to civilization. His chest tightened with the sense that real dangers lurked inside, and he left the cave to start his actual mission.

∞

Zach grabbed the trunk of a felled tree with both hands and dragged the skeletal evergreen up a modest gradient. He circumvented patches of ice, boulders, shrubs, and trees. Near the halfway mark, his eyes caught a mass of brown fur and antlers atop a snow drift less than thirty feet off the trail.

A gnawing hunger compelled him to drop the tree and investigate. He salivated at the thought of devouring semi-fresh carrion directly from the carcass.

Reaching the four-point Mule Deer, Zach scanned the body. There were no obvious bullet or arrow wounds, nor flesh torn by fangs, claw, or beak. His stomach wrenched at the sight of teeth and jawbone exposed. The skin peeled away from mouth to neckline with surgical precision and charred around the edges. An empty eye socket and an ear cut away. Peering into its gaping mouth, he nearly vomited again at the missing tongue and esophagus. He grabbed the fore and hind legs to turn the beast on its back. Two precision-cut, golf ball-diameter holes in the chest and two in the abdomen were absent of blood.

"*Holy crap!*" Zach exclaimed. "*They took its freaking balls?*"

He flipped the buck over. The eye, ear, and lips were removed on that side, too. Zach examined the rear end with the anus and large intestine cored out of the beast. "They took its butthole! That's just wrong."

Zach stepped back to reevaluate the scene. He observed many animal carcasses up close with the unmistakable, putrid stench that only a vulture would find appetizing. Having been on the Wilkerson's annual elk hunt, Zack knew the blood and bowels from a freshly killed rudiment caused serious olfactory distress.

But not with this buck. The beast and surrounding snow were bloodless. The mutilations must have taken place somewhere else, with only Zach's tracks in the snow. Maybe the body dropped from the air to this remote location.

Zach's heart pounded, and his palms sweated as thoughts rushed through his mind:

Who would do this?

Who'd poach a buck, take its nuts, and leave its antlers?

Satanists in helicopters?

A serial deer killer in a Cessna?

Nazi veterinarians conducting illegal experiments from a Zeppelin?

He wanted to run back to camp, but there was a mission to complete.

∞

Zach crested the incline and hiked across the plateau. He stopped to make a confirming glance over the sandstone cliff, then rolled the tree off the edge. He made nine more round trips and rolled nine more trees over the cliff.

He avoided glancing at the buck with each lap, since the marred carcass was permanently burned into his memory. He'd have nightmares for months. Mainly, he couldn't stop obsessing about the current location of the killer. He needed to finish the mission and get back to camp before the *Deerinator in a Dirigible* returned to relish its kill.

∞

Book Cliffs
Emery County, Utah
Day 2

Liza returned to camp, thrilled for a waiting campfire. A pile of skeletal evergreens against the canyon wall reminded her of the post-yule bonfires on Golden Gate National Recreation Area's Ocean Beach and made her homesick.

Zach stirred and spied Liza sitting on the other side of the fire. He stood and jumped back in a single motion. "What the heck are you doing with a bear?"

Liza petted Jacob on her lap.

"He won't hurt you. While he's sleeping." She laughed.

Zach took another step back.

"I'm just kidding." Liza rubbed the cub's head. "He's just a baby. See, he won't hurt you."

He judiciously stepped toward the fire.

Liza held up the water pack. "Want some water?"

Zach walked around the fire and examined the beast. "He's really cute. I guess he can't hurt us, but what about his mother?"

Liza's head shook. "She's dead."

Zach put the water pack hose to his mouth and took a couple sips. He didn't want to consume more than his share.

"Drink all you want. We can get more," Liza said.

Zach greedily drank; more of an energy drink and soda guy; plain water never tasted so good.

Wilkie and Jeff arrived, their shoulders laden with a pole carrying a black, furry knapsack.

"What the heck's that?" Zach said.

"It's dinner," Wilkie said.

"That isn't an answer," Zach said.

"It's a man-eating bear. Tastes just like chicken," Jeff said.

Zach shifted to the opposite side of the fire. His mind shut down at the word *BEAR*. Until now, he convinced himself that bears were still in hibernation.

Wilkie shaved a thin piece from the makeshift spit and let the meat fall on the knife. He laid it in front of Liza. Her head shook vehemently.

He offered the morsel to Zach. "No thanks. I'm not eating any bear."

"Me either. I'll stick to tamarisk tea, thank you," Liza said.

"We're burning off calories exponentially," Wilkie said. "Tea won't cut it."

"I'll just have to survive off my fat stores," Liza said. "Humans can survive two to three weeks without food."

"If you stay in bed maybe, but with physical exertion in freezing temperatures only a few days," Wilkie said, "It will take two, maybe three, days to hike out of here. We need to keep our energy levels up. You can't wait until you're too exhausted or hypothermic to refuel out here."

"I don't care. Jeff says it tastes nasty," Liza said.

"A little salt's all it needs," Jeff said. "Wash it down with tea, and you hardly notice it."

"I'll take my chances," Liza said.

"She gave her life to save her other cub and failed," Jeff said. "Now she can save our lives. If we don't make it, your little buddy dies, too. Think about that?"

"We don't have any milk for Jacob," Liza said.

"The quicker we return to civilization, the quicker the critter can get some milk," Jeff said. "Who's going to carry Jacob when he gets too weak? It won't be me. You better keep your strength up. You'll be hiking for two."

∞

Despite the odor, resting on a bed of bear fur was damn comfortable for Jeff. A full belly and plenty of fluids didn't hurt, either. Although Jeff had initially loathed Jacob for taking Liza's affection away, he didn't turn away the cub's shared body heat for the night. Since Liza wouldn't join them, the bear cub would make do. Jeff longed to sleep on the bearskin more than he wanted Liza's affection, anyway.

Wilkie first offered Liza the bearskin bedroll. Jeff didn't hesitate for her to reject the offer twice or for Zach to make dibs. He didn't want to appear unchivalrous. Down deep, Jeff felt every man (and woman) for himself. Wilkie dressed the carcass, so he had every right to keep the skin for his bedroll. Jeff chalked up Wilkie's generosity as foolishness.

∞

Jeff woke to a pre-dawn sky as Wilkie tended strips of jerky on sticks dangling over the fire.

"Ready to hit the trail?" Jeff asked.

"Just about," Wilkie said. "You want some tea?"

Jeff nodded.

Wilkie pulled a sock over his hand to retrieve the metal cup from the fire.

Jeff grabbed it with a sleeve and took a sip. "Who thought tamarisk could be this good."

"As we climb in elevation, we should find more to eat," Wilkie said. "Hopefully, some wild onion or juniper berries to cover the bear fat."

"Wakey-wakey sleepy heads," Jeff said. "Let's go home."

∞

THE FOLLOWING MORNING

Unspecified Trail
Book Cliffs
Carbon County, Utah
Day 3

Liza couldn't believe she hadn't craved a cigarette since arriving at the Book Cliffs — or how much her stamina had dropped since yesterday. Her father called her, *living perpetual motion.* She disproved Dad's theory as her strength faded while trekking a day's worth of uneven ground since sunrise.

She watched Zach with amazement as he showed no signs of slowing throughout the day. They both ate the same spring grasses and juniper berries along the way. While Liza felt listless, he seemed to be rejuvenated with every morsel.

Liza wanted to stop and curl into a ball, but her desire to reach civilization for Jacob made her continue. As the day progressed, the cub walked less and slept more in Liza's arms. To distract from an aching back and arms, she made a counting game by putting one foot forward at a time, set a goal of a thousand steps, and reset the count once reaching the target. She'd lost track of the number of resets. With every new round, the effectiveness of the game diminished.

She was ready to stop for the night when Wilkie spoke. "Do you hear that?"

Jeff stopped in his tracks. "Hear what?"

"A stream. That's a good sign," Wilkie said.

Zach smirked. "Tell me something I don't know. It's the way we need to travel."

"Let's get going. It's all downhill from here," Wilkie said.

"We should make camp," Zach said.

"Let's keep going, Sideshow. We don't need your bogus psychic compass anymore," Jeff said.

"My correct internal GPS tells me we need to cross the stream soon. It's late in the day. We don't want to be soaked when the temperature drops."

The stream was farther away than expected. Descending a hill, they finally found the torrent of melting mountain snow-pack arriving from miles away.

"It's our guide to salvation," Zach said. "We must cross downstream about a hundred feet and two more times before we reach the valley."

They reached a copse of Gambel Oak, backing a derelict stone campfire ring.

Wilkie turned to the others. "Seems as good a place as any."

∞

Zach returned to camp with hands full of kindling. He smiled at the fresh-cut pinion pine boughs to sleep on tonight, and Liza and Jacob asleep on the remnant of the cub's mother. Zach snorted at how pissed DeBoer would be returning to find his bearskin bedroll taken. Zach might scream if DeBoer bragged once more about how comfortably he slept on the bearskin.

For Jeff DeBoer, the master of one-upmanship, the bearskin bedroll seemed less than an exclamation of personal enjoyment and more about rubbing their noses in bear fur. Zach withheld saying the pine bough mats smelled much better than rotten bear meat, but let it slide.

It drove Zach crazy that Wilkie seemed in denial about Jeff's superiority complex.

Why can't Wilkie see Jeff's a selfish jerk? He often thought.

Zach felt certain Jeff only hung out with Wilkie for status.

Others, great and small, seemed to gravitate toward Wilkie. He made them feel like the most important person in the world. The star wide receiver and junior class vice president practiced kindness and respect.

Jeff certainly didn't possess Wilkie's patience or altruism to be a special needs mentor at school.

When Alice Dautry, a classmate with Down's Syndrome, asked Wilkie to the Sadie Hawkins Dance, he said *yes* without hesitation.

Zach would always remember the beaming faces of Alice and Wilkie dressed as a cowgirl and cowboy, walking arm-in-arm into the school gymnasium. At the end of the date, he gave her a peck on the cheek. On Monday, Alice proudly let everyone know Wilkie had kissed her. He seemed to take the weak, lonely and shunned under his wing. He wasn't always that way.

Zach remembered when Wilkie was a bit of a hard-ass jock. He wasn't a bully, but held an air of superiority and was self-absorbed with a sense of invincibility and entitlement. His parents taught him to be honest and always courteous when dealing with others, but it didn't mean he had to acknowledge another's existence.

Since his mother's illness, Wilkie reevaluated his life priorities after watching her wither away from breast cancer.

For a time, Jeff and Wilkie outwardly seemed to be kindred spirits. The now enlightened Wilkie had moved on. Jeff just followed. Zach was unsure if Jeff even liked Wilkie.

Zach hid a smile as Jeffery J. DeBoer returned from gathering wood.

Jeff's face lacked emotion, but his gaze turned a cold, jet black at Liza and the cub asleep on the prized bearskin.

Zach grinned at Wilkie's triumphant return with an armload of wild spring greens and pockets full of pine nuts and juniper berries. After nibbling on young grasses all day, this was a glorious feast.

Jeff ate quickly and spooned with Jacob while Liza was away taking a wee. Zach felt confident that DeBoer feigned sleep when Liza returned.

∞

Jeff, Zach, and Liza cuddled at the campfire's edge. Unable to sleep, Wilkie stoked the flames through the night. With only jackets for warmth at a higher altitude, a robust fire would keep hypothermia at bay.

Wilkie sensed they were being watched. He was unsure if his subconscious picked up cues from below the conscious threshold or was an irrational fear brought on from being exposed out in the open, surrounded by shadow. Tending the fire calmed his anxiety. Besides, recurrent bouts of sharp abdominal pain didn't allow for much sleep.

A whisper came from the bearskin rug. "You can't sleep either? Gut ache?"

Wilkie nodded. "You?"

"Me, too. The trots, methinks," Jeff replied.

"Mama-Bear-Zuma's revenge."

Jeff snorted. "I can't sleep anymore. You want the bearskin?"

"Thanks, but only if you keep the fire going." Wilkie stared into the darkness. "I'm worried our food might attract unwanted guests."

"What are you thinking?"

"A cougar, maybe."

"A cougar wouldn't mess with us. Unless it's starving."

"That might be the case. Other than bears, have you noticed any other wildlife?"

"Come to think of it, I have seen no game at all."

"It's beyond strange," Wilkie said. "I've been to the Book Cliffs at least a dozen times, and it's always chucked full of wildlife. Tons of deer, pronghorn, elk, rabbits, birds, lizards, snakes. Some sections have herds of buffalo and wild horses. Don't you think it strange that our entire time here, have you seen any birds other than the vultures floating in the updrafts? It's as if the area's sterile of animal life."

Jeff nodded. "You may be right. Try to get some sleep. I'll keep the fire going."

Wilkie passed the survivalist knife to Jeff. "Goodnight."

∞

Campsite #2
Book Cliffs
Carbon County, Utah
Day 4

Zach repeatedly packed snow from the leeward base of trees and boulders into the aluminum cup. He eventually melted enough to top off the water pack. Afterward, he melted more for juniper berry tea and shared it with the others. Wilkie was savoring the last cup.

"We need to go soon," Zach said.

"Oh, crap. I need to go right *now*!" The sight of Jeff fleeing, waddling as an anal-retentive duck, made the rest of the crew snicker.

"Keep those cheeks tight, DeBoer," Zach yelled. "You don't want any spatter amongst your pitter-patter."

"Shut up, Sideshow!" Jeff replied.

The uproar drowned out Jeff's insult.

Away from the crew, Jeff found a secluded thicket of Mountain Mahogany at the base of a rocky cliff. With unbearable lower abdominal pain and pressure, he couldn't pull his jeans down fast enough.

Distant groans and the sound of flatulence made the crew back at the campsite laugh wholeheartedly.

"Be strong, Jeff. You can do it," Wilkie yelled.

"Shut up, Bruce. Go do something useful and find some toilet paper."

Jeff groaned with pain.

"Push harder, DeBoer. Give it all you got." Zach shouted.

An inhuman grunt muted their laughter, followed by a roar that reverberated from the hill above. Wilkie leaped over the fire to put some flames between him and a charging 300-pound cinnamon-colored bear. The boar's rapid descent left the crew too terrified to utter a sound.

Jacob ran toward Jeff.

The beast hesitated. As if debating whether to eat the juicy human main course or start with the cub appetizer first. He decided on the appetizer.

Wilkie's arms wrapped around Liza. For a split second, she hesitated. Feeling bare skin from a raised tee shirt, she dug fingernails into Wilkie's sides, placed a brutal knee to his crotch, and ran after Jacob.

Wilkie wanted to fall to the ground and writhe in the dirt, but picked up the chase with a Quasimodo-like stoop instead.

∞

Squatting with pants around his ankles, it surprised Jeff to see Jacob racing toward him. The cub positioned itself between him and the cliff face. Moments earlier, he heard a commotion from camp. A roar. Unintelligible screams. He finally understood as, less than sixty feet away, a black bear emerged from the trees on a direct course to them. Forgetting the task at hand, Jeff turned to run but fell hard as bunched-up boxer briefs and jeans constrained his ankles.

It was too early for Jeff to die in this real-life horror movie — vulnerable, thrashing on the ground with his bare butt in the air. Sideshow should be the first to die. Jeff would be second. It would kill Wilkie last. The stupid little bear and the hot little redhead would survive.

Jeff struggled to get up while simultaneously hefting pants. He recognized that something about this situation was all wrong. His fear dissipated, replaced with a psychotic rage. This freaking bear didn't have the right to kill him. Saturated with contempt, Jeff let loose a primal scream.

∞

Liza sprinted as thoughts flashed through her mind. *I hope Jacob climbed a tree. I'll throw rocks at it. Get it to chase me.*

She heard a blood-curdling scream, and the ground shook as she exited the grove of trees. Zach and Wilkie came up alongside as a waterfall of rocks and debris flew off the escarpment. The rumbling, seismic violence made them shudder as a dust cloud hid the impact zone from their eyes.

The trio's anxiety was boundless with visions of the possible aftermath of destruction and praying it did not bury Jeff and Jacob.

The crew cautiously entered the dust cloud. They halted, mortified by snapping teeth and ferocious roars. The beast tried in vain to crawl away as Zach ran in the opposite direction.

"Zach, wait!" Wilkie said. "It can't hurt us. Its hindquarters are under a boulder."

Zach returned. "How big a boulder?"

"At least seven hundred, maybe over a thousand pounds. I'm surprised it's still alive. It's not going anywhere. I doubt it will live much longer."

"Damn straight, it won't live any longer," a voice echoed from inside the dust cloud.

Jeff appeared covered in gray dust and hauling a basketball-size stone. He reached the growling head and raised the rock overhead with both hands. The beast roared, claws stretched in vain, and teeth snapped.

"Jeff, don't!" Liza pleaded. "I can help him transition peacefully."

Jeff screamed as he swung the stone downward with a single, vicious motion. The crunch of rock on bone made the others cringe. Jeff beamed.

The beast moaned once and collapsed. Its eyes glazed over, tongue dangled out of its mouth, and it breathed in rapid, shallow grunts. The bear's body convulsed for a moment, then released its final breath.

"Why did you do that?" Liza screamed.

"I was putting the poor creature out of its misery!" Jeff yelled.

"Bullshit! I can feel your hate."

"A bear about kills you. Let's see you all pumped up with adrenaline and shit and not bash its fucking head in."

Liza almost spoke again when a fur ball camouflaged in dust came running straight toward her.

"Jacob! I'm so glad you're okay." She lifted the cub into an embrace.

"She cares more about that damn bear than she does about me," Jeff muttered.

PART4-WHERE HAVE YOU BEEN LATELY?

"It has been said that civilization is twenty-four hours and two meals away from barbarism."
-Neil Gaiman

Mile Marker 200
U.S. Route 6
Carbon County, Utah
Day 4

Standing on the shoulder of a high desert highway, Idha Gupta felt disheartened that their holiday was nearly over. The American Southwest was so vast and open compared to her homeland. India's cities brimmed with people, and Maharashtra's mangroves and jungles stalked by criminals and man-eating tigers. After excursions to the Grand Canyon and Moab, she regretted spending an extra day in Las Vegas playing keno and slots instead of experiencing more natural wonders.

The vistas from atop mile-high Dead Horse Point this morning were incredible. Walking along the mesa's ridge, the red rock canyon scenery expanded and changed with every step. At the visitor's center, Idha felt great sorrow upon hearing the legend of the abandoned horses desperate from thirst, who plummeted to their deaths, trying to reach the Colorado River's water below.

As her husband kneeled to place the jack under the late model Toyota Camry, Idha gazed at the striated two-thousand vertical feet of Cretaceous sandstone that gave the Book Cliffs its name.

"Mohindar, those cliffs are like something from a John Ford movie," she said. "You can imagine a thousand natives standing on the top with bows and arrows."

"Yes, my dear."

Idha passed the time watching the brown and white spotted cattle grazing across the sparse prairie. Bits of brown grasses and puny brush didn't seem capable of providing a proper meal for such noble creatures—especially the nursing calves. Yet, the cattle grazed without want.

At first, she was unsure if her eyes were playing tricks. She'd seen Hollywood versions of mirages and hoped the four people bounding down the rangeland would fade away. With a kilometer of desert grasses and cacti between them, she prayed the wanderers would change direction before being impeded by the barbed wire fence ten meters from the road.

Unsure what it meant to have strangers appear at a stranded vehicle in America, she could only reference the same situation back home. Being stranded on a Maharashtra highway in the middle of nowhere was an open invitation to highwaymen for robbery, assault, and possibly murder—or, in her case, something much worse.

Idha turned to her husband as he removed the ruptured tire off the rear axle and rolled it toward the trunk. "Mohindar! They're getting closer."

He gazed upon the travelers. "Don't worry, my dear. There won't be any hooligans or bandits out here in the middle of nowhere. They're students on holiday."

Idha's brow furrowed. She didn't trust his local knowledge, even if he lived in America while working on his doctorate at

Stanford and returned twice a year on business.

Mohindar grinned at his wife's clenched fists and jaw, and arms crossed. "Please, my dear, trust me. America's big cities have some dangerous bits, but not out in the middle of Utah. They're just young people enjoying nature."

"I hope you are correct, Mohindar. I don't want to die in America."

∞

"Mohindar. Mohindar. They're almost here," Idha murmured frantically.

Mohindar tightened the last lug nut and stood upright. He faced the newcomers as Idha slid between him and the car.

Three young men and a young woman holding a bear cub stood at the base of the road berm.

"Nameste. Namaskar," Wilkie said.

"Nameste. Namaskra," Mohindar replied.

"Auprabhaat sar. Ham kho gee hain," Wilkie said. "Kya ham krpaya aapaka mobail phon udhaar le sakate hain?"

Idha was so nervous that she didn't notice that the blond American hooligan spoke in her native tongue.

"Were you born in Mumbai? You speak Hindi with a Maharashtra accent," Mohindar said.

"No, I was born in South Carolina," Wilkie said, and mumbled, "I don't speak Hindu."

A tan four-by-four pulled off the highway and stopped directly behind the rental car, deflecting Mohindar's attention.

Idha questioned the vehicle's timely appearance. Maybe the driver and the so-called ramblers were in cahoots. She flinched as red and blue lights pulsed from the four-by-four's grill and released a nervous laugh. If the four youths had ill intent, this police officer would scare them off.

"Look, Idha. No worries," Mohindar murmured. "John Wayne and the U.S. Cavalry have come to the rescue."

A lanky officer dressed in a tan uniform and olive slacks stepped from the truck. The badge patch on the breast pocket and holstered sidearm made Idha feel much safer.

Mohindar could not decode the patch on the officer's baseball cap. *DNR.*

Wilkie instantly recognized the emblem on the truck's door, *Utah Division of Natural Resources.* He side-glanced at Liza, holding Jacob. "Oh, crap."

"You folks need some help?" the officer asked.

"Thank you, officer. Only a flat tire. It's nearly fixed," Mohindar said. "However, these young people may need your help."

The officer did a double take and glared at Liza. "What the hell? Don't you know it's illegal to possess a black bear cub?"

"His mother's dead," Liza said. "He would have died without our help."

"Why can't you city slickers just leave wild things damn well alone?" the officer said.

"We have to help him," she said. "He's been unconscious for about an hour and hasn't eaten for a couple days."

"Quick, put it in the truck. We need to get it to the wildlife rehab center in Green River right away."

Liza moved deliberately toward the truck. The boys followed.

"Whoa, wait a minute, fellas. I only have room for the cub."

"I'm going with him," Liza said.

"Fine. What about your friends?"

"We can give the boys a ride to town, officer," Mohindar said.

"That would be greatly appreciated. Thank you," the officer said.

"Where is the nearest town on our way to Salt Lake City?"

he asked.

"Price, a few miles up the road, would be your best bet."

The officer reached into a shirt pocket. "Before I let you go, I need your full names, home addresses, and telephone numbers. I may have some questions for you boys later."

The officer hopped in the driver's seat and looked both ways. He made a U-turn on Highway 6 toward Green River and scanned his memory on the short drive.

"Ms. O'Reilly, you and your friends seem really familiar. Do I know you from somewhere?"

∞

Gulf Service Station
Price, Utah
Day 4

Zach patronized a convenience store restroom for only the sixth or seventh time in his life today. He only used public toilets in dire situations — and this was indeed an emergency. In his mind, hands permeated with wilderness grime were slightly more dangerous than public restroom germs left behind by strangers. Zach vigorously lathered and rinsed thrice. He used a blower to dry his hands and strategically placed a paper towel on the door handle before exiting.

Scarcely out the door, Zach faced tube-shaped convenience store victuals under glass. He ogled the fare with an uncharacteristic, mouth-watering lust for processed meat and cornmeal rolling on hot steel. Lasciviously, it turned.

Uncle George's slaughterhouse stories left an indelible impression on Zach. The occasional worker's finger or hand caught in the meat grinder — unable to retrieve the ground appendage before being mixed with the other meat. Uncle George had proof that USDA regulations allowed for traces of rat, feces, and cockroach in cold cuts and wieners.

Zach felt certain foodborne illness, possibly death, awaited those who consumed baloney and bratwurst. Yet, here he was with a strong desire to consume processed meat delights that had been rolling all day — and likely laced with finger, cockroach, rat, and poo.

After three days of sparse pickings as a non-hunting hunter-gatherer, convenience store staples were nearly as desirable as Zach's favorite meal, *surf-n-turf*. Since ribeye and lobster tail weren't on the menu, he'd have to make do.

There were several choices available from the roller-grill, but he decided on the triple crown of rolling carnal delights: a *corn dog*, *taquito*, and a *shriveled jumbo hot dog*. Zach selected the least dark of the latter. He figured after surviving the last couple of days on wild plants and grasses, an overcooked wiener wouldn't kill him. Enough ketchup and Pepsi could wash any nastiness away.

Near the cash register, Zach scanned the cell phone accessory display. Something gave him pause. *When did they release the iPhone 6S?* He grabbed an iPhone 5C charger, opened the package, and plugged in the connector to make sure it fit.

Wilkie's and Jeff's debit cards declined. Zach checked his wallet for cash — thrilled to have enough to avoid being forced to decide between his three-course meal or calling home — and still able to spot Wilkie and Jeff a few bucks, too. Zach approached Wilkie and Jeff, already chowing down at a booth. Wilkie's choice in condiment made Zach want to sit elsewhere, but the only electrical outlet was at that table.

"Ranch dressing on egg rolls? Gross," Zach said. "I don't understand how you can put that crap on everything."

"You don't know what you're missing," Wilkie said. "It's nectar for the gods."

"For Hades, maybe. That stuff's nasty."

Zach slid into the booth, had Wilkie plug the phone

charger in the outlet, and wolfed down a ketchup-drenched hot dog while waiting for a bit of charge.

"I see your ketchup addiction isn't getting any better," Wilkie said.

"Ketchup is so much more normal than ranch dressing."

"At least I don't ruin good steaks with ketchup. To each his own, I guess."

"Let's see if this bad boy starts," Zach said. He held the button and hit speed dial. It rang three times before going to voicemail.

"Hi, Mom, it's Zach. We're in Price. Call me right back. I love you. Talk to you soon."

Jeff reached for the phone. "Let me call my mom," he said as flecks of bean burrito spewed before swallowing.

Zach pulled it away. "I'm calling the house phone first. Mom doesn't answer her cell at home."

He dialed the number from memory and, shortly thereafter, had a puzzled look on his face.

"I must have dialed the wrong number," he said and selected the correct number from the phone's address book.

"That's weird. The message says the phone is no longer in service. Maybe mom didn't pay the bill."

"It's my turn," Jeff said.

Jeff dialed and hit send. He also had a puzzled look and dialed again. "That's too weird. My home phone is disconnected, too."

"Call your mom's cell phone," Wilkie said.

"Honestly, I don't know. I just hit the redial on my phone."

Zach's phone rang. The caller ID showed *ICE-Mom*. "Hi, Mom. Yeah, it's me. What's wrong? Why are you crying?"

∞

Wilkie's patience wore thin. Mrs. Davidson's crying dominated the call. Zach could only say, *I'm sorry. Mom, don't cry. Everything will be alright.*

Wilkie knew his dad would be equally worried and needed to let him know they were okay. He remembered spotting a mythical payphone out front.

We're at the Gulf convenience store in Price, Wilkie heard as he exited the door.

Being a huge fan of 1970s muscle cars, he gave only a passing glance at a mint-condition 1972 Corvette Stingray parked out front. He dialed zero on the payphone and waited for an operator.

∞

"Collect call from Bruce Wilkerson Jr. for Bruce Wilkerson Sr," the operator said. "Do you accept the charges?"

"Wilkie?"

"Dad."

"Do you accept the charges?"

"What a bunch of malarkey," Dad said. "This is a lollygagger. My son wouldn't engage in such foolishness. I won't accept the charges."

Wilkie hung up the phone in disbelief.

Dad, the retired US Army Special Forces Operator, had used the keywords: *lollygagger, malarkey.* He believed the phone line wasn't secure.

Wilkie always thought Dad was a bit paranoid for implementing family code words for calls home when deployed overseas. The idea of using this scheme at home made little sense. Yet, Dad's message was obvious. It wasn't safe to talk on the phone. Someone might be listening. *But why would that matter?*

Some leaflets taped on the side of the payphone carrel caught Wilkie's attention. He pulled one free and purposely headed to the nearby Carbon County Sun Advocate vending rack. He scanned the newspaper's front page and shuddered with recognition.

Zach and Jeff, both unusually pallid, exited the convenience store and sprinted to Wilkie.

"Holy crap, Wilkie!" Zach said. "My mom said we've been missing for two years."

"I know." He handed Jeff the fliers. "Look at these missing kids. It's us."

∞

Stigler Wildlife Rehabilitation Center
Emery County, Utah
Monday, April 13, 2015

Seated in the veterinary office waiting room, Liza clenched her waist from a sudden wave of nausea. The boys were in trouble. She didn't know why. She just knew. On the waiting room LCD TV, the Salt Lake City NBC affiliate's news broadcast opened with a graphic with today's date. Liza's mind muddled — unsure if she had read the date correctly.

No way it's 2015? Liza thought.

Officer Wells returned from outside with a folder and handed a bulletin to Liza. "I knew your names were familiar."

Liza scanned the flier's details.

Missing: Bruce 'Wilkie' Wilkerson, Liza O'Reilly, Jeff DeBoer, Zach Davidson.

Possible interstate abduction.

Fifty-thousand-dollar reward.

Immediately contact the FBI, local police, or call 911.

She handed the papers back to Wells. Her brain became overloaded.

"We need to notify your parents," Wells said. "Where've you and your friends been?"

The ranger's words didn't register as a red banner graphic flashed across the television, drawing Liza's attention: *Breaking News!*

"We have breaking news from Price," the co-anchor said. "Eyewitnesses told NewsFirst of an unusual incident that looked like a scene from an Arnold Schwarzenegger movie."

Liza's stomach lurched. "Oh, *shit*!"

∞

Gulf Service Station
Price, Utah
Monday, April 13, 2015

Zach, Wilkie, and Jeff paced in front of the convenience store.

"This doesn't make sense." Zach stared trance-like at the sidewalk, muttering to himself. "This is too freaking weird. Too freaking weird. Too freaking weird."

"How the hell did we lose two years?" Jeff asked.

"Too freaking weird. Too freaking weird."

"I'm clueless. I got nothing," Wilkie said.

"Too freaking weird. Too freaking weird." Zach's mutterings stopped as a queasiness overcame him. He stood still and closed his eyes.

Wilkie noticed a missing wingman and turned back toward him. "You, okay?"

Zach shook his head. "Something's wrong."

"What?"

Zach's pulse thumped in his ears. "I'm not sure, but it's bad."

Jeff sneered. "You've lost it, Sideshow Bob."

The blurry vision of a danger flying from the south became clearer in Zach's mind. "We need to leave right *now!*"

"Hold your horses," Jeff said. "Your mom said she'd be here in ninety minutes."

Wilkie and Jeff's jaws dropped as Zach took off, sprinted past the gas pumps, turned left, and continued down the shoulder of the road.

They turned toward a muted thumping noise. Their mouths were agape as an unmarked charcoal-colored helicopter descended parallel and across the street from Zach.

Wilkie stared at a sniper prone in the open gunner door and screamed, "Zach! Drop for cover!"

Wilkie cringed at the telltale signs of rifle recoil and wafting smoke.

Zach reached behind with one hand, touching the entry point, but kept running. A few steps later, he staggered and dropped to his hands and knees. He wobbled side-to-side before tipping over on the road, motionless.

"No!" Wilkie shouted.

Jeff shook with rage. "You bastards! I'll kill you!"

"Ouch! What the heck?" Wilkie said. He found a red dart sticking in his shoulder, pulled it out, and plopped down on the concrete. He turned toward Jeff and mumbled, "r-u-, r-u-, r-u-u-u-n," before toppling to his side.

Jeff looked toward the projectile's origin. Preoccupied by the first helicopter, he missed two new ones hovering across the highway — a sniper prone in each.

With Wilkie and Zach down, Jeff was determined not to let the bastards get him. He beheld a stronghold and sprinted. A classic red Corvette would be one classy dart shield. The moment before he dove behind the Vette, he felt a prick in his neck.

∞

Stigler Wildlife Rehabilitation Center
Emery County, Utah
Monday, April 13, 2015

"Ms. O'Reilly, where have you been?" Wells asked.

Liza pointed at the television. "Hold on. This has something to do with the boys."

"*Exit two-forty on highway six is closed and cordoned off for a two-mile radius. Because of the possibility of more explosive devices, authorities have cleared the area."*

Wells turned up the volume.

"We have what seems to be a military-type operation here in Price. Eyewitnesses describe a scene from a Hollywood action movie. A sniper from a helicopter taking down a suspected terrorist. Another helicopter being hit by a projectile, crashing and exploding in a fireball as it hit the ground. The authorities aren't allowing us near the crash site or providing any details. However, we have video shot by bystanders. We need to remind viewers this video is extremely graphic and may not be suitable for all viewers."

A shaky video showed three charcoal helicopters flying in the Echelon Formation tracing the highway. One separated from the others and descended, barely clearing high-tension power lines. The camera tracked the lone craft without insignia or markings flying parallel to the street. It descended until it cruised about thirty feet above the asphalt.

From the way this craft maneuvered, Wells was certain it wasn't a law enforcement pilot. These craft had similar dimensions to an MH-60M Black Hawk but with the angular composite panels of a stealth jet. Black Hawk meets B-1 bomber. As a reserve member of the 3rd Ranger Battalion, Wells heard whispers among special forces operators about a Stealth Hawk but never saw one before.

His patriot blood boiled. A black op on American soil. *Posse Comitatus be damned,* he thought.

The amateur videographer's smartphone followed the decelerating craft until capturing a young man with curly red hair running on the opposite side of the road.

"It's Zach!" Liza said.

Wells recognized the white puff of smokeless gunpowder wafting from the mystery craft.

Liza cried out. "No. Please, God. No."

"Holy (bleep) (bleep). They (bleep) shot the (bleep) dude!" the amateur cameraman screamed.

After the boy lay still on the ground, the craft started its descent.

Off-screen, violent metal-crashing-into-metal entered the audio as the cameraman pivoted toward the sound. The camera caught another helicopter, dark gray with a large red blotch embedded into one side of the craft. Its rotors trailed upward, and flames licked skyward as the aircraft plummeted.

"Holy (bleep) (bleep)!"

Following the impact with the ground, the camera shook as a fireball engulfed the craft. The camera immediately changed direction. The video bounced rapidly, capturing bits of retail buildings, blue jeans, pavement, and fast-moving tennis shoes — assumed to be running away from the craft. *"Holy (bleep) (bleep)! The (bleep) (bleep) helicopter blew up!"*

"Kent and Julie, the authorities have asked us to discontinue our remote broadcast for a briefing," Kjar said. *"Back to you."*

"Thank you, Marty Kjar, reporting live from Price," co-anchor Kent said. *"Do we have the second video ready?"*

"Yes, we have video footage submitted by another eyewitness," co-anchor Julie said. *"Again, this footage may not be suitable for some viewers."*

Liza and Wells locked eyes on the screen.

Recording from the side of the Gulf convenience store, an employee, during a cigarette break, captured video of two helicopters hovering over the other side of the street. Another gas station, a big box store, and a strip mall in the background.

Originating from the store's parking lot, a large red object came into view, hurdling over the fuel island canopy toward the craft. The woman's iPhone remained steady when the object collided with a helicopter. The camera wobbled from the crash landing's fireball but stayed on target.

"Wow, what a surreal scene from Price. This footage seems unbelievable," co-anchor Julie said.

"It certainly looks to me that an older model Corvette collided with the helicopter. If this video proves genuine, someone must have built one gigantic trebuchet," Kent said.

"We have word from Price that authorities are about to start a live briefing," Julie said. *"Back to Marty Kjar, live from Price."*

∞

"My friends aren't terrorists!" Liza said. "They barely had the clothes on their backs, let alone explosives for a car bomb."

"I believe you, Ms. O'Reilly," Wells said.

"We need to tell them."

"Tell who?"

"The ATF. They're mistaken."

"That's not the ATF. It was military. I believe you're in grave danger if you go near them. They'll be looking for you."

Liza's face twisted.

"I know people that can protect you, Ms. O'Reilly, but we need to get you to them ASAP."

"What about my friends? We need to help them."

"Let me worry about them. Let's get you to safety first."

"What about my dad? He needs to know I'm alright."

"I'll make sure he knows," Wells said. "Trust me."

Liza had observed that platitudes of confidence often preceded disingenuous people's actions. *Trust me,* or *believe me,* was often a big red flag. However, something about Wells effused trust. His anger was equal to hers—but he was still holding something back.

"I've got good news," the veterinarian said as he entered the waiting room. "After a couple I.V.s, little Jacob is going to be fine. You saved his life."

PART 5-NIGHTMARES END?

"Never attempt to win by force what can be won by deception."
- Niccolò Machiavelli

Utah State Hospital
Unspecified Date

From his bed, Wilkie looked past the stainless-steel toilet and washbasin mounted on the opposite wall, preoccupied with thoughts of home. He'd prefer to daydream through a window or, even better, a few minutes outside for a little fresh air and sunshine. One of many carrots dangled just out of reach by Dr. Jones.

Wilkie dreaded his daily therapy sessions. He thought, *What a waste of time. Same crap, different day.* He grimaced at the doctor's arrival in his obligatory white lab coat with two orderlies in white scrubs that entered through the clear acrylic door of his cell (as the staff called the accommodations).

"Hello, Wilkie," Jones said.

Wilkie nodded.

Two nurse's aides set up folding chairs for Jones and Wilkie, then stood in the corners. Their hands set near their holstered TASERs.

"Where are the books you promised?" Wilkie asked.

"When you remember what happened at Blue Lake, you

can have all the books you desire," Jones said.

"More lies, I see. When can I see my family?"

"Answer my questions, and I'll see what I can do."

Wilkie's lips crinkled as if he had eaten something vile.

"Why do you think you're at the State Hospital?" Jones asked.

"A helicopter brought me against my will, but you already know that, Doctor Jones."

"What I know is that you arrived at the State Hospital in a sheriff's van. I know nothing about any helicopters."

"So, if I'm under arrest, when do I get my phone call and get to speak with my lawyer."

"We've been over this before. You need to be isolated to recover your memories. Do you know why you are here?"

"You claim by court order. Something about an incident at Blue Lake."

"So, tell me, what happened at Blue Lake?"

Wilkie groaned. "We were there to scuba dive. We fished the night before."

"Did you go scuba diving? Tell me about going scuba diving."

"As I've told you a dozen times before, we never dived. I don't see the need to discuss this anymore."

"Yes, you've told me that's what you believe happened. However, that's not what others with intimate knowledge of the situation have reported."

"I stand by my story."

"Let me review what you told me from prior sessions." Jones glanced at his notes. "You were fishing with your friends, Zach Davidson and Jeff DeBoer, at Blue Lake. You later met a young woman named Liza O'Reilly. She went skinny dipping with Jeff. You don't remember leaving the lake, but the next morning, you woke up in a cave with your friends hundreds of miles away. You encountered bears. One tried to attack Jeff. Liza brought an orphaned bear cub with you. You returned to civilization and learned two years had passed, only to be abducted by commandos in helicopters. Next thing you remember is waking up at the State Hospital."

"That's generally accurate."

"Okay, Wilkie, put yourself in my shoes. You're a therapist. Your patient tells you about a two-year lapse of time with no recollection. He also claims to wake up in a cave on the other side of the state also with no recollection of how he got there. This person also claimed to be abducted by men in helicopters. How would that story sound to you?"

"Crazy, I know, but I'm not crazy."

"Sometimes, the human mind can create elaborate constructs to avoid facing painful truths. To avoid the shame and guilt of facing something horrific."

"I know what I experienced." Wilkie leaned in, looking intently at Jones. "Please stop trying to get me to admit to things that didn't happen."

"I need you to remember what happened at Blue Lake. Something terrible happened that night, and your story doesn't match what others, including the police, say happened."

Jones nodded. The larger orderly approached Wilkie with a TASER. The other with a syringe.

"Not again," Wilkie murmured.

The smaller orderly reached him. "We can do this a hard way — or the easy way."

Wilkie held out his arm. He didn't like the hard way. Although the manufacturer claims a TASER is harmless, it didn't feel harmless.

The smaller orderly sterilized the injection site and administered the clear liquid in the crook of his arm.

He felt a burning sensation flow up his arm. When it

reached his shoulder, everything went blurry.

"Take him to treatment room two," Jones said.

∞

THE FOLLOWING DAY

Utah State Hospital

Wilkie spent much of each day in exercise and meditation. With every push-up, he'd review the truths as he understood. Missing for two years. Abducted by the government. Placed in solitary confinement without a window or recreation and visitation privileges.

With every squat-thrust, he'd review the conversations with the liar Jones. With every crunch, he tried to remember what happened during the drug-induced haze of treatments. The terror of being restrained. Confusion of the strobe lights. Whispers from the shadows. Screams from the adjacent rooms. The lingering mind fog.

Qigong meditations not only cleared Wilkie's mind, but gave him hope.

Master Ng taught the posture and breathing techniques used during meditation would improve Wilkie's Qi—and over time, it proved correct.

Today, Wilkie's life force, or Qi, flowed unrestricted, and for the first time, he savored the bland cafeteria-style lunch. A dry tuna salad sandwich, plain potato chips, and green gelatin. Even the orange juice from a foil-sealed plastic cup tasted like freshly squeezed. He looked forward to meeting with Dr. Jones for a change.

∞

Jones and the orderlies entered the cell.

Wilkie remained seated cross-legged on the cold floor, eyes closed, focused on breathing. He inhaled through the nose, visualized the air flow entering his sinuses, curled downward along the spine and into the stomach before circling up the chest to be exhaled through the mouth.

"Good afternoon, Wilkie," Jones said. "You seem relaxed."

Wilkie remained still. "I'm quite at peace."

Jones sat and extended a hand toward the other chair. "Please take a seat."

Wilkie opened his eyes and rose from the floor. He reached into the chair, folded it shut, and flipped it over. With the legs in his hands, he made a professional wrestler-like move by hammering the chair's backrest into the head of the linebacker-sized orderly. The orderly slumped next to the bed, motionless.

Wilkie shifted left as electrode darts hit the wall. He grabbed the TASER's wires and yanked firmly, causing the normal-sized orderly to teeter a bit. He lunged and administered a jab to the larynx with the free hand. The man gasped, grabbed his throat, and dropped to the floor.

Wilkie threw Jones onto the bed, retrieved a TASER, and lifted Jones by the scruff of the neck. They exited the cell and secured the door with the orderlies inside.

Wilkie felt absolute freedom. Until this moment, he only left his cell sedated for treatment and returned in a semi-conscious state. His daily schedule was determined by others. Told when to eat. When to sleep. His intelligence was insulted by Jones' incessant questions about false memories. The staff may have attempted to control everything, but Wilkie never let them have his heart and soul. The resistance had started. Now, he had the power.

They moved down the hall and passed other cells, each with a single occupant.

"You can't escape. They won't allow you to leave," Jones said.

"I don't care about escaping. Where are my friends?"

"You can't see them."

"Stop lying! You're taking me to them."

"That's impossible."

"Bullcrap!"

"They're dead."

Wilkie slammed Jones into a wall. "Liar! They're here! I've heard them!"

"You're making a mistake, Wilkie. You really don't want to hurt anyone else."

Jones winced as his arm was twisted nearly to a shoulder blade.

"I can do you real harm," Wilkie said. "You'll cooperate if you want to get through this without any broken bones."

"I believe you, Wilkie. Hurting me like you did to Zach and Jeff will not do either of us any good?"

Wilkie paused at Smith's new ploy. "I never hurt my friends."

"Fine, but those men you attacked need medical attention. Please let me get help."

At a secure door, Wilkie scanned Jones' badge. They scarcely entered the hallway when the alarm's red lights flashed, and *ANG... ANG... ANG* of sirens started its repetitive cycle.

Wilkie still felt free. He was in charge. They couldn't stop him from his objective.

An assault team entered another door down the hallway. Wilkie hugged the wall and used Jones as a shield.

As the commandos neared, Wilkie held the weapon to Jones' temple. "Stand back! A TASER to the head can kill."

Wilkie didn't know if his claim was valid, but thought it was worth a try.

"Don't hurt him. That's an order," Jones said.

"We have our own orders, sir."

Wilkie inched down the hall with his back to the wall. He

had to look into the cells. The assault team followed in lockstep.

Wilkie moved with purpose toward the clear Lexan wall panels. He missed the electrode barbs being deployed as he took a glance toward a cell but didn't miss the jolt of high-voltage electricity.

He had never expected that they'd tase Jones. The voltage flowed through Jones into him. Wilkie's muscles contracted the same and didn't allow him to let go. His finger involuntarily pulled the trigger and released his TASER's metal barbs into Jones' side. With the pain and muscle contractions intensified by two TASERS, Wilkie hardly noticed the prick from a tranquilizer dart. As Wilkie slumped to the floor toward unconsciousness, he caught a blurred glimpse of the familiar outline of a scrawny kid with red curly hair in the next cell.

∞

TWO NIGHTS LATER

Utah State Hospital
Unspecified Date

Wilkie lay in a cold sweat. The dream started innocuously enough. He walked down the hospital hallway made of burnished metallic blocks with Roman archway ceilings alongside Jones with two orderlies in tow. He'd never walked the state hospital's square concrete halls sealed with a white high-gloss paint unaccompanied.

"You are a natural born leader," Jones said. "With our training, you're destined to rule the world."

Wilkie jumped to a darkened room, naked, alone, lying on an examination table hewed from purple stone. A subtle blue light surrounded the immediate area. A rhythmic pulse filled the room, and clicks emanated from the shadows. It reminded Wilkie of katydids trying to attract a mate. He sensed the clicks were communications.

Metal straps restrained his wrists and ankles, and rounded metal bars held his chest and thighs. His head turned left to right. Light surrounded each table, contrasting the perfect darkness in between. To his right, Jeff DeBoer and strangers were in the same predicament. On his left, Liza O'Reilly and two others. The enormous feet and red hair of Zach Davidson revealed him in the farthest corner.

His head tilted back, allowing for a glimpse of others on exam tables behind. He looked past his feet to find others. He tried but failed to scream as he discovered two robotic arms working metallic instruments through an incision in Wilkie's navel. It looked as if the robot surgeon was using shiny metal chopsticks to root out a piece of chicken hidden under vegetables — or maybe an appendix. With minimal pain, Wilkie relaxed and watched with fascination.

∞

Wilkie awoke. *That was one heck of a weird dream.*

It must have been the chicken chow mein from last night's dinner that made him capable of ruling the world. Dream Jones had such high hopes for his future. Prostate on the bed, Wilkie had nowhere to go but to wait for Jones.

Since his attempted escape, four new orderlies armed with Thomas A. Smith Electric Rifles, commonly known as TASER, arrived daily to fit his straightjacket. Two orderlies would return with plastic lawn chairs that replaced the metal folding ones. Another placed a small resin table between the chairs.

Jones entered with a thick manila folder and sat. "Would you like to take a seat today, Wilkie?"

"No, thank you. I feel like taking my punishment lying down."

"Showing humor. That's good. Did you have nightmares again last night?"

"How would you know?"

"The orderlies said that you tossed and turned in your sleep."

"You already have the answer, so why ask?"

"I'm afraid we must take a different path with your treatment. A more direct, less gentle path. I've been trying to allow your psyche to heal and give you time to recover your memories."

"You mean for the last two years?"

"It's been a little over two months since you were at Blue Lake. This two-year time-lapse that you claim never occurred."

Wilkie glared at Jones. "It occurred alright."

Jones sighed. "Wilkie, neither you nor I question you assaulted the two orderlies . Is that correct?"

"Sure. You're correct on that point."

"What I've kept from you are the consequences of your actions. Mr. Gunderson, the one you hit in the head with a chair, passed away that night. The other orderly, McNamara, is on a ventilator. He's expected to survive, but the extent of his brain damage is still unknown. Even with the emergency tracheotomy performed by our staff, the doctors still give him little chance of making a full recovery."

The color drained from Wilkie's face. "No, it can't be. I didn't hit them that hard."

Wilkie envisioned the unconscious Gunderson with a clear fluid draining from the ears, an outward sign of a fractured skull. The punch to the other could have crushed the larynx — but unlikely to have done such.

"You saw the condition they were in after you assaulted them." Jones said. "They didn't receive immediate medical attention because of your premeditated acts."

"I'm going to puke," Wilkie said.

The two orderlies hoisted the straight-jacketed Wilkie

off the bed and over the stainless-steel sink just in time to retch. When the dry heaves stopped, an orderly wiped Wilkie's mouth and gave a sip of water before placing him on a chair in front of Jones.

Tears streamed down Wilkie's face. "I'm sorry. I'm sorry. I didn't mean to kill him."

"I believe you, Wilkie. Yet, you've proven that you can administer excessive violence," Jones said. "What happened at Blue Lake?"

"I don't remember."

"What happened to Zach and Jeff?" Jones asked.

"I don't know. I don't know."

Seeing his bowels in a stranglehold of agony, Jones waited. "What did you do to them?"

"I don't know. I don't remember."

"What did you do to your friends?"

"I don't know. Why don't you tell me?"

"Good. Good. Now we're making progress."

Jones laid an open file folder on the table.

∞

30+ YEARS EARLIER

Mongkok District
Kowloon, Hong Kong
1984

Ng Wai Keung's three older brothers were Fei Jai, or Flyboys — low-level thugs for the largest Hong Kong-based triad. Weeks before his birth, Ng's father abandoned the family, leaving his mother to raise four boys alone in Mongkok — the most densely populated slum on the planet. Ng seemed destined to follow in his brothers' footsteps until a plea from a concerned auntie to an enigmatic Kung Fu teacher rescued Ng from the corrupting streets of Mongkok.

The Fei Jai spoke Master Lam's name with soft, reverential tones. Similar to the Cosa Nostra, considering the clergy a protected class, the Sun Yee On and other triads gave Master Lam's students a *hands-off* status.

Lam expected nothing less than total commitment from his disciples. They would live at home and not a monastic life. Yet, Lam's training would be equally rigorous to that of any Shaolin monk. Follow your master's teachings with discipline and integrity, and one day, the disciple will not become a master of Kung Fu — moreover, the master of his own heart and mind.

∞

After Ng became a Kung Fu master, he immigrated to America and founded the *Abundance Kung Fu, Meditation & Acupuncture Center.*

Translated as hard work, Kung Fu was so much more than fighting skills. Ng expected his students to do well at school, serve the community, and commit to a discipleship that placed art, meditation, morals, poetry, learning, and philosophy as important as any physical ability.

Even though Master Ng lowered his standards slightly for Americans, he only admitted half of the applicants. Twenty-five percent left the program after a month or two. Half again quit within six months.

A practitioner of Wing Chun, an external or physical style of Kung Fu, Master Ng also gave near equal weight to the spiritual elements and mental mastery of the Wudang internal style — focusing on strengthening the mind first, and the body will follow.

Master Ng's students had committed to daily physical disconnection through Tai Chi and meditation and a scholarly commitment to learn and live by the time-tested ancient philosophies to make one not only a better martial artist but, more importantly, a better person.

∞

TWO WEEKS LATER

Utah State Hospital
Unspecified Date

Wilkie focused on breathing while he sat cross-legged on a concrete floor with perfect posture and arms crossed. He tipped over numerous times before obtaining lotus-position while wearing a straightjacket.

Seven years of training with Master Ng had Chang Tzu quotes burned into his memory. *Breathing control gives man strength, vitality, inspiration, and magical powers.*

Meditation normally created an unencumbered space for clarity, but Wilkie's tortured mind couldn't shake Jones' words.

"If conditions are right, there is still a primitive man inside all of us. We are all capable of horrific, sometimes senseless violence."

A Confucian teaching came to Wilkie's mind:

Fish is what I want, bear's palm is also what I want. If I cannot have both, I would rather take bear's palm than fish. Life is what I want; being honorable is also what I want. If I cannot have both, I would rather take an honorable death than life. On the one hand, though life is what I want, there is something I want more than life. That is why I do not cling to life at all cost. On the other hand, though death is what I loathe, there is something I loathe more than death.

Confucius taught it was better to die with honor than live without. Wilkie's religious tradition taught suicide was a mortal sin next to murder in gravity. One didn't have the right to take a life — your own or others. He knew suicide for a Confucian or a Latter-Day Saint, in this case, wasn't honorable. Yet, murder also flew in the face of those values.

Unbearable images replaced Wilkie's false memories. He struggled to believe he had pummeled Zach into a bloody pulp or stabbed Jeff thirty-seven times. Yet, the crime scene photos didn't lie. The bloody carnage on the dive dock. Their mutilated bodies were placed in body bags. His two best friend's gray, lifeless corpses lay on morgue slabs. He killed another man for just doing his job. Another might have permanent brain damage.

Jones' attempt to bring comfort failed. "You experienced a psychotic episode. You were not to blame."

Wilkie recollected nothing about the events at Blue Lake, but the evidence presented was clear. He was a murderer and needed to pay for his sins and end his pain.

Still, in modified-lotus posture, Wilkie worked on a plan. His head was still vulnerable. He envisioned raising from meditation and toppling headfirst on the rim of the stainless-steel commode. If still conscious, he could repeat the process or shift to jumping noggin-first into the concrete walls. Hopefully, this would be enough. If it didn't work, he'd enact a second phase in the hospital infirmary.

He focused on breathing and reviewed the plan repeatedly until he was ready to act.

A voice entered Wilkie's mind. *Suicide isn't the answer. Understanding is.*

He pushed the crazy voice aside, focused on breathing, and reviewed the plan.

Be not afraid. Open your eyes.

Wilkie's eyes opened, but was unsure if he was dreaming or having a psychotic episode.

Hovering above the floor was a well-built man dressed in a flowing white robe with sleeves to wrists and hem to ankles. His wavy platinum mane was almost as impressive as his piercing sapphire eyes.

Wilkie felt much like Ebenezer Scrooge in *A Christmas*

Carol, being visited by the tortured spirit of his dead business partner. Instead of being seated on a four-poster bed surrounded by bed curtains and dressed in a Georgian-era nightgown and cap, he sat on a cold, polished concrete floor, dressed in prison issue tighty-whities and a straightjacket.

Make haste. Touch my robe. They're coming, entered Wilkie's mind.

Assuming it was a dream, Wilkie reached out with a toe.

Scarcely touching the robe, Wilkie found himself also dressed in a white robe, standing between rows of long wooden tables in a rustic, great hall where grand feasts took place. He scanned the artistically carved polished tree trunk columns supporting rough-hewn timber roof beams and beds covered in animal skins lining the walls. There was a stone fire pit in the center of the lodge with a steady fire.

An iron kettle hung over the flames. A sweet, savory aroma wafted through the room.

"What smells so delicious?" Wilkie asked.

"Lapskause," the man said. "Caribou and lingonberry stew. Would you care for some?"

"Yes, please. You don't know how bad hospital food can be."

The man's hand extended toward a wooden table and two stools. Scarcely seated, a maiden came from nowhere with hand-carved wooden bowls filled with lapskause.

Wilkie dug in as if he hadn't eaten for days. "This is amazing."

"I'm glad you like it. We may speak freely now."

"Who are you? The Ghost of Christmas Past?" Wilkie took another bite.

The man chuckled. "I am Arild of the Chájehit, a multidimensional being of light."

You may be an undigested bit of beef, a blot of mustard, a crumb of cheese, a fragment of an underdone potato, Wilkie thought.

After a hearty Ghost-of-Christmas-Present-like laugh, Arild said, "I'm not the spirit of Jacob Marley. However, I am a messenger sent to warn you."

"Warn me of what? That I'm going insane? To confirm that I hallucinate about visits from angels?"

"You're not mad! As Ebenezer Scrooge, you're tormented—not by avarice and indifference—but bound by the chains of ignorance and self-doubt. You're caught between rival conspiracies. A multitude of human and alien tormentors vying for your enlistment."

"*Aliens*, huh?" Wilkie snickered. "Who are these *alien* conspirators?"

"Your world knows nothing of their existence. Soon, you will be among a select few to learn the names of the different alien-human factions and their competing agendas."

"Why are you helping me? How do I know you aren't manipulating me?"

Arild leaned forward with his arms on the table and locked eyes on Wilkie.

"My people are moderators—referees in an intergalactic competition. Our defining principles restrict how and when we might intervene in the competition, but you are a unique case that gives us some latitude.

"We'll reveal things to you as unbiasedly as possible and point you in the right direction so you can figure out most on your own.

"What we are offering today is to unlock a natural gift to aid your quest for truth. The gift of memory."

Arild sat up. "Your current tormentors, the Dumal, and their human cohorts, the Thule Society, have attempted to conceal your memories, but no more. If you choose to have your memories restored, be careful to whom you share them—and only during a proper place and time. If you choose to remember, you must follow this command with exactness: *never let your tormentors know you remember.*"

"Why?"

"Your tormentors may be hidden from the world, yet are powerful. They have infiltrated all areas of your society. If you become a threat to their aims, they will harm you and your loved ones to keep their agendas secret."

"How?"

"Some will discredit you—make you irrelevant. Your proclamations about spacemen will become the rantings of a lunatic. It's not beyond your tormentors to use extortion, blackmail, or threats against your family. If that doesn't work, they will imprison you or make you disappear."

Wilkie gulped. "As in, kill me?"

Arild nodded. "You could end up at the bottom of the Marianas Trench—and others will consume you."

Wilkie's eyes opened wide. "As in, eat me?"

Arild smirked. "With your memories intact, you will learn the true intentions of your tormentors."

"For what purpose, may I ask?"

"One day, you will proclaim their sins to the world. Not today, but many years in the future. Your proclamations of their treachery will allow the people of Earth to choose."

"Choose what?"

"Choose their own destiny—but first, you will need to make two choices."

"What choices?"

"First, you must choose to remember."

"Why wouldn't I want to remember?"

"Because memories are often bitter—and it will be difficult for you not to proclaim your tormentor's sinful existence from the rooftops."

Initially, the concept of regaining lost memories appealed to Wilkie, but he hesitated. He had too many painful memories: mom withering away, suffering, gone — and the knowledge that he murdered his two best friends.

Arild continued. "Second, eventually, you will have to choose a side."

"Which side should I choose?"

"You must first understand their many individual designs before you can make an informed choice. We hope you choose not to bind your heart to any of them at this time. However, you have your agency. You are free to choose. We hope you choose to do the right thing."

"Why are you doing this?"

"I cannot say more than you are a descendant of my people, the Chájehit. One of my brothers lived among your people and fell in love with a mortal woman. Your great-great-grandmother was the result, giving us the right to intercede on your behalf. Your tormentors must never know that you are Chájehit. You must go back soon. Do you want to remember?"

Wilkie nodded. "I do."

"Close your eyes and repeat after me. Volo recordabor."

"Volo recordabor," Wilkie said and opened his eyes

Still in lotus position on the cell floor, Wilkie immediately questioned his sanity. It didn't take long to realize his hands were resting on his lap, and his straight jacket lay neatly folded on the floor next to him.

∞

FOUR WEEKS LATER

Utah State Hospital
Unspecified Date

Wilkie's criminal defense attorney had never been late — until now. Shackled to the tabletop with nowhere to go, he struggled to keep his eyes open. Barely laying his head on the table, fatigue overcame him, and rapid eye movements sent him back to Blue Lake.

He sat on the dive dock with Zach. They tried to ignore the splashing and giggling outside their peripheral vision.

"We should call the cops," Zach said.

"Why?" Wilkie asked.

"DeBoer's molesting a ten-year-old. Possibly, a boy."

"Really? That's the best you got? Why don't you try killing Jeff with kindness for a change? You'll make him seem petty if you quit reacting to him."

"I've tried. I think he hates me. He tolerates me at best."

"He's just teasing you," Wilkie said. "If he pushes your buttons and you don't react, he'll stop."

"Back on topic. As scouts, we have a civic duty to report crime. We still don't know her age—and you said she's built like a boy. I think we should call the cops." Zach chortled. "I'm serious."

Wilkie grinned while shaking his head. "Go ahead if you must. It could be the other way around. Liza might be twenty-four, and DeBoer's only sixteen, so it's statutory rape on her part. Most likely, it's just two horny teenagers, so you'll piss off the cops for making them drive all the way out here—and give you a ticket for wasting their time."

Zach looked across the lake. "What in the heck's that?"

"Where?"

Zach pointed. "Those three lights coming toward us."

Wilkie closely tracked the objects' flight pattern. "Probably some F16s from Hill Airforce Base.

The illuminated craft came to a stop at the edge of the bombing range—hovering less than a quarter mile from the dive dock. Without a word, Zach and Wilkie stood up to watch.

"Mother puss bucket!" Zach said. "Is that what I think it is?"

"If you're thinking what I'm thinking," Wilkie said.

The three objects wove in a silent, fluid motion. A sight more mesmerizing than a campfire. The dive dock rocked in unison with the slosh of someone coming out of the water — but didn't divert their attention.

"Huh, hum," Liza said.

"Shh!"

Liza passed in front of Wilke and Zach. Being too short to block their view, she failed to move their eyes off the horizon. She turned toward the waltz of light with the same fascination as the boys.

"Zach, throw me my towel," Jeff said.

"Shh," came in unison from the dock.

"What the heck? Throw me my damn towel, Sideshow!"

The towel shot over Jeff's head into the water. He couldn't believe the little douche could be so insolent. "You fuckin' clown! I should kick your scrawny black ass."

He crawled onto the dive dock and stood. The sight of the three cigar-shaped objects immersed in a vanilla glow made him quickly forget about punching Zach.

"What is that?" Jeff asked.

"UFOs, dumbass," Zach said.

The objects continued to weave for a few more minutes and vanished. Only moments later, a pair of low-flying F22s streaked past the area where the craft had hovered.

∞

The boys left Liza at the lake and traversed the dusty road back to camp with Zach's flashlight leading the way.

"Were the UFOs putting on a show for us?" Jeff asked.

"Yeah, *Mystery UFO Theater 3000*." Wilkie laughed.

"That's stupid. It makes no sense," Jeff said.

Zach laughed. "I get it. That's funny, Wilkie. No one at camp is going to believe us. What are we going to tell them?"

Jeff glared at Zach. "Who cares? We know what we saw."

"We tell the truth," Wilkie answered. "Like Jeff said, *we know what we saw.*"

"I guess we can finally answer the question," Zach said.

"What question?" Wilkie asked.

"Are we alone in the universe?"

At that moment, an overhead blue beam engulfed them. An intense electric hum. Ionized air crackled. They floated in the luminescence full of warmth and peace and desire and submission.

∞

The trio awoke surrounded by towering nude beings with silvery, smooth skin and spindly, long limbs. No visible genitalia, a slit for a mouth, and holes for ears. Dark blue bubble eyes seemed filled with contempt. The tallest creature distinguished by a charcoal-colored, four-point natal star over his left eye.

Jeff and Zach only heard clicks emitted from the creatures.

Wilkie heard the largest alien say, "Put them with the female."

Boney fingers wrapped around Zach's arms and dragged him through the archway.

"Ouch, that hurts!" Zach said.

"Silence, human trash!" Wilkie heard the escort bark as they dragged Zack out of the room.

"Why are you doing this to us?" Wilkie asked.

"Because we can," the leader said.

While being dragged toward the hall, Wilkie said, "Just because you can doesn't mean you should."

"Bring that one back," the leader called.

They made Wilkie kneel before the leader.

"You understand our language. We may have a special

use for you, Wilkie."

Wilkie wondered how the alien knew his name.

∞

"Come, walk with me," the leader said.

Wilkie walked alongside the creature down a long hall. The two guards followed behind to protect their charge. Yet far enough away to avoid eavesdropping. The hallway was composed of perfectly fit, silvery metallic blocks that formed an arched ceiling able to accommodate the tallest members of the crew.

"I am Admiral Cerculus. You are my guest on the vessel Ergonea, the flagship of the Dumal Federation fleet."

"I don't want to sound rude, but I don't feel like a guest."

"We mean you no harm. Our interactions with your species are as much for your benefit as ours."

"But why are you abducting humans? We aren't lab rats."

"Lab rats? I do not understand the meaning of this, *lab rats*?"

"Rodents used in laboratory experiments. So, why are you abducting humans? I assume it's for experimentation."

"My people are explorers. We have learned from millions of years of diaspora to avoid contacting the inhabitants of new planets until we fully understand the endemic species. To reveal ourselves too soon could have disastrous results. We need time to prepare."

"Disastrous? How?" Wilkie asked.

"Infectious diseases can decimate the host planet's population or devastate my people. Much of our research focuses on harmful pathogens and developing immunities. Your own Earth history has shown the introduction of new microbes by invaders can conquer nations better than any army."

"So, you plan to conquer Earth?" Wilkie asked.

"No, no, my dear boy." Cerculus put a hand on Wilkie's

shoulder. "We will wait and prepare, so we are welcomed as guests. Our experience has taught that the local governments must invite us, or there may be disastrous results for both our peoples."

Wilkie followed him through an archway into a cavernous, unfurnished room with dozens of Dumal spread throughout. He glanced around the room and audibly gasped at an infamous red symbol prominently displayed on the forward bulkhead.

"The red double Swastika has been the symbol of the Dumal for over three hundred million years," Cerculus said. "For less than twelve thousand years, multiple cultures from around Earth have adopted a single Swastika in various forms from the Dumal. Mostly positive in meaning. The Nazis gave the Swastika a bad name."

Wilkie's gaze tracked a couple petite gray aliens meandering the room with crude metallic platters held above their heads. The much taller Dumal crew grabbed the long, brown ribbons from the serving plates and devoured the jerky-like strips with a loud and messy slurp like a five-year-old child eating spaghetti.

He glanced overhead through a transparent dome and gasped again.

"Earth is beautiful. I never tire of this view," Cerculus said.

Wilkie just nodded—dumbfounded by the bright blue planet.

"You may be helpful in the preparation for the return of my people to our home world."

Wilkie snapped out of his trance. "*Your whaaaaat?*"

"Earth, or as my people call it, Oh, is the Dumal aboriginal home world," Cerculus said. "We've come to reclaim our birthright."

"If that's true, why did you leave in the first place? You're obviously far more technologically advanced than us."

"A ruthless and power-hungry race, the Chájehit and their proxies, the Mai, forced the Dumal to leave. They gave humans our place on Oh. The Dumal can only return to Oh on condition that Earth governments welcome our return to dwell on uninhabited lands. We have done much, and have much left to do to prepare your people."

"How long have you been preparing?" Wilkie asked.

"Tens of thousands of years," Cerculus said, "but we hope to approach your leaders within the next decade."

"So, why do you need me?"

"You have a gift few humans possess, the ability to understand our language."

Wilkie's eyebrows raised. After four years of junior high and high school Spanish, he still couldn't hold a meaningful conversation with a native speaker. He highly doubted he was conversing in an extraterrestrial language.

"The Ergonea has the unique ability to develop latent talents. Your coming aboard allowed the ship's cybernetic intelligence to unlock your natural xenoglossia or omnilingual ability."

"What language are we speaking now? Aren't we conversing in English?"

"No, our entire conversation has been in Dumal. We've been monitoring you and hoped that xenoglossia was part of your makeup. Your innate leadership qualities complement your gift. If you are willing, you may be helpful in preparing the human governments to welcome our return home to Oh."

"Why do you need to prepare? Why don't you just go introduce yourselves? *We come in peace* or something to that effect?"

"Humans have a tendency to be hostile toward newcomers," Cerculus said. "Your history with the Jewish people is a good example. Forced from their motherland to live among other peoples. Subject to persecution for being different. The solution to return the Jews to their homeland seemed simple enough and initially worked — but shortly after their return to Palestine, the land wasn't large enough for both Jew and Palestinian to co-exist. The modern blood feud between the sons of Abraham over birthright occurred because cultures and religions diverged. Can you imagine the outcome of a non-human species arriving on Oh to reclaim their home, and we didn't prepare the current population to accept our return?

"Internment camps, war, and genocide against those that are different have been commonplace throughout human history. Class, cultural, racial, and religious differences among humans will seem like minor issues compared to the perceived threat from technologically advanced, non-human newcomers from other planets. Yet, the Dumal are the true indigenous species of Oh — but we will be considered extraterrestrial by the different nations and numerous cultures of a non-unified Earth."

"How can I help?" Wilkie asked.

"You will need to return regularly to the Ergonea for training and testing. We will prepare you to be an influential leader and unifier of your people."

"When do we begin?"

"You've already begun," Cerculus said. "You need to go to our testing laboratory to see if we can help you unlock more of your natural abilities. Once this series of tests is complete, we will bury your short-term memory for your own protection. You'll return to Earth to resume your life as if we never met. We'll have you return from time to time for more training and testing."

"Why do I need protection?"

"Because our mutual enemies, the Chájehit and the Mai, must never know of your role in the Dumal's repatriation. One day, we will return your memories to understand our righteous cause."

Wilkie nodded. "I feel for your people. My forefathers endured persecution and were driven from their homes for being different."

"My comrades will escort you to the testing center. I look forward to meeting with you again, Wilkie."

The two gray escorts were about to grab Wilkie by the arms, but sensed Cerculus's disapproval.

"Come with us," one escort said.

Wilkie had scarcely left the room. "Comrades, my apologies for the stench. I hope it didn't ruin your appetite."

Cerculus entered a station at the far corner of the room. A fan of disinfecting light scoured him from top to bottom.

PART 6-WAKE UP MR. WILKERSON

"The Truth Shall Set You Free."
-John 8:32

Utah State Hospital
Unspecified Date

Two men wearing slim-fit black suits and matching skinny ties accenting their anemic complexions and dark, close-cropped hair entered the interrogation room.

The brawny, short one pounded a fist on the table. "Mr. Wilkerson, wake up."

The two sat opposite of Wilkie as he raised his head off the table. He yawned and had to lean forward to rub his eyes with shackled hands. "You aren't my attorney. Where's Mr. Black?"

Each man pulled an ID from inside their jackets.

The lithe, tall man spoke. "I'm Deputy Assistant Attorney General Smith with the U.S. Department of Justice. This is Major Jones from the Defense Intelligence Agency."

There are a lot of Joneses, Smiths, and Blacks around here, Wilkie thought while trying to contain a smile. "Mr. Black advised me not to talk to anyone without him present."

"Mr. Wilkerson, we're here to make a deal," Smith said. "The State of Utah wants to execute you, and now they've deemed you mentally competent to stand trial, a death sentence conviction is highly likely. Utah doesn't allow for the insanity defense."

"So, I've heard. So, why would you guys have an interest in me?"

"A federal grand jury will indict you on murder charges. Since the alleged murders occurred on federal land, federal courts have a clear jurisdictional claim over the State of Utah. Pleading *not guilty by reason of insanity* is allowable under federal murder statutes."

Wilkie fixated on Smith. "I still won't speak to you without Mr. Black."

"I don't think you understand what we're prepared to offer. If you agree, we will try your case in federal court. You will enter a plea of *not guilty by reason of insanity*. After a quick trial, the judge will find you not guilty and will order you committed to a secure mental health facility. One run by Major Jones. The Eighth Circuit Court of Appeals ruled in Archuleta versus Hedrick that persons found not guilty by reason of insanity cannot be detained indefinitely. Once you're deemed safe to re-enter society, they must release you. Major Jones will decide when you are safe to re-enter society."

A line from a Walter Scott poem came to Wilkie's mind: *Oh, what a tangled web we weave when first we practice to deceive.*

"We know your insanity was temporary," Jones said, "and your country needs you."

"Why would you need me?"

"We understand you have special skill sets. Expert in martial arts, survival skills, and proficient in languages."

Wilkie's eyebrow rose while he rubbed his chin. "So, let me get this straight. I speak languages, know Kung Fu, and can live off bark and twigs—and the federal government wants to save me from the State of Utah giving me the needle? I still don't understand why."

"You come from a long line of American patriots," Jones said. "Your grandfather was 101st Airborne, one of only one-hundred-thirty-seven men to receive the Medal of Honor in the Korean conflict. Your father is a highly decorated Special Forces soldier. His highest commendations are classified. We believe you possess the DNA to follow in their footsteps. The service you provide your country will make theirs' pale in comparison."

Wilkie put his arms on the table and eyeballed Jones. "Are you expecting a major military conflict, Major? World War III?"

Jones matched Wilkie's actions. "Our country has never faced such an enemy before. More than ever, our country needs patriots like yourself to fight the coming war."

Wilkie sat upright. "I still want my lawyer, and I want it in writing."

"Mr. Black doesn't possess the proper security clearance," Smith said. "If we secure you qualified defense counsel, will you accept the offer?"

"Maybe."

They were all startled by a *William Tell Overture* ringtone.

Jones reached into his jacket as he walked to a corner. "Jones."

He listened intently before replying. "Confirm: Golf-Echo-November-Golf-Hotel-India-Sierra,   Kilo-Hotel-Alpha-November."

Jones paced back and forth with a furloughed brow as Smith bit his lip.

"Evac 13:06. Roger that." Jones hung up. "We need to hoof it. Our transport is leaving with or without us in five minutes.";

Smith stood, flung a business card on the table, and turned. "We'll be in touch." The pair rushed out the door without closing it.

The staff barking orders and rapid footfalls up and down the hospital halls weren't something Wilkie had heard before.

The mere rumor of Mongol hordes caused Slavic peasants to flee the fields to the illusionary protection of the castle.

The Mongols, the original masters of siege warfare and shock-and-awe wouldn't let mere fortress walls stand in the way of making an example of merchant and peasant, master and apprentice, prince and pauper — only keeping a few artisans alive.

The peasants would have been safer fleeing into the woods, waiting for the horde to move on, than seeking a short-lived refuge from their noble protector.

The code name of Genghis Khan spelled out on Jones' call invoked a Slavic peasant-like response in both men — and the rest of the state hospital staff.

∞

Green River Launch Complex (decommissioned)
White Sands Missile Range
Grand County, Utah
Wednesday, June 17, 2015

A pair of elevator doors opened into an abandoned corrugated steel warehouse and its rust-peppered faded gray walls. Cracks and divots canvassed the concrete floor.

Wilkie glanced back at the elevator camouflaged inside a parts shed as four commando handlers kept him moving along. He exited the building and stopped in his tracks. His eyes opened wide at the sparse desert landscape with a handful of dilapidated steel buildings.

He spied a dozen Sikorsky-made helicopters around the perimeter and realized this wasn't the state hospital in Orem. A few large troop transports, ambulances, and Humvees formed the inner perimeter.

Wilkie's rescued cohorts dressed in hospital gowns and slippers waited inside vehicles, and nearly a hundred men and women, many in lab coats and scrubs, kneeling on the ground surrounded by commandos.

He did a double-take, passing the dead orderly Gunderson—apparently resurrected, and the vegetative orderly McNamara—now miraculously recovered and breathing on his own. A wide grin overcame Wilkie's face, seeing their arms incapacitated by zip ties behind their backs. He scanned the sea of the detained for the Doctor and Major Jones and Deputy Assistant Attorney General Smith without luck. A restrained Mr. Black, however, would soon need his own defense attorney.

Wilkie watched his hero run from a crowd of suits and uniforms and shouted, "*Dad!*"

Bruce embraced Bruce Jr. and wouldn't let go.

Wilkie noticed Dad weeping. The only other time he'd seen Dad cry was when Mom passed.

A man in an Armani suit walked toward the Wilkerson's. "Bruce, we need to move out."

"Wilkie, you remember Representative Callahan?"

He responded in kind to the congressman's grin and extended hand. "Wilkie, we're so glad you're alright. We never gave up looking for you."

Father and son beamed, arms around each other's shoulders, and followed Callahan to a waiting Blackhawk helicopter.

Wilkie's knees collapsed as he reached the cabin's sliding door. Hands reached from the cabin and hoisted him inside.

"I knew it! I knew you were alive," Wilkie blubbered.

Zach and Jeff pulled Wilkie in tight. None wanted the group hug to end.

PART 7-WAKE UP MR. WOLSTENHOLME

"The Truth is Scary, but Not Knowing is Terrifying"
-Becca Fitzpatrick

Green River Launch Complex (Decommissioned)
White Sands Missile Range
Grand County, Utah
Wednesday, June 17, 2015

Jardine Wolstenholme hung out the parked helicopter door. A sea of military organization before him. He watched soldiers escort hospital gown-wearing victims to helicopters and ambulances while marines detained the victims' former captors.

The far end was beset with smiling politicians and administrators mingled with combat uniforms adorned with stars, birds, and oak clusters like the staging area for a 4th of July parade. A glorious public occasion for senators and generals to pat each other's back. They took every opportunity to remind citizens that America was still the land of the free and home of the brave—because of selfless public servants and courageous military officers.

The parade floats, horses, marching bands, and Model-T convertibles were replaced by a fleet of modern helicopters, ambulances, and some large Jeep-esque vehicles parked around the grounds.

THE HEROES OF FEBRUARY 22ND, VOLUME 1 125

"What do you call those vehicles?" Wolstenholme asked a passing soldier.

"Those? They're Humvees."

"Does the Army still use Jeeps?"

"Are you kidding? The Army hasn't used Jeeps since the eighties."

Wolstenholme's knees buckled. He grabbed a handhold just in time to keep from toppling to the ground. *I'm twenty-three, dammit. Only twenty-three,* he thought. *I can't be ninety-two.*

A pilot popped his head in from the cockpit. "Please get in your jump seat, sir. We're about to lift off."

∞

TWO DAYS LATER

U.S. Army Dugway Proving Ground
Dugway, Utah
Friday, June 19, 2015

Jardine Wolstenholme grinned non-stop since the helicopter ride.

After spending two years housed underground in a faux sanitarium, being in the high desert, fresh air, and sunlight seemed like heaven. Arriving at a top-secret weapons development base and changing into military fatigues brought a bigger smile.

A mission briefing in an aircraft hangar the next morning made it seem like little had changed from his previous life.

A General shuffled to the rostrum. His brow furrowed as he scanned the 128 men and 44 women seated eight rows deep before him.

"Welcome to Dugway Proving Ground. As members of the United States armed forces, we have chosen you to be part of a special program to acclimate you back into society. We've scheduled training for eight weeks here at Dugway, and later, we will relocate you to a place of your choosing to transition you back into the modern world." He extended a hand toward a man seated. "Let me introduce the man who made this all possible. Congressman James R. Callahan from the great State of New Mexico. He will now address you."

Callahan reached the podium. "My fellow Americans. Along with General Wilson and the rest of the staff, I want to welcome you to Dugway Proving Ground—and also to the year two thousand fifteen."

A low murmur passed through the hangar.

"I can't imagine how difficult this is for you. It's hard for us to comprehend how you've arrived at this particular time from various points in history. I wish we knew how to send you back to your time, but the best we can do is to help you transition to resume your lives in today's America. We're early in our investigation, but we will do our best to answer your questions. We'll now open the floor to your questions?"

The soldiers looked at each other. One stood. "What the hell happened?"

"I'm sorry, we can't hear you," Callahan said, and pointed. "There's a microphone stand right there. Also, please state your name, rank, service branch, and the date and last place you remember before your abduction."

A queue formed down the middle aisle.

"Second Lieutenant Delbert Washington, West Point class of nineteen hundred and seventeen. Before everything changed, I remember being on patrol near Verdun, France, on the night of the six April nineteen-hundred eighteen. Pardon me, sir—but what the hell happened? How did I end up back home and in the future?"

"Welcome, fellow West Pointer," Callahan said. "From what we have pieced together, lieutenant, a hostile force from another planet kidnapped you. We've yet to determine why they returned you nearly a century later. We simply do not know."

A lanky soldier gave a couple of taps on the microphone with a finger. "Corporal Gordon Murphy, U.S. Army Air Forces. We disappeared on the twenty-sixth of May, nineteen forty-five. What happened at the end of World War Two? Did America invade Japan? We won. Right?"

"General Douglas MacArthur accepted Japan's unconditional surrender on the second of September, nineteen forty-five," Callahan said.

"Praise God. May I ask how it ended?"

Callahan rubbed his chin. Some terms would be unfamiliar to many of the soldiers. "America deployed a new class of high-explosive that destroyed the Japanese cities of Hiroshima and Nagasaki."

"Atom bombs? Which planes dropped the bombs?" Murphy asked.

Callahan nodded—the scholar of military history was a bit puzzled. "Your abduction occurred when only a privileged few knew of the atomic bomb's existence. Were you associated with the Manhattan Project?"

"Yes, sir. Which B-29 flight crews had the privilege of dropping the atom bomb on the Nips, might I ask?"

Callahan refrained from correcting Murphy's racial slur. The abductee had much to learn about accepted social convention since the war. It was something to cover during re-acclimation training.

"The Enola Gay and the Bockscar flew those missions," Callahan said.

"Captain's Tibbetts and Bock. Good officers. Good crews. What about the crew of the Lucinda?"

"I've never heard of the Lucinda," Callahan said. "Were you based at Wendover Airfield?"

"Yes, sir," Murphy said and pointed toward Anders, Wolstenholme, and Hosek seated. "My three colleagues and I were the senior ordinance crew of the fifteen ordinance specialist crews assigned to the 509th Composite Group."

"For your information, the second atom bomb was mistakenly loaded on the Bockscar, so Major Sweeny and crew of the Great Aristotle crew piloted the Bockscar," Callahan said.

"Also, good men. Thank you, Sir." Murphy said and sat next to Hosek.

"Gunnery Sergeant Christopher Bryant, United States Marine Corps. The last thing I remember was driving back to Pendleton from Vegas on the night of July seventh, nineteen-sixty-nine. Were those spacemen operating that so-called mental hospital?"

"Semper Fi, Sergeant. That's a great question. I'm ashamed to say that those holding you at the White Sands facility were part of a rogue element of our government. They were operating an unsanctioned facility as part of a conspiracy with the aliens. For what end, we don't know. It's still early in our investigation."

A murmur rippled throughout the hangar.

Callahan continued. "Now, I must tell the two-fold purpose for you being brought to Dugway. Our primary purpose is to help you rejoin society.

"However, we have legitimate concerns about how the public will react to learning creatures from other planets exist, let alone if they find out loyal Americans have been abducted by them with the aid of a secret cabal within the United States government.

"If we made such things public, we strongly believe that it will lead to mass panic, riots, and anarchy. We promise your individual stories will be documented as part of the overall picture and then will provide you with a cover story and training on how to avoid letting the proverbial cat-out-of-the-bag when you are reassigned from Dugway."

Bryant's arms shook as his hand clamped down on the

microphone. "Pardon me, sir, but we want justice! We want these traitors and spacemen to pay for their crimes. They stole our lives with the help of our government."

A rumbling rolled through the abductees.

Callahan nodded. "We have no intention of leaving any of you without justice. Most of the human perpetrators are in custody and will face a secret military tribunal. I assure you they will pay for their treason. We're gathering ongoing intelligence to best counter both our internal and external enemies. Now, the second part for you being here today. We hope you are also willing to continue to serve your country to defeat these enemies of not only the United States of America but of all humanity. The aliens must not go unchecked — but it has to be done in secret. We must protect the general public from the knowledge that we are not alone in the galaxy."

$$\infty$$

ONE DAY LATER

US Army Proving Ground
Dugway, Utah
Saturday, June 20, 2015

Jardine Wolstenholme lay awake on his bunk, unable to get his widowed mother out of his mind. She had to be gone. He reckoned she'd be a hundred and twenty-eight by now.

Miss Eileen Stewart might still be around. The once fair maiden would be an ancient woman. He wondered to whom she married. *How many children, grandchildren, even great-grandchildren did she have*? He didn't expect her to keep a vow made in jest. She was quite a catch. He hoped his former fiancé had led a full and happy life.

Someone whispered, "Jardine."

Wolstenholme checked on his squadmates. Hosek

remained asleep on the adjacent top bunk. Sawing logs on the bottom bunks, Anders and Murphy were clear-cutting a rainforest.

"Over here," the voice whispered.

He quivered with a start. He sighed and smiled back at the jolly face. "Arild!"

The Chájehit put a finger to his lips and extended an arm.

Wolstenholme instantly sat cross-legged inside a Lavvu, a teepee-like structure constructed with a lattice of spruce poles and animal skins pulled taut over the outside. The floor was layered with the hides of large rudiments. He faced Arild seated across the fire from him.

"Where are we?" he asked.

"On Earth—but not your Earth," Arild said. "We are on my Earth's equivalent of Norway."

"I'm a tad bit confused."

"I dwell in a universe parallel to your own."

Wolstenholme nodded. "Your lodge was far roomier than this teepee. Do you go camping often?"

"I enjoy being amongst God's creations. This is the time of year for us to gather our herds."

"This teepee still beats sleeping six stories underground in what the Army calls a *habitat ring*."

"I'd rather sleep above ground, too. Let's go outside to enjoy the morning."

Wolstenholme bent over to exit the Lavvu. He shielded his eyes as the sunrise reflected off the snowpack. He stood upright. "Wow!"

Before him, a pristine mountain valley with a herd of caribou wandering among a village of people and Lavvu. The sun warmed his face in the crisp air. He didn't remember changing from skivvies into clothing made from animal skins. *Arild is full of surprises*. He relished the fresh air. Hints of campfire and reindeer manure had more substance than the manufactured air of Dugway's habitat ring.

Wolstenholme grinned as a boy led a caribou, ridden by two small children, passed him. "Who are these people?"

"This is my clan. We live off the land and from our herds."

"Do all Chájehit live like this?"

"Our Earth is similar to your Earth; we've adapted to living in different environments and have evolved into different cultures. Some are farmers, some fishermen, some traders, some builders — but we are all Chájehit."

"I thought you were guardians of the universe?"

"We consider ourselves servants of the Prime Mover," Arild said.

"The Prime Mover?"

"Jardine, you will find the answer to that question in your own due time. Now, for the reason you are here. You have the power to travel where you please."

"Thank you, but I don't know if I want to wander too far from camp." Wolstenholme tapped his foot. "Do you have wolves in your Norway?"

"We have moose and polar bears, too, but none will harm you. However, you don't understand. We have provided another gift of the Chájehit to you, the ability to travel by desire."

At first, Wolstenholme's brow furrowed, then his eyes opened wide. "I can travel from your Earth to my Earth by just thinking about it?"

"Yes, and much more, but you must learn to focus on your desire and will," Arild said. "Are you hungry?"

"A bit."

"Last time we met, you found the lapskause delicious, no? Do you want some?"

"Yes, sir."

Arild pointed across the village. "It's over there. Go, eat."

Wolstenholme stepped toward the cooking fire.

A firm yet gentle hand held him back. "Use your desire instead of your feet."

Wolstenholme thought about traveling to the stew—but didn't move. He closed his eyes and wished. The method worked in fairy tales.

"Jiminy Cricket, it didn't work."

"Be patient, Jardine. Focus on the result. With a little faith and desire, you can move through space," Arild said. "Focus on your hunger. Aren't you hungry? Doesn't your body need sustenance to survive?"

With his eyes closed, Wolstenholme concentrated on an empty stomach as much as reaching the cauldron.

"Open your eyes, Jardine. Look at the man. He's fifty paces away, dishing up the rich stew. His mouth will soon savor the tender meat, seasoned with wild onion and herbs, and the subtle bitter-sweetness of the lingonberry. His mouth is joyful with every bite. His belly warmed and satisfied. It's yours with a wish."

Wolstenholme closed his eyes again. He remembered the last time he ate the stew—delicious and associated with freedom—a reprieve from the holding cell at the secret prison, aka sanitarium. His mouth watered as the breeze carried a whiff of the stew. His mind became clear and focused. Background noise disappeared.

Only his thoughts and Arild's voice remained. "Believe you can do it. Desire to be with the man. Desire to be near the kettle. Imagine the Lapskause in your mouth. Now open your eyes."

Wolstenholme didn't feel like he moved but knew he had. He opened his eyes and found himself next to the cauldron, with Arild as envisioned.

"Jardine, let me introduce you to my brother Bjorn."

Bjorn handed the bowl of stew to Arild and clutched both of Wolstenholme's forearms.

"It's a pleasure to meet you, Spencer Jardine Wolstenholme of the Chájehit. Welcome to our home. We expect to sing songs about your great and heroic adventures."

∞

Arild patted Wolstenholme's shoulder and smiled. "You've worked hard today. Your training is complete. You are welcome to stay but may go back to your Earth anytime you wish."

"Thank you, Arild. I always enjoy our time together. However, I should get going."

"Remember to use your gifts for good and not for personal gain or glory. You shouldn't squander them either, but use them in the service of humanity."

Wolstenholme slouched.

"What is bothering you, my brother?" Arild asked.

"I'm unsure if I should ask. I'm sure the answer is *no*."

"You may always speak freely with Arild."

"You know how you said time travel might be part of my abilities?" His head turned slightly to avoid eye contact. "I want to see Eileen. Tell her to not wait for me."

"You are free to choose. However, the Chájehit follow eternal principles. Linear time moves forward with, or without, us. We should choose not to live in the past but learn from our mistakes. A better future happens through the choices made today. Trying to change the past always has unintended and often less desirable consequences. Best to let destiny run its natural course. Again, you are free to choose."

"Thank you for everything," Wolstenholme said.

They clutched each other's forearms.

"Goodbye, my friend."

"Goodbye, Arild."

∞

Steward Home
265 Dogwood Circle
Stewartville, Georgia

Jardine Wolstenholme exhaled and grinned. He arrived in the correct universe, the right planet, and the desired location.

From the sidewalk, he scanned the house, which was like his second home. The whitewash clapboard siding was now a light peach. A medium-sized maple replaced the stately elm. The porch swing brought a smile. Eileen and he would sit on it for hours. Watching sunsets, holding hands, small talk with passing neighbors, smooching — and lots of laughter. He loved to make her laugh. He missed Eileen's laugh.

He bound up the front porch steps and checked his reflection in the picture window. *Arild's full of all kinds of surprises.*

Gone were the Sami herder outerwear, replaced by neatly pressed denim dungarees, long-sleeved gingham shirt, and black penny loafers — regular come-a-courting clothes for Wolstenholme. Arild didn't provide a comb, so he ran his fingers from the part and pressed down out-of-place hairs. Finally presentable, he knocked.

An unfamiliar girl answered the door. She bore a resemblance to a ten-year-old Eileen in pigtails.

"Hello, is Miss Eileen Stewart home?"

"May I ask who's calling?"

"Mr. Jardine Wolstenholme."

"Please wait here. I'll go fetch Aunt Eileen."

Wolstenholme wondered why she failed to invite a family friend in. Leaving a stranger on the porch was barely acceptable in the South. No offer of cold lemonade or sweet tea on a sweltering summer afternoon, stranger or not, was uncouth at best. He didn't know Eileen had a niece. Her married sister only had sons. The girl must have been the daughter of Mrs. Stuart's friend or cousin.

The girl returned. "Aunt Eileen's coming. Are you her friend?"

"Yes, young lady. Are you visiting your Aunt Eileen?"

The girl cocked her head back and said, "I live here."

The girl left before a familiar silver-haired woman hunched with a cane, mindful of every shuffled step, approached the screen door and laughed. "Jardine Wolstenholme, I haven't heard that name in ages."

"It's good to see you, ma'am. I'm home on leave," Wolstenholme said.

She stopped at the door and used her cane to straighten up. Her eyes opened wide. "Oh, good Lord. It's really you."

She lost her balance. Wolstenholme quickly opened the screen door and caught her in time. "Let's find you a seat, Nana Stewart."

He escorted and eased her onto the porch swing. She clutched his hands and bade him to sit.

"You haven't changed a bit," she said. Her shriveled hands touched the contours of his face. "Is it really you?"

"Where's Miss Eileen, Nana Stewart? I've come a long way to see her, ma'am."

"Is it my time to go? Have you come to take me home? I've prayed for the Lord to take me for oh so long."

Nana Stewart's memory faltered before his enlistment. *Her dementia must be getting worse,* he thought.

"*Wolsty*, is it really *you*?"

Wolstenholme gave pause. Nana Stewart and Eileen's mother were proper Southern ladies. Being betrothed to Eileen still didn't allow for a level of informality to call either lady by their given names, and conversely, they hadn't called Jardine by his childhood nickname — since childhood.

She gazed into his eyes.

Uncomfortable, he looked toward the street as a modern pickup truck backed out of the driveway next door. He turned back, now recognizing his favorite hazel eyes. "*Eileen*?"

"Yes. It's me. I've been waiting for you my entire life, sweet boy."

"What's today's date?"

"August twenty-fourth."

"What year?"

"Two-thousand-fourteen."

He paused in thought before speaking again. "Did you ever marry?"

"No, you were the only boy for me."

Wolstenholme's stomach hurt. She waited a lifetime for nothing.

"Am I being called home? I'm ready to go with you," Eileen said.

"I'm sorry, sweetheart, but I'm not a spirit. It's me in the flesh."

She clutched her face, and her eyes opened wide. "B-b-but, the Army said you died in that airplane crash back in forty-five—and you've not aged a day." Her hands clutched the sides of Wolstenholme's face, and she looked intently into his eyes. "How can this be?"

The burden overwhelmed him. Eileen had been the only person he ever fully trusted. "It's a long story. Do you have time?"

"I'm all ears."

PART 8-WAKE UP MR. WILKERSON PART II

"The more things change, the more they are the same."
-Alphonse Karr

EIGHT WEEKS LATER

Tooele County, Utah
Friday, August 14, 2015

After returning home from his illegal confinement, Wilkie became laser-focused on making up his last three semesters of high school. The six-week General Educational Development (GED) preparation class was all-consuming. Between Monday through Friday class, homework, his weekend job, church activities, and the occasional abductee support group meeting gave him little time for himself. He had a knot in his stomach before arriving at the GED testing center. Seven and a half hours later, he felt a great weight lift from his shoulders as he walked away with a high school equivalency diploma in his hands and his first weekend free since coming home.

Jeff DeBoer arrived at the Wilkerson home from Provo around 7pm and, together with Zach, headed toward the Pony Express Trail in Wilkie's Jeep Wrangler.

They paused on the graded dirt road, taking some video of wild mustangs grazing on the open range, and continued until passing a sign pointing toward a 3-foot-tall stone wall:

Aunt Libby's Dog Cemetery.

The four by four ascended the trail a few hundred feet short of the stone cairn, marking the location of the former Lookout Pass Pony Express Station. Wilkie pulled off onto an unimproved trail until reaching a semi-level area and parked. He lowered the Jeep's tailgate and tossed sleeping bags and bed pads to his friends.

They set up camp while stereo speakers on the roll bar resonated a classic rock playlist.

"Shall I start a fire?" Jeff asked.

"Not unless you want a ticket," Wilkie said. "There's a fire ban in effect."

Wilkie brought out his camp stove and prepared dinner. They watched the sunset while they ate.

∞

Wilkie lay on his back, enjoying the night sky, and background music quieted his mind. A streak of light caught his attention. His eyes tracked the falling star's arc crossing the Milky Way's plasmatic mists.

"Man, I've missed the outdoors," he whispered.

The ambient noise of crickets, Zach's intermittent snoring, and the occasional coyote howls blended into the background as Aerosmith's Sweet Emotion played.

"Jeff, I'm ready to turn in." Wilkie looked toward him. "Are you awake?"

Jeff didn't move. Wilkie got up and headed toward the Jeep to grab his mobile and keys.

He nearly returned to his bedroll when Zach shot upright and screamed, "Run! Aliens!"

He promptly fell back onto his pillow.

Wilkie stopped in his tracks. "Zach, you're having a bad dream."

A beam of blue-green light surrounded their sleeping bags.

Wilkie shuddered. "Oh, crap. Not again."

∞

Duml Fleet Flagship Ergonea
Orbiting 1,339 Miles Above Earth
Friday, June 5, 2015

Wilkie floated above the ship's metallic floor and moved in concert with Cerculus's finger. The Admiral gazed into Wilkie's eyes and pointed his digit downward. Two Dumal bodyguards caught Wilkie before he reached the floor and held him upright.

"Your strength will return shortly," Cerculus said. "Do you remember my name?"

Wilkie grunted and nodded.

"Keep trying to speak. You should have vocal capabilities before you can stand on your own. I've unlocked your memories of previous visits."

Wilkie's voice creaked like a boy starting puberty. "I have a question."

Cerculus nodded.

"Why did I lose time on my first visit?" Wilkie rubbed the back of his neck. "I can't lose two years again."

"I was wondering when you would ask me. A computer virus randomly disrupts the Ergonea's time-warp circuits and navigation systems and only moves forward in time."

Wilkie's mouth hung open. "*A virus*? How did that happen?"

"A subversive element hacked our systems. Mujar terrorists seeking to destroy harmony among the member races."

"Don't you have anti-virus software?"

"We do. However, the sophistication of this virus is admirable. We can't determine where it hides when dormant. As the ship's time-warp circuits activate, the virus randomly comes out of dormancy and disappears again."

"If it's random, that shouldn't matter. Send me back in time and drop me off. How hard should that be for you?"

"Per Intergalactic Council rules, our ships have one chance to return our guests to the original time and point of departure."

"I lost two years of my life because a virus sent your ship forward in time and some stupid rule? That's B.S."

"It's unlikely it will happen again. Time-loss episodes are extremely rare, and when they occur, there's usually only a few hours difference."

Wilkie's lips pursed. "Virus or no virus, I don't want to lose any more time. Not on this visit or any others. It's too big a sacrifice to ask."

The timely arrival of two gray aliens brought Cerculus some relief. "Your escorts have arrived. I will see you again soon."

∞

The hypnotic gaze of the gray technician made Wilkie, already secured to the table, paralyzed from head to toe. This was one of those times Wilkie wished he couldn't remember.

The prick of the cranial sensors was the least painful and intrusive test. Spreaders forced open his eyes for strobing images that gave him the beginnings of a migraine. He dreaded the requisite physiological testing: a mix of tissue and fluid collection, cavity-invading probes, and exploratory surgeries.

The ocular probes were exquisitely painful. He debated which of the robotic probes were the next most dreaded: *oral or anal*. One made him dry heave, and the other violated. Nasal and auditory probes felt much less intrusive.

The high-energy robotic scalpel made nearly painless incisions. Wilkie winced when the probes touched a nerve. Each exploratory surgery seemed random—as if investigating a different organ or body part for each incursion. His physiology couldn't be that unique among the hundreds of other abductees undergoing the same procedures.

The one consistent with every Ergonea *"visit"* involved a gray waving a handheld scanner over his left foot—as if the appendage produced some kind of unique phenomena.

With the procedures completed, the technician gazed again into Wilkie's eyes, and things went dark.

Once awake, the Dumal expected Wilkie wouldn't remember the procedures. Wilkie still didn't know if the Chájehit's remittance of memories were a gift or a curse. After each trip to the Ergonea, he hoped to return to his own bed and own time, his migraine gone—but he didn't count on it.

∞

THE FOLLOWING DAY

Near the Arctic Circle
Greenland
Saturday, June 6, 2015

Wilkie woke on a hard mattress, surrounded by familiar stainless-steel fixtures, detained behind a clear Lexan wall. *"What the heck? I thought they closed this hellhole."*

He expected the two chair-bearing and TASER-carrying thugs, Gunderson and McNamara, to arrive with Dr. Jones to torment him at any moment.

"I'm out of here." He instantaneously stood outside the cell. "Time to free the hostages."

The *ang-ang-ang* of an alarm blared as Wilkie ran down the hallway. Captives approached the Plexiglas walls of their enclosures, but there was no sign of Zach or Jeff among them. He reached the hallway's end and passed through a steel door as if it didn't exist. He turned right and barreled toward a waiting squadron, three across and three deep—vanished before they could deploy their non-lethal weapons—and reappeared behind the men, never breaking stride. To his left a glimpse of curly red hair. He bound toward Zach's cell and disappeared.

Wilkie stood next to Zach. "Grab my arm. Where's DeBoer?"

"Next door," Jeff yelled.

They arrived in an instant.

"Am I glad to see you," Jeff said, and extended a middle finger toward the hostile force outside, "but not you dickwads!"

"No time to dilly-dally," Wilkie said. "Let's get the hell out of here."

"Wilkie, teleporting and cussing," Zach said. "What's this world coming to?"

∞

On the fly, Wilkie could only think of only one destination—a place of joy, contentment, and fond memories.

The rush on Christmas mornings to make a cursory validation that the annual North Pole delivery occurred—and the reciprocal gift devoured. For Wilkie, there were few better childhood memories than playing with new toys, sipping mom's secret recipe hot cocoa swirled with an island of whipped cream and chocolate shavings—and beholding mom content on dad's lap.

He had fond recollections of weekly family nights, including song and devotion and the aroma of fresh-baked cookies wafting from the kitchen. The countless hours spent playing Scrabble, Catan, Risk, and chess. It was a place of tedium, too. Youngsters forced to sit still for eons, receiving guests and enduring adult conversations.

Mostly, it was a quiet place, which Wilkie grew to appreciate as he got older. The off-white sofa was an ideal locale for a weekend nap or undisturbed adventures to Arrakis, Hogwarts, and Middle Earth. Mom often brought a sandwich or snack as provisions for the journey to fantasy worlds.

∞

Wilkerson Home
Abundance, Utah
Saturday, June 6, 2015

The living room wasn't quite the same since Mom passed. Wilkie never considered they'd be teleporting in the middle of visitors.

Zach's eyes went wide. "Oh, crap!"

Jeff faced a middle-aged man on a loveseat. *"Ta-dah!* I bet you've never seen such an amazing act of illusion before?"

From the sofa next to Jenny, Bruce shook his head and glared at the boys. "Be more careful in the future, men. Luckily, you're with people who understand. They have something interesting to share with you."

"How was your campout?" Jenny Wilkerson asked.

"Pretty typical, Mom," Zach smirked. "Alien abduction. Secret underground government laboratory."

Jenny's milky complexion turned whiter.

Bruce Wilkerson's head turned with a snap. *"What*? The Green River facility?"

Wilkie nodded.

"No, not Green River... Greenland," Zach said. "The design was identical, but it's not White Sands."

"We need to call Jim Callahan when we're finished and get it shut down."

"We're just glad you're back home safe." Jenny rose from a sofa and pulled the three boys into her arms.

"Okay, Mom. That's enough," Zach said.

He released and spied two petite redheads seated on a facing sofa. It was hard to determine the age of the older one. Zach knew the other was in her early twenties but still looked every bit a pre-teen.

The one who knew Zach stood up. "Look at you. All tall and grown-up."

"Where have you been?" Zach asked.

"Is that all you can say? Get over here," Liza O'Reilly said.

After Zach and Liza embraced, she hugged Jeff and Wilkie.

"I've missed you guys," Liza said.

"So, where have you been?" Jeff asked.

"We'll get to that later. Let me introduce my mom, Heather, and my dad, Michael. And our chaperone… uh, Warren."

At first glance, Wilkie thought Liza and her mom might be sisters about ten years apart.

Michael, seated on the loveseat, looked only a couple inches taller than his daughter. He stood up to shake the boy's hands and met Wilkie eye-to-eye.

All legs and no torso, Wilkie thought.

A man in a dark suit and yellow power tie sat on a kitchen chair near the entrance of the foyer. His eyes continuously scanned the room.

Jeff DeBoer faced a female version of Jekyll and Hyde side-by-side on the sofa, both with green eyes and feathery ginger hair.

Liza glowered as she rested against the couch back with crossed arms and feet dangling off the edge.

Heather grinned from ear to ear. She rocked back and forth non-stop on the edge of the sofa — the balls of her feet barely reaching the carpet.

Jeff found Liza's mother, with tight blue jeans and a low-cut blouse, quite attractive. She looked like a slightly older, curvy, and busty version of her daughter. Heather stopped rocking and leaned forward, placing her hands on her knees. Jeff's eyes focused on the more exposed cleavage, but raised his eyes when caught.

Heather gave him a quick look over, followed by a mischievous, *I don't mind smile.*

She sat upright and said, "Liza and I have traveled all the way from Montana to meet you." Her gaze alternated between Jeff and Wilkie. "Thirteen years ago, aliens abducted me. It ruined my life. I traveled the country looking for answers but found none—until I met Dupre seven years ago. He invited me to join with fellow abductees at Aryana Ranch. Dupre negotiated a safe harbor agreement with the IGC and Dumal to discontinue abductions for those that dwell within our community."

Wilkie's mouth hung open. He'd never heard the names ICG and Dumal outside of conversations with Cerculus and Arild.

"Liza, how long have you lived there?" Wilkie asked.

"About nine months. An older couple near Moab kept me safe before I moved to Montana."

Wilkie tilted his head. A month ago, he walked a corridor of the Ergonea with Cerculus. While passing the surgery, he glanced through a doorway. A petite redhead was at the far end of the surgical stations. He assumed it was Liza—but now he wasn't entirely sure.

"You can't believe my excitement at being reunited with Eliza," Heather said.

"Ugh," Liza sighed. "It's Liza, Heather."

"Sorry, dear." She patted Liza's knee. "I want to invite you to enjoy the freedom, safety, and security of Aryana—to be free from alien intrusions in your lives."

Liza's lips scrunched as if she had eaten something vile.

Heather continued. "Dupre's network has discovered a planned escalation of human experimentation by the Dumal and rumors of something much worse. Since you're Liza's friends, we want you to be safe with us."

Wilkie and Jeff noticed Liza's head oscillated ever-so-slightly.

Zach never took his eyes off Heather. He couldn't imagine

anything more wonderful than a life free of abductions — except for being with Joy.

"Can we bring our families with us?" Wilkie asked.

"The invitation is only for you and Jeff to live at Aryana," Heather said.

"You forgot me," Zach said.

Heather frowned. "I'm sorry, dear. I don't think you'd fit in. There is another survivor's group in Georgia that would welcome *your kind*."

Zach's heart broke on two fronts: first, he longed for sanctuary more than anything, and second, he knew all about *your kind*. "Mrs. O'Reilly?"

"It's now Mrs. Dupre," Heather said. "Mrs. Winston Dupre."

"Mrs. Dupre, with all due respect, my hometown's Abundance, Utah. It doesn't get any whiter than Abundance. Inside this freckly milk chocolate exterior is a creamy white center. I don't want to be abducted anymore."

"I feel for you, honey. I really do," Heather said. "I tell you what. I'll put in a kind word with Dupre. Maybe he can make an exception in your case — or introduce you to Liddell, the commandant at the Memnon School. They'd welcome you without a doubt."

Bruce Wilkerson stood up. "Thank you, Heather, but speaking for my family, and I believe I also speak for Jeff's mother, we must decline your offer."

"But the boys will continue to be abducted," Heather said. "You don't want them abducted, do you?"

"Of course not. However, I don't want either of my sons, Zach or Wilkie, to live away from home with a bunch of strangers that appear to be racists."

Zach beamed. *Bruce called me his son.*

"Eliza, tell them we're not that way. We aren't racists.

We're survivors," Heather said.

"It's Liza—and it is that way. Your so-called husband's a racist sonofabitch." She looked at Wilkie and Zach. "Did you know Aryana in the Zoroastrian religion is the Aryan homeland?"

"These boys, as you call them, are men to me. Maybe they should decide for themselves," Heather said. "Wilkie, don't you want to be free from abductions?"

"I'm not interested. No, Zach. No me."

"What if we made an exemption for Zach's admission to Aryana?" Heather said.

"It's still not likely."

"Jeff, what about you?" Heather bent over to reveal her ample bosom and stared into his eyes. "Think about it. No more abductions, headaches, or lost time. Besides, we need more strong young men like you at Aryana. The ratio of women to men is almost three-to-one. We simply don't have enough able-bodied young men."

"I'm going to be sick," Liza said.

"Just ignore Eliza. She's on her period," Heather said.

Liza rolled her eyes and groaned.

"What do you want, Jeff?"

"Can I have a few days to decide? It's a big decision."

"I understand, but I have to be clear. This offer won't stand forever. Here's my card for when you're ready."

Wilkie refused the offering. Heather let her fingers linger as Jeff took the card.

"I think you're making a mistake, Wilkie," Heather said. "If you change your mind, Jeff has my card."

"Still not interested," Wilkie said.

"Thank you for your time. I hope you change your mind, Wilkie." Heather caught Jeff's gaze and smiled. "Don't wait too long to decide, Jeff. I could use a man like you at Aryana. Let's go, Eliza. It's time to go home."

"My name's Liza, and Aryana isn't my home. My home's with my dad."

"Don't talk that way to me, dear. I'm still your mother."

Michael O'Reilly stood, beet-red face, fists clenched. "You crazy bitch! You stopped being Liza's mom the minute you abandoned her. She's an adult and can make her own decisions."

"Well done, Dad. I couldn't have said it better," Liza said.

Heather clenched her arms around her stomach and rocked in her seat. "But you promised Dupre you'd come back."

"I'm not going back," Liza said.

From across the living room, a baritone voice spoke up. "You don't have a choice in the matter, Liza. You're going back to Aryana."

Michael glared at Warren. "If my daughter wants to stay, she stays."

Warren stood as his right hand pushed back a suit jacket, revealing a holstered sidearm.

"How dare you threaten guests in my home!" Bruce snapped. "You'd be wise to close that coat and be on your way."

"I have my orders. Come along, Liza."

"I won't go. You're going to have to shoot me first."

Warren stepped toward Liza as Wilkie stepped between. Bruce rose and flanked.

Warren drew the Glock G21 and pointed it alternately between Wilkie and Bruce. "Stand aside."

"You better think twice about pulling a gun on us," Bruce said.

Warren's aim shifted on Wilkie as he took a half step forward and disappeared. Wilkie appeared behind and, with a lightning motion, twisted the gun away and trained it on a bewildered Warren.

"You don't have the guts to shoot me, kid.

"But I have no compunction about placing three rounds

in your center mass," Bruce said, aiming a .45 caliber Colt Model 1911 retrieved from the drawer of a nearby credenza. "Step back, *asshole!*"

Wilkie and Zach didn't know if they should laugh or show shock. It was so out of character for *Mr. Positive* (as some call Bruce) to speak derogatorily of others in private, let alone call anyone an *asshole* to their face.

"Interlace your fingers behind your head. Kneel on the ground." Warren complied with Bruce's command. "Zach, there's a bag of large zip ties in my electrical toolbox in the garage. Please get them. Honey, call 911."

Heather inched toward the front door.

Michael blocked her way. "Where do you think you're going, Mrs. Duupreeee?"

"I can't take all this negative energy. I need some fresh air," Heather said.

"You stay put!"

"Get out of my way, Mike. You can't stop me."

"You can't run away this time. If anyone has held Liza against her will, I'll make sure the authorities press charges."

Heather disappeared.

"What the—" Michael said. "Where'd she go?"

Wilkie looked at Liza. "Does your mom teleport?"

"I don't know. This is a first, but she's still here. Heather, show yourself."

"Where is she?" Wilkie asked

"I can feel her. She's terrified," Liza said. "Listen for panicked breathing."

Returning from the garage, Zach noticed a change. The tick-tock of the grandfather clock was the only sound.

"Got a mouse on the loose?" Zach asked.

Everyone *shushed* in unison.

"Thanks, Zach. Give those here," Bruce said. "Wilkie, keep

your sights trained on this scumbag's head."

Bruce pulled out three zip ties. He formed two into large loops. The third he interlocked between the other two to form flex cuffs.

"Hands behind your back," Bruce ordered.

Warren lay still. Bruce placed a knee on Warren's back and used three fingers to pull Warren's hand behind his back. Bruce put a nylon loop around the hand and cinched it. Warren resisted with the other hand. Bruce dug the knee deeper and used the same three-finger pressure point hold, making the hand compliant. He pulled the zip ties tighter and double-checked their worthiness.

"She's still here," Liza said.

"Who's still here?" Zach asked.

"Heather. She's invisible or something. Listen for her," Liza said.

"I haven't heard nothing. I think she left," Jeff said.

The wail of police sirens neared.

"She's panicked. Her heart's racing a hundred miles a minute," Liza said.

Warren lifted his head off the floor. "Get away, Heather!"

From the far corner of the room, mirage-like colored waves caught Zach's eye. It faded away before he pointed. "I saw something right there."

Two officers with guns drawn approached the front door. "Abundance police! Keep your hands free and visible at all times. We're coming in."

"It's all clear. The perpetrator's subdued," Bruce yelled.

"She's gone," Liza said.

"Who's gone?" Bruce asked.

"Heather. I can't feel her anymore."

PART 9-NEW BEGINNINGS

"Our duty is to be useful, not according to our desires but according to our powers."
-Henri Frederic Amiel

FORTY-FIVE DAYS LATER

World War II Memorial
Washington Mall
Washington, D.C.
Saturday, August 22, 2015

Fifty-six granite pillars of the World War II Memorial surrounded Deputy Director Smith and Major Jones, both dressed as Beltway bureaucrats. Jones's ill-fitting, off-the-rack suit and polyester tie were typical of a Pentagon employee. His immaculately polished Florsheim oxfords matched that of a career soldier. Smith's tailored suit and dress shirt, Gucci tie, and handmade Italian shoes made him look the part of a Wall Street lawyer or high-ranking Justice Department official. Regardless of the apparel's cost, sweat pooled under both men's coats on this sweltering summer evening.

They stood near a concave wall as the setting sun reflected off the 4048 gold stars mounted thereon. Each star represented a hundred Americans who paid the ultimate price to defeat the

Axis powers during *The War*. The inscription underneath stated: *Here We Mark the Price of Freedom.*

A nonagenarian, his wheelchair pushed by a septuagenarian son, approached the Freedom Wall with three generations of family in tow. The veteran rose to his feet as the son and a grandson provided balance. He did his best to straighten an arthritic back before raising his arm to salute fallen comrades.

Smith breathed a sigh of relief when the veteran and his posterity left.

"It's getting late. Do you think they'll show?" Jones asked.

"Being late may be part of their strategy."

Jones touched his earpiece and turned around. "Speak of the devil. Four o'clock on a direct course."

An athletic figure and petite redhead swayed arm-in-arm. Typical for their age, they wore summer-break attire. Shorts, tee shirts, flip-flops. They rounded the reflecting pool toward Smith and Jones.

"See, I told you they'd come. Have your men maintain their position," Smith said.

Liza and Wilkie reached the men.

"Mr. Smith." Wilkie smiled and extended a hand.

As Smith shook Wilkie's hand, Liza grabbed Jones's arm, and they all vanished.

∞

The sudden transition from the outdoor memorial to inside a modern log cabin left Jones disoriented.

Heat radiated from a river rock fireplace into a room decorated in a southwest motif and furnished with log-frame furniture. Smith stepped to the nearest window.

"Where the *hell* have you taken us?" Jones demanded.

"The Northwest Territories of Canada," Liza said.

"How dare you take us without our consent!"

Wilkie tilted his head back and hooted. Liza laughed, too.

Jones' face turned red as he shook.

The pair laughed so hard that tears formed in their eyes.

"Stop laughing! You insubordinate little shits!" Jones reached behind his back and aimed a pistol at Wilkie. "Take us back to Washington now!"

The pistol immediately wiped the smile off of Wilkie's face. "You agreed to come to the memorial unarmed and alone. You've broken both those agreements, and you're in no position to bargain right now."

"I could just shoot you and be done with it. Smith can call for a chopper anytime."

Smith spoke from the window. "Willard, put that away. Mr. Wilkerson and Ms. O'Reilly have the upper hand."

"I'll holster my sidearm when we're back in Washington."

"*Major*, relinquish your weapon."

Jones's eyes opened wide, and he tilted his head. "Sir, please."

Smith approached and held out his hand. "That's an order."

Jones hesitated momentarily before handing his Sig Sauer M17 to Smith. Who in turn handed the pistol to Wilkie.

"You're a wise man, Mr. Smith," Liza said.

Jones glared at Smith. "You're making a mistake, sir."

"We're the ones that made the mistake," Smith said. "Take a peek out the window."

Jones walked to the window. Outside, an evergreen wilderness with chest-deep virgin snow. His gaze shifted to the clear night sky and shivered with a newfound realization.

"My sat phone won't work here, will it, Mr. Wilkerson?" Smith asked.

"I doubt it."

Jones returned from the window. His face was now as pale as the snow outside.

"We are in the Northwest Territories of Canada—but it's safe to assume, Mr. Wilkerson, that we're on Earth in a parallel universe?" Smith asked.

"How did you figure that out?"

"The two moons kind of gave it away."

Liza gestured for Jones and Smith to sit at the kitchen dinette.

"So, why are we here?" Smith asked.

"We are meeting with you as a favor to Admiral Cerculus. He asked us to consider working with you," Wilkie said. "The odds are slim that we'd get involved with dishonorable men."

"Dishonorable? You're the ones that kidnapped us." Jones snapped.

Liza cackled. *"You gotta be kidding me*? Your thugs were ready to kidnap us again."

"We did no such thing," Jones said.

Liza rolled her eyes and groaned. "You really have some big cajones to deny it."

Wilkie took over. "You started with zero credibility after unlawfully imprisoning us and committing crimes against our minds and bodies at White Sands. Remember, it's us who contacted you for a meeting, and you agreed to our terms of coming alone and unarmed. You now have less-than-zero credibility with us, Jones. We're still talking because we believe the plight of the Dumal is just, but we won't be played."

"Your people were wrong. We came alone," Jones said, as flopped sweat formed on his brow.

"Enough with the lies already," Wilkie exclaimed. "We had our own people scout your agents. Our Plan A was to talk with you at the memorial, but you forced our Plan B."

"Give it a rest, Willard. These kids aren't fools," Smith said, as Jones glared at him.

"We can't work with habitual liars. There has to be an

element of trust," Liza said. "Wilkie, let's give the Major a lift home. Mr. Smith, we'll be right back."

Jones's brow furrowed. "I won't leave you, Sir."

Smith straightened his posture and looked Jones in the eyes. "Go without me. That's an order."

"Yes, sir."

Wilkie and Liza looked at each other, locked arms, and reached across the table to touch Jones and disappeared.

∞

"You have everything you need to find your way back." Liza handed Jones a device, grabbed Wilkie's arm, and left Jones behind.

Jones pulled a cell phone from his suit coat. The signal indicator showed no bars. *Where the hell am I?*

He tried to get his bearings in the darkness. The crystalline and expansive night sky left him feeling insignificant and only fueled his anger. The Milky Way illuminated silhouettes of rectangular objects on the ground nearby, but not much else. He fumbled with the device in his hands until he found a switch. The LED headlamp revealed a hard-crusted white surface at Jones's feet. He walked toward the objects. The lamp shone on identical pairs of hiking backpacks, 5-gallon plastic water jugs, and sleeping bags laid out on pads.

His wilderness survival training demanded he'd stay put for the night. He laid atop a sleeping bag to think. A pan-salt dry lake bed. Hot and dry at night. The feel of near sea-level air. This eliminated the Andes, Asia, and Bonneville. Most likely some salt flats in Africa or the American Southwest. Maybe Death Valley. He could sleep soundly if he was in Texas, Arizona, or California. If in Africa, Jones would have to stay up all night to repel attacks from man-eating predators.

Damn those kids!

∞

Liza, Wilkie, and Smith sat around the kitchenette.

"Which one of you can teleport?" Smith asked.

"Does it matter?" Liza said.

"For my cooperation with the Dumal, it's a critical question," Smith said. "Let me rephrase. Is the Teleporter a leaper or a warper?"

"A what?" Wilkie said.

"A leaper or a warper?"

"I don't understand," Wilkie said.

"A leaper's ability is to teleport through space only. Warpers can move through both time and space," Smith said.

"Why does it matter?" Wilkie asked.

"Because a warper once violated our trust and tried to change the past. He was unsuccessful, thank God."

"You don't have to worry, Mr. Smith," Liza said. "We can only teleport through space."

"And across dimensions. Are you sure you can't travel through time?"

"I'm pretty sure we can't," Wilkie said.

"So, what are your terms to assist us with the Dumal reintegration?" Smith asked.

"Here you go." Liza handed a manila envelope to Smith. "We'll return you to your office now and contact you in a few days."

Smith wondered how they knew the location of his office.

∞

Robert F Kennedy Building
Washington, D.C.
Saturday, August 22, 2015

Smith reread the official diplomatic notice printed in both Dumal and English. It wasn't what he expected, but if he wanted to maintain the alliance, he had little choice.

The Dumal Federation hereby appoints Eliza Helen O'Reilly and Bruce Cowley Wilkerson, Jr. as emissaries of the Dumal Federation with all diplomatic rights and privileges.

As official Ambassadors of the Crown Prince, Ms. O'Reilly and Mr. Wilkerson are to be extended the same rights, courtesy, deference, access, and accommodations provided to the Crown Prince, Conference of Sovereigns, Cerculus, or any Dumal diplomatic official.

The bottom of the document showed the Crown Prince's signature and was embossed with the royal seal. A photocopy of Wilkie and Liza's diplomatic passports included a handwritten note on the back.

Dear Misters Smith and Jones,
We hope you understand the concept of diplomatic rights, but just in case you don't understand, we better explain. Your people may never detain or threaten us again. We consider any offense made against us an aggression against the Crown Prince and the Dumal Federation.
We just wanted to make sure you and Major Jones understood.
XOXO,
Liza and Wilkie.

Why weren't these submitted through official channels? Smith thought. He figured Cerculus allowed Liza and Wilkie to let him have a taste of his own medicine.

∞

TEN DAYS LATER

West Central, Alabama
Tuesday, September 1, 2015

Zach's redeye flight from Salt Lake City to Birmingham didn't allow for much sleep. He hoped for a solid six hours of shuteye on the Greyhound bus ride from Birmingham to Eutaw.

Finding an empty row, he threw a carry-on bag in the overhead bin and slid into the window seat. He positioned a pillow between the headrest and window, laid his long legs diagonally, and closed his eyes.

"Excuse me. Is this seat taken?"

Zach startled and sat upright. Before him, a smiling, wrinkly face wearing thick bifocals. Her age-spot-covered mahogany skin complimented her downy silver hair. In one arm was a kitchen sink-toting handbag, and the other carried a cane. She reminded Zach of his Nana Dee.

"No, ma'am." *I hope she doesn't want to talk. Please let me sleep.*

Like Nana Dee did with strangers, Mrs. Ford treated Zach like an old family friend by providing updates on her children, grandchildren, and great-grandchildren and talked about Jesus as if he was her best friend.

She reminisced how life growing up on a tenant farm was hard, and yet, was a simpler, joyful time. Although her sharecropper parents had little money for raising seven children, their home was rich with love, music, and laughter.

Other than not sleeping, Zach was glad for the extra-gabby, extra-sweet company. It kept his mind off his break-up with Joy.

Halfway between Eutaw and Livingston, Zach said goodbye to Mrs. Ford. He exited the air-conditioned Greyhound bus onto the roadside. His shirt quickly drenched and felt similar to the forty-pound weight vest he wore during plyometric exercises. He wished his ride would arrive shortly and had well-functioning air conditioning.

At the rural junction, Zach scanned the lush landscape. Utah's desert valleys and foothills were brown during its wettest summers. Zach still couldn't believe Alabama's farmers were experiencing a drought with so much green around.

The humid, rural landscape brought fond recollections of spending a few weeks each summer, together with Seth, in their father's hometown, Deweyville, Mississippi — a small town north of Tupelo and Oxford.

Although Zach's father rarely set foot in Deweyville, there was a boatload of caring uncles, aunties, and cousins — and neighbors who treated the boys as one of their own. Except for the humidity, Deweyville was like a second home to Zach because of his grandmother, Delilah Davidson.

Although lacking in height and nearly as wide, Nana Dee was a powerhouse. The glue that held the family together, a pillar of the church and community — and how she loved her Utah grandsons who stayed with her each summer.

The summer before his first abduction, Zach stayed almost the entire school break with Nana Dee. He had grown out his hair since the previous fall, and much to Nana Dee's vexation, he didn't cut it all summer. Proud of his Dr. J afro, Zach couldn't wait to show all his friends back home in Utah.

Returning to Abundance that summer, Zach arrived early to the neighborhood wardhouse gym before the weekly church youth activity started. Other boys from the ward noticed Zach shooting hoops dressed in his customary color-coordinated headband, wristbands, shorts, and sneaks. They said nothing about the elongated ginger curls pushed up in a bouquet-like bunch by the headband. The gym was full by the time Wilkie and Jeff arrived.

"Better warn Bart Simpson," Wilkie said, doing a Chief Clancy Wiggum imitation. "*Sideshow Bob's* escaped from prison. Ooh, is that a donut, Lou?"

The entire gym howled. Zach felt tempted to punch Wilkie in the face before going straight away to his barber. Although

Wilkie only said so once, the *Sideshow Bob* nickname instantly stuck.

Nana Dee had forewarned, "Folks will poke fun at that abomination of a hairdo."

She was always right.

∞

Widowed a year before Zach's birth, Nana Dee was actually Zach and Seth's great-grandmother.

An abusive boyfriend had murdered Zach's grandmother, making his father, Ezekiel, an orphan at age seven.

Reverend Davidson and Nana Dee had raised Zeke to be a hard-working, honest, and God-fearing person. She was heartbroken that her grandson would abandon his devoted wife, Jennifer, two sons, and an NBA career for the devil's drug. She prayed daily for Ezekiel to return to his senses.

Jenny Davidson had court-mandated full custody of Seth and Zach. Even though her ex-husband didn't seem to want any part of the boy's lives, she felt it imperative for her boys to connect with their father's side of the family. Besides, Jenny loved Delilah Davidson and valued her positive influence on her sons. Jenny didn't want to deny her boys the special relationship children have with their grandparents.

∞

Zach reminisced about riding bikes all summer long in Deweyville with Seth and cousins Gabriel and Caleb.

The neighbors called them *the Four Horsemen of the Apocalypse*.

Zach grinned with memories of Nana Dee calling the grandchildren and friends inside during the heat of the afternoon. Upon entry, the children would see Nana seated in her favorite wingback chair, a glass of iced tea on an end table, and reading glasses on the tip of her nose, ready for business.

"Y'all go get a drink of water in the kitchen, and come set

yourselves down at Nana Dee's feet," she'd say every time.

The congregation of children sat on a large Victorian parlor rug mesmerized as Nana Dee read from the Bible, but mostly to hear the most entertaining stories and also tales about her childhood — which older kids believed Nana also made up and were equally enjoyable.

Zach laughed with memories of her falling asleep mid-story. Moments later, she'd wake herself up with the first snort of a snore — or sometimes to children snickering. Nonplussed for only a moment, she continued right where she left off — as if nothing ever happened. Caleb often timed Nana's mid-story naps and claimed the record was four minutes and twenty-one seconds.

Zach had warm, fond memories of the extended family post-church potluck dinners. His mouth watered with thoughts of Aunt Hope's smoky and savory red beans and Nana's hot out of the oven cornbread. Mostly, he missed the sense of belonging, the laughter, the love. He found nothing more satisfying to the belly and soul than sharing a Sunday feast with the Davidson clan.

A sudden sadness overcame him. He never got to say goodbye to Nana Dee. She passed while he was missing.

Damn aliens.

His mourning shifted to the thought of Joy and the pain of their breakup. He was on the verge of bawling when a honk startled him.

"You, Zach?" the driver asked. "This is your chariot to Memnon."

Zach swiped his forearm across his eyes and nodded before noticing all four of the luxury sedan's windows open and mumbled, "Great. No air conditioning."

He contained surprise that transportation to Memnon School was an American-made, late-seventies boat of a car.

Given the militaristic tone of the staff from previous emails and telephone conversations, Memnon seemed more like a military academy and not a regular preparatory college. He had envisioned a five-ton troop carrier, Humvee, or a tank would be the standard mode of transportation.

Good thing that's a Lincoln, and not a Prius, entered his mind seeing a giant man in the driver's seat. His gargantuan smile dominated his pockmarked, mocha baby face — and made Zach feel at ease.

∞

Memnon Preparatory College
Sumter County, Alabama
Tuesday, September 1, 2015

A rectangular sign over the school entrance proclaimed:

WELCOME TO MEMNON PREPARATORY COLLEGE FOR
THE GIFTED
PRIDE • DUTY • HONOR • LOYALTY • COMMUNITY
Visitor Check-in Required

Big Dennis deftly maneuvered the two-ton Lincoln Mark VI around concrete pylons before being forced to a stop by a hardened steel boom bar.

Three male guards approached. One stood behind the vehicle. The others took positions on the sides. A female guard with an assault rifle crossing her body faced the Lincoln from beyond the gate. A Humvee parked to the side.

Dennis smiled as a guard approached. "Hey, Jordan."

"Hey, Big D." Jordan bent down to the driver's window and exchanged a fist bump with Dennis. "You know the drill."

"Zach, we need to get out," Dennis said and stepped out of the Lincoln. "Be gentle with the old girl, Jordan."

"We always are."

The guard with the Kalashnikov watched Zach closely while two others searched the car's interior, trunk, and engine compartment. The last checked under the vehicle with a mirror on a telescoping rod.

"Sir, please come here. You need to check in," she said.

Zach approached the guard.

With a form-fitting uniform, she seemed the epitome of an Amazon warrior. She removed a pair of aviator sunglasses to reveal a pair of breathtaking eyes: hazel, almond-shaped, and bright. Her wavy hair was tucked under a helmet. A golden ringlet dangled on both sides, enhancing her blemish-free almond face.

"Hey, Big D," she said.

"Hey, Azalea," Dennis said.

Azalea? I'm going to marry that girl, Zach thought.

The guard turned her head away from his gaze.

"Sergeant LaBatier. This is Mr. Davidson," Dennis said.

Azalea nodded. "Your ID, please, sir."

She compared the driver's license picture to Zach's face. "Thank you, Mr. Davison. I'll be right back."

She walked into the guard station and returned a few minutes later. "Mr. Davidson. Welcome to Memnon School. Here's your visitor's badge and lanyard. Please wear it at all times and always stay with your escort. Enjoy your visit."

"Thank you, Azalea," Zach said.

Azalea's scowl made Zach wince.

"It's Sergeant LaBatier. Thank you, Mr. Davison."

"Sergeant LaBatier. Yes, ma'am."

∞

Zach sat at an aluminum cafeteria table inside an empty gymnasium. On the front wall were three portraits in a row with quotes that sounded positive and patriotic.

The script under Malcolm X's portrait read:

*You can't separate peace from freedom because
no one can be at peace unless he has his freedom.*

George Washington stated:

The harder the conflict, the greater the triumph.

Martin Luther King Jr. said:

*Life's most persistent and urgent question is,
'What are you doing for others?'*

Centered above the portraits of the three American icons hung a larger portrait of a man in uniform with a quote underneath.

*Being united in the struggle for justice, liberty, and
survival of our race is our great and only cause*
- Commandant Eric Liddell

Liddell's likeness prominently displayed above such renowned leaders sent Zach a coherent message.

Shortly thereafter, a guard on rounds glanced into the gymnasium/mess hall of the Multipurpose Center. He turned to leave before doing a double-take and made a beeline toward Zach.

"Why are you sitting here?"

"I was told to sit here," Zach said.

"Where's your ID badge?"

Zach lifted his lanyard.

"Where's your escort?"

"Dennis went to get some food," Zach said.

"You in the kitchen, Big D?" the guard yelled.

Dennis poked his head out the kitchen door. "I'm making some ham sandwiches. You want some Marcus — I mean Sargent Landry?"

Landry walked toward the kitchen.

"You shouldn't leave civilians with visitor's badges out of your sight, Big D. You know that."

"Zach's alright. He'll wear a cadet uniform soon enough. He's meeting the Commandant right after we eat. He's the dude the Commandant been talking about."

"Davidson?" Landry asked.

Big Dennis nodded. "Yep."

∞

Administration Building
Memnon Preparatory College
Sumter County, Alabama
Tuesday, September 1, 2015

The tiny office seemed smaller as the interview dragged on.

I'm a fraud, and he knows it, Zach thought.

Across the desk, a gray-haired and fit man exuded an air of authority, and a grandfatherly demeanor interviewed Zach for nearly an hour.

As the questions ended, Zach was relieved for a moment, but a nascent fear emerged as he realized his journey had just started.

Why did I say 'yes'? he thought.

"Congratulations, Cadet Davidson," Commandant Liddell said.

Both men stood and shook hands.

"It's been a pleasure to meet you, Zach. Thank you for making the long trek from Utah to join us. I believe you will be an excellent fit at Memnon Prep. I hope we are for you, too."

"It's nice to meet you too, sir. I look forward to starting classes on Monday."

"Good man." Liddell smiled. "Well, I'm off to a meeting. Please take a seat. There's someone that's been waiting to meet you."

Zach studied the contents of the modest office during the long wait. On the left wall, he examined Liddell's framed diplomas.

One from the U.S. Military Academy at West Point, masters from Georgetown and the London School of Economics, and a doctorate from Yale. One frame held a certificate from the Army War College stating *Distinguished Teaching Fellow*. Another displayed a Certificate of Retirement from the United States Army.

Photographs upon the credenza on the right showed a young Liddell with other soldiers wearing combat fatigues with jungles and tarmacs as backdrops. Zach locked eyes on the moment President Lyndon B Johnson placed a medal over Liddell's bowed head. Near-retirement photos showed Liddell at official functions dressed in formal blues, posing with generals, politicians, and bureaucrats.

Zach moved behind Liddell's desk to inspect the fine-tip cursive quotes on the wall.

— flying saucers from another solar system are real — manned by intelligent observers who are members of a race that may have been investigating our Earth for centuries
- Professor Hermann Oberth

"That's why I'm here," Zach whispered. His chest tightened as he read the next.

One death is a tragedy; one million is a statistic
- Joseph Stalin

What we affirm is that we must proceed along the path of liberation, even if this costs millions of atomic victims
- Che Guevara

He shivered. "What the hell?"

(White) Christians are merely a tool used by the Devil to keep you, the Nubian man, woman, and child, blind to your true heritage and perfect way of life. It is another means of slavery
- Dr. Malachi Z K York

"What the freak?"

The tree of liberty must be refreshed from time to time with the blood of patriots and tyrants
- Thomas Jefferson

The Mother Wheel is a heavily armed spaceship the size of a city, which will rain destruction upon white America
- Louis Farrakhan

Zach shook his head and whispered, "What the heck have I gotten myself into?"

Liddell seemed a living contradiction for a learned and successful man. The professor of history and economics and retired full-bird colonel had some 'weird-ass' sayings right behind him. Zach couldn't determine if Liddell was a patriot, communist revolutionary, UFO conspiracist, black separatist — or all of the above.

"Hello, Zach."

Zach flinched and turned toward a towering, gaunt, and utterly bald man with a salt and pepper goatee-mustache, who filled the doorway. Something about him seemed vaguely familiar.

"You look as nervous as a long-tail cat in a room full of rocking chairs," the man said.

Zach had only heard that saying from one other person, *Nana Dee.*

He reimagined the man with a younger, clean-shaven face, a full head of hair, and fainter crow's feet around his eyes — then Zach's eyes opened wide. *"Dad?"*

∞

SIXTY-FOUR DAYS LATER

Camp Memnon
Kemper County, Mississippi
Sunday, October 25, 2015

Zach Davidson kept his eyes closed as hot water rolled off his shoulders. He thought about the times he almost quit and returned home during the first three weeks of boot camp. Now, nine weeks in, he still missed his bed and Mom, Seth, Wilkie, and more, but the bonds he formed with members of his platoon made his homesickness manageable.

A drill sergeant yelled into the dormitory shower area, "Time to quit jerking it and finish up, peons. You got 30 minutes till breakfast and 90 minutes until inspection."

As Zach's eyes opened, he found the same nine squadmates as before, also enjoying their last hot shower for seven days. He closed the shower valve, toweled off, and headed to the nearest full-length mirror.

In his nude reflection, he hardly recognized the scrawny kid from nine weeks ago. The first week, he struggled with completing 25 sit-ups or push-ups. Now, he didn't balk when ordered to give a 100 of either. He ran his fingers across the lines of his stomach. It took seven weeks of intense abdominal work and inedible mess hall chow to create the six-pack abs he always dreamed about. The constant drilling outdoors created more face freckles, but Zach was only a tad tanner—and was still the fairest-skinned and only ginger cadet in boot camp.

"Looking good," Zach said, and pirouetted in the opposite direction, looked over his shoulder, examined his back and calves in the mirror, and decided they needed more work. Looking down, he realized his size-sixteen feet hadn't grown for quite some time, although his height had caught up by two more inches since his arrival at Memnon.

The drill sergeant turned the corner and yelled, "Davidson, your junk ain't getting any bigger staring at it. Get a move on."

∞

Cadet Zach Davidson didn't notice the weight of his battle gear for the first nine kilometers of the march across woods, fields, and hills. He fumed since being called *son* by Major Ezekiel Davidson during the executive officer's pre-field exercises inspection and the last big event's rah-rah speeches. On his first day at Memnon, Zach had made it clear he wouldn't acknowledge Major Davidson as his father, but would keep things professional.

Sergeant Morris stuck his head out of the Humvee's passenger window toward the ten-man unit at the rear. "Phoenix Squad, pick up the pace! Ranger standard time." The Humvee increased its speed from 5.5kph to 6.4kph.

The sergeant's order and the Humvee's increased speed roused Zach from his resentful cruise control. It felt like his gear doubled in weight, and he noticed the burn in his shoulders, quads, and calves for the first time.

A few kilometers later, the Humvee stopped at the base of a hill, and Sergeant Morris stuck his head out the passenger window. "Phoenix Squad, halt!" The driver, Corporal Zafar, and Morris exited the vehicle and moved near the tailgate. "Gather round and listen up."

Zach and his squadmates broke formation and huddled up near their non-commissioned officers.

"You humped 75 pounds of combat gear for 15 klicks and look like shit," Morris said. "It's definitely an improvement."

The squad chuckled.

"Well done." Morris nodded at the cadets. "We're breaking for lunch. Return here at 1230 hours, and Corporal Zafar will explain your exercises for the rest of our afternoon. Enjoy your MREs, and get some rest. We have a long day ahead. Dismissed."

∞

Soon after returning to bivouac, Zach popped two extra-strength ibuprofen tablets in his mouth, dry swallowed, and joined the others at the campfire. Zach was too tired for conversation and didn't notice the others' silence.

He sat next to his battle buddy, Charles Minns, as Minns poured water into the plastic pouch containing a flameless ration heater and Meal-Ready-to-Eat. The water-activated chemical reaction would provide a hot dinner in twelve minutes.

Zach observed Minns nosh throughout the afternoon's activities. He figured Minns required a lot of fuel to power his six foot five inch NFL defensive lineman-like body. Zach's lunch MRE felt like dead weight in his stomach and could keep hunger at bay for a couple of days. He assumed the others avoiding dinner felt the same way as him; MRE bloated and too exhausted to eat.

Sergeant Morris and Corporal Zafar walked up to the group.

"Let's have a little post-mortem about this afternoon's exercises. First, the field orientation course." Morris shook his head. "Davidson, Minns, I don't know how you did it."

A lone cadet stood. "Permission to ask a question, sir."

"Take a seat, Thompson. Let's keep this informal. Raise your hand next time."

"Yes, sir."

"What's your question?"

Thompson, by instinct, almost stood but caught a glare from Morris and remained seated. "Did Minns and Davidson cheat?"

"Kind of, and no." Morris said. "The gruesome twosome arrived at the rendezvous point twice. The first time was under eight minutes. GPS tracking confirmed they arrived at each waypoint and the rendezvous point as instructed with the key phrases."

There were murmurs among the cadets.

"Their second attempt took one hour, fifty-two minutes, including about ten minutes wasted to restart their course—and they still beat the rest of your sorry asses. Care to explain how you did it the first time, Cadet Minns?"

A huge grin overcame Minns's face. "We used the compass from waypoint to waypoint on the map and wrote the key phrase from each on our map, then arrived at the rendezvous as Corporal Zafar instructed. Technically, we didn't cheat. Corporal Jafar did not tell us to complete the course on foot."

"So, explain to your squadmates how you improvised your first time."

"We oriented the compass on the map as instructed, then Zach eagle-eyed each waypoint location, and we teleported to it, and wrote the key phrases—and teleported to you at the live fire range from the last waypoint. We should have got there faster." Minns grimaced. "You then cussed us out and instructed us to leap back to camp and start over on foot."

Morris stared at Zach. "Alright, Davidson, with your return to the starting point and a ten-minute delay, how did you still beat the other battle buddies?"

"I can't help it if I'm the only eagle-eye in the squad." Zach shrugged. "I can't unsee what I've already seen."

Morris glared at Zach. "Care to elaborate?"

"Since I already knew the route and had already written the key phrase from each waypoint, it allowed us to hoof it straight through.

"It still doesn't seem fair." Morris shook his head, then alternated his stare between Minns and Davidson. "You two dominated in the live fire exercise as well. Any E.T. powers we don't know about that gave you an edge?"

"No, sir," Zach and Minns said in unison.

"Phoenix Squadron, good work today. Tomorrow, we meet up with the rest of our platoon. Revelry will be at 0400, and we march at 0500. Lights out at 2100 hours, but from experience, you won't make it until then.

"Before we break." Morris's lips curled upward. "Three cheers for Cadets Minns and Davidson."

"Hoorah, hoorah, hoorah," the squadron shouted.

A huge grin came over Morris's face. "Corporal Zafar, can you please tell Minns and Davidson what they won for finishing first in both of today's exercises."

"Phoenix Squad, starting at 2100, here are tonight's 2-hour watch assignments: Minns and Jackson. First watch. Davidson and Thomas. Second watch…"

∞

The waxing gibbous moon neared its apogee as Cadet Jackson noticed the camp being its most illuminated of the night. He approached Minns on the opposite side of the camp.

"Hey, big fella. It's 2241," Jackson whispered. "We should rouse second watch soon."

"22:50?"

Jackson nodded. "Sounds good."

Both cadets jumped as someone screamed from a nearby two-man tent. "Aliens. They're coming. Run!"

They turned, scanned the perimeter and the camp—then chuckled.

"Zach and his damn nightmares," Minns said. "Gee."

Moments later, a blue light engulfed the camp and dust blew in all directions, startling Jackson and Minns again. They looked skyward at the beam emitted by a disc-shaped object hovering about 40 feet overhead. Minns attempted to run, but his legs wouldn't move. Jackson tried to speak but couldn't. They felt weightless as their feet left the ground, and they floated until almost reaching the vessel—before passing out.

∞

Zach Davidson's stoic mien hid a rage burning inside. *No more abductions, my ass!*

He noticed the Ergonea possessed an odd medicinal smell as two grays led him down the passageway. It reminded him more experimentation was coming—and made him angrier. They reached and stopped at the control room's arched entrance.

Three Dumal officers remained at their stations. After a long, awkward pause, one turned around and extended his spindly arm.

Please enter, the voice entered Zach's mind.

Zach froze until both grays shoved him over the threshold. The petite aliens blocked the exit as he approached the Being.

He stared intently at the charcoal-gray natal star mark over its eye, figured this Dumal had to be nearly eight feet tall, and thought, *Wilkie's description is spot on.*

Welcome to the Ergonea, Cadet Davidson. The alien tilted his head and made eye contact. *I have not formally introduced myself. I am Cerculus, Fleet Admiral of the Dumal Federation Expeditionary Forces.*

Zach nodded, being afraid of what he might say.

May I call you Zach?

Zach nodded again.

Cerculus extended his hand. *Shall we walk?*

They headed out the control room door into an arched hallway made with silvery blocks and walked for what seemed a mile until reaching the mess hall.

Zach glanced at the red double swastika over the archway and thought, *Just like Wilkie said.*

Upon entry, he gasped, and any anger he held dissipated by the view of the bright blue orb seen via the transparent dome. He almost spoke aloud, *'Seeing earth from space is more amazing than Wilkie said,'* but caught himself before revealing that he and Wilkie could remember all their previous abductions after the memory-burying procedures.

Are you hungry? Cerculus asked.

"Kind of," Zach said.

Cerculus made eye contact with a gray, who weaved through other gray servers holding silver platters above their heads and the Dumal crew members that surrounded them. He disappeared behind a curtain on the far end of the dining hall and soon returned with a carbon fiber-like pub table and placed it between Zach and Cerculus.

Two Grays, each carrying a platter, exited the curtain and approached the table. One placed a plate on the table in front of Cerculus. A coil of a jerky-like material filled the plate.

Zach's eyes opened wide, then he smiled as the gray placed the plate in front of him. *How did they know?* (A baked potato with butter and chives, ribeye steak, and steamed lobster tail with a ramekin of clarified butter was Zach's favorite meal).

Zach observed Cerculus hoist the outer end of the spiral, aligned it with his mouth-slit, and slurped the food upward like a stock ticker paper into a ticker tape machine.

Cerculus continued to eat and noticed Zach staring. *Please, eat.*

Zach hesitated as he picked up his fork and steak knife. He'd never eaten this meal outside a fine dining establishment and never standing up. He finally cut a piece of beef and held it up for examination. Not seeing a hint of pink flesh, Zach popped it into his mouth and savored the chew.

How is your steak? The coil continuously unwound into Cerculus's mouth.

Zach swallowed. "Fantastic. How did you know I like it well done?"

We pay great individual attention in accommodating all our guests.

"Thank you for your hospitality." Zach looked Cerculus in the eyes. "You've never fed me before. Why now?"

I have something important to discuss with you.

Cerculus didn't register Zach's raised eyelids and eyebrows and jaw dropping as surprise, but the Dumal's psychic empathy did instead.

In our study of Earth's cultures, we've observed when humans eat together, they create bonds with those sharing a meal.

"So, what do you want to discuss?"

I don't believe it's a mistake for your ability to sense future danger and being a remote viewer. They perfectly complement Wilkie's and Liza's abilities.

"You want to talk to me about that?" Zach took a bite of lobster.

Wilkie will become an important leader, but he can't do so without your and Liza's help. You must stand with Wilkie and assist and protect him at all costs.

Zach stopped chewing, looked at Cerculus, and swallowed. "Wilkie's like a brother to me. I'll always stick by him."

∞

Zach froze as he stood in the examination chamber entryway and counted sixteen stone-slab tables. Four tables were empty, and his squad's two NCOs, medic, and nine other cadets occupied the remaining tables, each attended by gray technicians and robotic arms.

Zach felt his pulse race. *I can't do this again.*

His two gray escorts each grabbed an arm and hauled him to the exam table. Zach couldn't believe that two hominids less than half his size could be so strong.

∞

Day 2 – Field Exercises
Camp Memnon
Kemper County, Mississippi
Monday, October 26, 2015

Platoon Sergeant Davis stomped back and forth across the platoon's rendezvous point as a trace of pre-dawn light burnished the horizon. Davis reminisced on Sergeant Morris's oft-quoted expression for new cadets: *Ten minutes early is on time.*

"Early, my ass," he murmured before entering the command tent.

"Where the hell is Phoenix Squadron?" Davis threw his arms in the air and frowned at Sergeant Bryant.

"I still can't get Morris or Zafar on the horn." Bryant shrugged. "… or track their geolocation."

"Keep trying," Davis said. "Give them ten more minutes before we start our field exercise."

"Yes, sir."

"This isn't like Sergeant Morris."

Davis exited the tent and continued stomping around camp, reviewing his alternative plan with only two of the three squadrons present, and checked his watch periodically. He realized fifteen minutes had passed and entered the command center tent. "Any luck, Aaron?"

Bryant looked up from his laptop. "The situation's still the same."

"Alright. Sergeant Uche and Sergeant Adams, looks like we go with Plan Bravo. Assemble your squads. Formation in five."

"Yes, sir."

∞

"Alright, platoon. You know your assignments. Move out!" Davis said.

"Hold on! I found them!" Bryant shouted as he ran out of the tent toward the other drill sergeants. He reached the others, short of breath. "Their geolocators just pinged."

Davis huddled the sergeants an earshot away from the cadets, and asked. "Where are they?"

"Still at bivouac." Bryant shook his head. "And I'm worried."

"Why?"

"Because there's no movement. Their geolocators are scattered around their camp and all stationary."

Davis paused in thought for a moment. "Sergeant Uche, you're acting platoon sergeant until I return. Go ahead with maneuvers without us."

He turned toward a medic and called, "Bring your gear. You're with me." He faced Bryant. "Get HQ on the horn, update our situation, then bring your GPS tablet. You're navigating."

Davis hopped in the driver's seat of the Humvee and brought the 6.5L turbo diesel to life as the medic loaded his bags in the back.

Bryant approached the driver's side window a couple of minutes later. "HQ's sending choppers and medics. They ordered us to stay with the platoon and continue with the field exercises."

"Bullshit!" Davis pounded his hands on the steering wheel. "Get HQ back on the horn. We're closer."

"This came directly from Commandant Liddle." Bryant's lips pursed. "Besides, we can't beat the helos."

Davis rubbed his chin and turned off the engine. "Damn it!"

∞

One of two Sikorsky S-92 helicopters circled the site and maintained enough altitude so as not to disturb the area with rotor downwash as Commandant Liddle and Major Davidson scanned below.

They observed tents strewn around the campsite and one caught hanging in a red maple tree on the edge of the clearing.

Davidson searched for the fair skin and ginger crewcut of his son, but didn't see signs of any men.

The Commandant noticed the worry lines on Davidson's brow, then patted his shoulder. "I'm sure they're going to be alright, Zeke."

The pilot's voice came over the headsets. "Commandant, we need to land on that ridge on our three o'clock."

"You can't get us any closer."

"Not unless you want to zipline."

"The ridge it is. I'm too old to jump out of this bird."

∞

Steam came off Commandant Liddell's breath as he found a quiet edge of the abandoned camp and dialed a number into the satellite phone. It rang twice.

"Deputy Director Smith's office. How may I help you?"

"Hello Martel, Eric Liddell here. I need to speak with Mr. Smith ASAP."

"I'm sorry, Commandant Liddell. Mr. Smith is out of pocket until Thursday and cannot be reached. Is it possible to leave a message with me, or I can send you to voicemail?"

"It's priority alpha, Martel."

"Let me see if I can reach him. One moment, please."

Liddell marched in place to fend off anxiety and the cold.

"Commandant Liddell, I'm transferring you to the Air Force One operator," Martel said. "I hope you can resolve your issue with Mr. Smith quickly."

"Thank you, Martel. You've been very helpful."

Liddell's heart raced in anticipation. Five seconds seemed like thirty after the transfer.

"Commandant Liddell," the operator said. "Deputy Director Smith will be with you momentarily."

The ten second pause seemed like minutes.

"Eric. What's so urgent you needed to interrupt my meeting with the president?" Smith asked.

Liddell took a deep breath and calmed his mind before he spoke. "G.W., the Dumal took thirteen of my men, including 10 cadets, in their last week of boot camp."

"Are you sure they didn't just get lost? The woods at Camp Memnon are pretty thick." Smith's eyebrow raised. "The Dumal were the ones to suggest the moratorium."

"Come on, G.W. It's the Dumal. We confirmed the men were accounted for last evening and disappeared before morning, leaving their weapons, equipment, and GPS trackers behind. And the kicker—ambient residual magnetism is a match for Dumal transport."

"Remanence. You determined by compass?"

"Initially, yes, but it wasn't endemic magnetic deviation. Abduction forensics verified this as Dumal by magnetometer and computer analysis."

"I must get back to you. We're halfway across the Atlantic, and I won't be able to contact the Dumal until after we reach Moscow."

Liddell raised an eyebrow. "Can't someone else contact the Dumal, given the circumstance?"

"Only if I'm dead. Dumal diplomatic protocols for contact

with the Crown Prince and the Sovereigns are strict. Resumption of Dumal experimentation on FAS cadets could only come from the highest levels."

∞

THREE DAYS LATER

Memnon Preparatory College
Sumter County, Alabama
Thursday, October 29, 2015

Goddamn Mujar malware! How can I explain this to their families? Liddell thought as his fingers tapped on his office desk. *They need to be returned soon.*

Unable to focus on the academic status reports, Liddell fretted on how a possible extended gap might hinder the recruitment of new cadets for months — maybe years.

His desk phone rang once before he picked up the handset. "Liddell."

A huge grin formed as he listened. "That's great news. Proceed as planned."

Liddle put his finger on the disconnect button and pushed another. "Dennis, get me G.W. Smith on a secure line. Priority alpha."

Liddle continued to tap his fingers on the desk and maintained his smile as he waited. He expected rings when a voice interrupted his bliss.

"Eric. Any updates?"

"We found them only moments ago. Unconscious, but safe." Liddell's smile faded. "Let's be happy it was three days and not two years like the last time."

"You can say that again," Smith said. "Are you sticking with the carbon monoxide poisoning cover story?"

"We are. They're being transferred to the field hospital as

we speak."

"How are you holding up?"

"I'm furious at the Dumal for resuming procedures on my cadets — and more so for Cerculus not notifying us. I thought this was a partnership."

"I have made a formal complaint with the ministry," Smith said. "The reason they gave me is our behavioral and psychic enhancements are not as comprehensive as those conducted on Ergonea."

"Rubbish. It's the same tech." Liddell shook his head. "This is about control. Their arrogance risked delaying Restoration Day."

∞

Field Hospital
Camp Memnon
Kemper County, Mississippi
Thursday, October 29, 2015

Zach Davidson fought waking up, but the din of pumping and beeping machines and roaming voices got the best of his curiosity. He opened his eyes toward the white polycarbonate ceiling and an aluminum frame supporting the canvas. His head turned toward three other squadmates in their hospital beds. They seemed asleep, with wires protruding from all over their bodies and respirators emanating from their mouths. He touched the endotracheal tube protruding from his mouth and followed it down the ventilator hose, realizing he was in the same situation.

The sounds of zipper opening drew his attention to a young woman wearing surgical garb, mask, and gloves entering.

She reached Zach's bedside and keyed a device on her scrubs. "Cadet Davidson's conscious."

Three other medical professionals rushed to his bedside and immediately checked the monitors. They took his blood pressure, pulse, and respirations and tested the reaction from Zach's pupils and reflexes.

It felt odd seeing an entirely black hospital staff for Zach. His weeklong hospitalization in Salt Lake a few years ago, the staff was mostly white, with a handful of Hispanic and Asian staff, but he only remembered one black doctor.

A woman with well-defined crow's feet around her eyes and an air of authority touched Zach's face. "Mr. Davidson. You're breathing on your own now. We'll get you off the ventilator shortly, honey."

∞

Zach heard a muted debate through the vinyl walls as a nurse escorted him back to his room. Minns, Jackson, and Thomas sat on the edge of their beds and became silent as Zack entered.

"How was your hyperbaric treatment?" Minns asked.

"Boring," Zach said, and sat on his bed. "What was I missing?"

Thomas broke the silence. "We were debating if our current predicament was really carbon monoxide poisoning or something else." Thomas rubbed his chin. "It doesn't seem plausible to me."

"It's plausible," Minns said. "It's the only thing that makes sense."

Thomas shook his head. "Since I'm the only one here with a degree in biochemistry, let me make sense of it for you. Diesel doesn't produce high levels of carbon monoxide, and we were out in the open. One idling Humvee at the base of a dell couldn't knock us all out unless we were inside the Humvee."

"The doctors are MDs, and you're not," Minns said and smirked. "If they say it was carbon monoxide, I trust them over your chemistry degree."

Bullshit! Zach thought, then said aloud, "I think the Dumal abducted us."

I don't think. I know.

"That's cray, cray," Minns said. "We all know the Dumal don't abduct folks from Memnon."

"Remember how I told you I have vivid dreams about my abductions."

"Yeah."

"I had one while we were in our comas."

"You can't dream while in a coma," said an unexpected voice. A new doctor standing in the door flap startled Zach and his squadmates.

"You shouldn't spread false information around." He approached Zach's bedside, put a hand on his shoulder, bent down, and locked eyes. "You don't want to be the one who starts a baseless conspiracy theory, do you?"

"Well, no." Zach felt tempted to say, *it's not baseless or a theory*, but held his tongue, knowing the medical personnel were culpable in the deception.

PART 10-DUTY CALLS

"When someone shows you who they are, believe them the first time."
- Maya Angelou

FIVE MONTHS LATER

Aryana Ranch
Lincoln County, Montana
Wednesday, February 3, 2016

Eric Anders parked his four-wheeler about a mile away and hefted a pack and AR-15 on opposite shoulders for the trek along the east perimeter fence. A wave of homesickness rolled over as his boots crunched on the crusty snow. The armed walk in the woods invoked memories of hunting on the family estate with Gracie and George, raised from pups to flush out pheasant and grouse.

Montana's sub-zero temperatures, evergreen forests, and the distant howls of wolves were also reminiscent of Minnesota. Anders didn't fear wolves, but brown bears were another issue. He'd never dealt with the fearless brutes back home and was grateful to avoid Montana grizzlies so far. After completing the bear safety course, he carried a can of bear mace when on patrol, but hoped never to use the device.

Near the middle of the patrol area, Anders tapped the two-way radio earpiece. "Soothsayer to base. Base, do you copy?"

"Base to Soothsayer. Go ahead."

Anders tapped the device again. "Sections two-zero-one, two-zero-two, and two-zero-three are all clear. Taking my lunch."

"Roger, Soothsayer. Confirmed. Sections two-zero-one, two-zero-two, and two-zero-three all-clear. On lunch break. Next report at twenty-three-hundred."

"Roger, base. Report back at twenty-three-hundred. Soothsayer out." Anders sighed, closed his eyes, and scanned the woods and the fence line track. He opened his eyes to search again.

He unclipped and hung the walkie-talkie on the bough of a Ponderosa Pine and trod thirty-odd yards into the woods until reaching a small clearing. He paused and made a 360-degree turn with his eyes open, then closed his eyes and did so in his mind. The coast was both visually and empathically clear.

After ten minutes, Anders was about ready to leave when the forest illuminated in a blue glow behind him. He turned toward an ancient, professionally dressed man in a wheelchair, a plaited wool blanket across his lap. The light surrounded his body and made his downy silver hair glow blue. Behind the man stood two serious-looking men dressed in black suits, white shirts, and skinny black ties. Anders wished he had a pair of their aviator sunglasses to filter the glare.

"General, it's good to see you," Ander said. "I wasn't certain you'd come."

Fishburn smiled. "How are you holding up, son?"

"Very well, thank you, sir."

"Are you ready to report?"

"Yes, sir." Anders cleared his throat. "Dupre is what we think he is. Another honest-to-God fascist working directly with the Dumal. Like Hitler, Dupre believes the world's a better place without Jews — and if he ruled that world. I don't think the man's insane, but he is highly intelligent, calculating, and patient. He's also suspicious about Aryana being infiltrated by MJ-12 and IGC agents."

"Is your unit free from any suspicion of being Majestic-12?" Fishburn asked.

Anders looked up for a moment. "Empathically speaking, we're not considered active threats."

"If you ever feel in any danger of being discovered, I want your unit to amscray ASAP." Fishburn wiped the corner of his mouth with a folded handkerchief. "What's the status of Dupre's relationship with the Dumal?"

"He doesn't trust the Dumal, but sees them as an end to his means. He claims, based on Dumal intelligence, that an IGC-led Armageddon is coming soon."

"That's a load of hooey." Fishburn snorted. "When does this supposed Apocalypse occur?"

"Senior staff speak in broad generalities and don't give any specifics."

Fishburn's brow furrowed. "What is Dupre's vision for his post-apocalyptic world?"

"It's pretty simple. Blacks, whites, Mexicans, and Dumal living in separate regions of North America."

"Is that all?"

"The fascists want a world without Jews and Mai — or IGC interference. Also, Asians should live in Asia and Arabs in the Middle East."

"How was your leap training with Ms. O'Reilly and Mr. Wilkerson?"

A ghost of a smile passed over his face. "Excellent, sir. Ironically, jump teams may come in handy one day against the fascists."

"Are Ms. O'Reilly and Mr. Wilkerson as committed to the aims of the Dumal as they claim?"

He gently bit his lip for a moment. "It's uncertain, sir. I can't read them."

Fishburn cocked his head. "Really? It's not uncommon for empaths like you and Miss O'Reilly not being able to read each other. Is Wilkerson empathic, too?"

"Not that I know of."

"Empaths often struggle to get a read on psychopaths." His eyes narrowed. "Is the Wilkerson boy a psychopath?"

"I don't believe so, sir. He seems altruistic to a fault."

"It could be an act. A psychopath with his abilities is a frightening proposition."

Ander sighed and stared intensely. "I've spent a lot of time with Wilkie and Liza. They're intelligent and decent folk and not fools or monsters, either. I don't need to be empathic to observe a person's character."

"On a first-name basis, I see. That's good."

"I need to disclose one thing." Anders ran an open palm down from his cheek and held his chin for a moment. "My relationship with Liza is moving a bit toward the romantic side."

Fishburn's left eyebrow rose. "Can you keep emotions from clouding your judgment, Lieutenant?"

"Yes, sir. I can."

Fishburn nodded. "Is the feeling mutual?"

"Yes, sir. I believe so."

"Thank you for being forthright." Fishburn rubbed his chin and then raised a finger. "This could work to our advantage." He leaned toward his charge. "Are you certain you can fulfill your mission without being emotionally compromised in this case, son?"

Anders bent over to meet Fishburn's stare. "Yes, sir. I made an oath to the United States of America to defend our nation against all enemies—foreign and domestic. I'm duty-bound to put my personal feelings aside. If we find she's a traitor, you can sign me up to lead the firing squad."

"How are your men?"

∞

Anders put two fingers on a molar and twisted it. "Before I forget, here's the camp roster, photographs, and maps of the Montana side of camp."

He handed the tooth to one man in a black suit. The other gave Anders a replacement tooth, which he twisted back in place.

Anders continued. "Once Sargent Wolstenholme returns from officer candidate school, we can gather intelligence on the Idaho and Canadian sides of base."

Fishburn pursed his lips and nodded twice. "Excellent work, Lieutenant Anders. I look forward to your next report. Godspeed, son."

∞

THREE MONTHS, TWO WEEKS LATER

Memnon Preparatory College
Sumter County, Alabama
Saturday, May 14, 2016

Part of Zach didn't expect Azalea LaBatier to show up. His courage struggled back and forth along a steep, switchback mountain pass, but eventually, hope crested the summit as he rounded the corner of the administrative building.

His *Azalea Sitting Under the Elm Tree at the Far End of Commons Fantasy* was being fulfilled with a sunset behind her.

He crossed the quad to reach the park bench and focused on a gorgeous face surrounded by golden, curly locks draped across bare, caramel shoulders.

"Hey, Davidson," Azalea said.

"Hey, LaBatier," he said, before being distracted by a pair of long, toned legs protruding from a floral sundress to slender feet with painted nails in flip-flops.

"Eyes up here, Davidson."

Zach grinned. Her hazel eyes were more alluring than her legs.

She returned a quick upward glance. *Man, he's gotten tall.* She paused on his Tardis t-shirt. *He'd get along with Dad.*

"How much have you grown since you got here?" she asked.

Zach shrugged. "Five and a half inches. I think I'm about done. Six-six is about it."

"It's too bad your melon didn't like keep up with those legs." She chuckled.

"Despite the insults, I'm glad you're here."

"I'm glad I came, too." Azalea snickered. "Despite the company."

"What changed your mind?"

"I figured you're safe, Davidson. Like you said, we're not on a date. We're just hanging out."

"You feel safe with me. Do I give off a safe-vibe?"

"You're like religious, and I heard through the grapevine that you're like a virgin."

Zach turned away and blushed. "I guess I shouldn't tell my secrets to Dennis anymore."

Azalea laughed. "Big D means no harm. He's been playing matchmaker for me, since like I've arrived. I guess he figured telling would like get me here with you—*but this isn't a date.*"

Zach turned and gazed at her. "F-Y-I, I'm a virgin by choice. I'm saving myself for marriage."

She nodded. "I've been like saving myself, too. Not necessarily for marriage, but at least for love."

"Aren't you putting yourself at risk hanging out with a stud like me?" He released a nervous chuckle.

Azalea smirked. "You're like such an idiot, Davidson."

"It seems like a valid point."

"That you're an *idiot*?" Azalea chortled.

"No! That you're living on the wild side, hanging out with a tall virgin idiot. You never know where the heart might lead."

"I'm still safe hanging out with you. You're off to Officer Candidate School (OCS) in like two weeks. You know, extracurricular relationships between officers and non-commissioned officers (NCO) are prohibited."

"What if I don't go to OCS? You'd be in trouble."

She glared at him. "Don't be an idiot, Davidson. You'd be a fool to miss the opportunity."

"Maybe I'd prefer to stay a non-commissioned officer."

"You know you're only like the second one they've invited to OCS. If you graduate, you'll be like the first to receive a commission."

Zach's brow furloughed. "Second, what?"

"Stop being such an idiot. Haven't you noticed there's like no mixed-race officers?"

The statement left Zach nonplussed. He mentally scanned through the faces of officers, unsure who was mixed race. He'd never given it any thought before.

Azalea continued. "Landry like went to OCS. He was like top in his class — until like the last two exams. He was certain he aced both, but he failed miserably. No matter how well he did, they'd like not let him graduate."

Zach's head warbled back and forth. "We're all mixed race. Almost all African-Americans have genes from European ancestors and vice versa."

"Like you better not let the Commandant hear you talk like that."

Zach frowned. "I've been uncomfortable with the whole Aryana, Memnon, and Xiuhcoatl segregation thing. We're all human beings and abductees. Race shouldn't matter."

"Race matters. They say I'm black, but truth be told, I'm multiracial, and the executives know it. I'll never be an officer." Her lips scrunched, and she paused for a moment. "It's like rumored that nepotism played a role in your rapid advancement."

Zach gripped the bench's backrest and glared at her. "*The Major*? No way! I'm so damn sick and tired of people saying that I rode the bastard's coattails."

Azalea shifted back in her seat with eyes wide. "Like that's the rumor."

Zach released his grip on the bench and sighed. "Look, I haven't spoken with the Sperm Donor since my first day, and it wasn't a meeting of my choice. I told him to go have sex with himself."

"You told the Major to go eff himself, and they still admitted you to the academy? Definitely nepotism."

He shifted side-to-side in his seat. "We-el-l, not really, but I wanted to. I made it clear I didn't want to have a relationship with him."

"The Commandant must have like really wanted you," she said while nodding. "Like anyone else shows that level of disrespect to a senior officer would have been like tossed out the gate—ASAP."

"The Sperm Donor understood why I won't acknowledge him as my father. With little involvement for most of my life, you'd think he expected it."

She tilted her head to the side and raised an eyebrow. "Did he say why he abandoned you?"

"He claimed to protect me from the aliens. Lot of good that did." Zach scoffed. "He chose drugs over his family. Like a typical addict, he doesn't take responsibility for his choices."

Azalea shook her head. "That's sad. I can't understand how a man can like abandon his family. My father and grandfathers are a huge part of my life."

"I'm blessed to have incredible grandparents and a great man, my best friend's father, who's been a father figure to me. During my two-year absence, he married my mom—so I guess he is my dad."

"I'm happy for you. Family is everything."

Zach nodded. "Enough about my sorry life. Tell me about where you grew up. Montana, wasn't it?"

"Hold on a minute." She waved her hand back and forth. "I heard you like have a fiancée back in Utah." She sensed a bit of hesitation.

"Damn, big-mouthed Big D!" Zach laughed. "She never was my fiancée, and it's long since over."

"Like what happened?"

Zach smirked. "You seem to overuse *like*. Did I just miss it, or is it something new to your vocabulary?"

"You're li—avoiding the question."

"You, first."

"No, I asked first. Ask me again later. So, what happened?"

His head rolled back. "I asked for her father's blessing, and he said, *yes*—with conditions."

"Like what conditions?"

A boyish grin overcame Zach. "He made me like promise we wouldn't like marry until she like finished college, and I like served a mission."

"You're such a turd." She glared at him. "What's a mission?"

"A church mission. Two years preaching, white shirt and ties, name tags, going door-to-door, bicycles. You know?" Zach shrugged.

"Oh, that. I thought you were li—a Baptist or something. Being from Utah, I guess I should have known." They sat in silence for a moment before Azalea broke the silence. "So, what did you do?"

"I promised her dad."

"How did she take it?"

"She was furious. She wanted to elope without her father's blessing. When I refused to break my promise, she said she never wanted to see me again."

"I see. You keep referring to your ex by personal pronoun. What's her name?"

"Joy — but I don't want to talk about her anymore. I don't dwell on the past."

Azalea felt Zach's anguish and knew he told the truth. Her father lived by the code of your word is your bond. Zach reminded her a bit of her dad.

"Now, on to you," Zach said. "You said you're racially diverse. How so?"

"On my father's side, grandpa's African-American and grandma's Vietnamese. My mom's side grandpa's white and grandma's Anglo, Navajo, and Mexican."

"You're from a small town," Zach said. "Mostly white people, right?"

Azalea nodded. "Yep."

"How did the locals take a black man and an Asian woman living in rural Montana?"

"Except for a few idiots, they've been pretty much accepted as one of their own," Azalea said. "My grandfather's a third-generation rancher in Deer Grove County, where the LaBatier name is known and respected. He's been treated as one of their own his entire life."

"Same for me," Zach said. "Being light-skinned, I experienced more racial crap here at Memnon than I ever experienced in Abundance."

"Me, too. The racist attitudes I've experienced here are almost new to me."

"How did your mom and dad meet?"

"They were childhood sweethearts. They grew up on adjoining ranches. In fact, my two granddads are lifelong besties. My folks say it was destiny." She beamed. "I always tell them their dads arranged the marriage before they were born."

"You know about my ex," Zach said. "How about you? Did you leave someone back in Deer Grove?"

"It's been over for a while." Her voice broke with emotion. "Like the cheating bastard broke my heart."

Zach patted her hand. "I'm sorry. I won't bring it up again."

"It's alright. It's kind of why I'm like so careful about dating and sex. You know, sex like complicates everything."

"I wouldn't know about that, but I hope one day my life gets complicated." Zach deadpanned and then beamed. "… Very complicated."

Azalea howled. "Oh god. Oh god. Thank you. It's been a long time since I laughed like that." Azalea wiped her eyes. "But don't expect to get complicated with me."

They both roared.

"You're back to overusing, like, again," Zach said. "You usually talk so professionally."

"I speak that way when I'm nervous; brings out the thirteen-year-old girl in me."

"What are you nervous about?"

Azalea clutched Zach's face with both hands and drew his lips to hers. He was initially unsure what had happened before he returned the gesture.

She pushed Zach's face back and looked deeply into his eyes. "Damn you, Zach! Damn you! *Why did you come to Memnon*?"

∞

THE FOLLOWING DAY

Memnon Preparatory College

Sumter County, Alabama
Sunday, May 15, 2016

Euphoria nearly overwhelmed Zach as he held Azalea's hand along a trail through the woods on their second "hanging out."

"Before you came, I planned to return home on my next leave and never come back," Azalea said.

"Why?"

"I hate this place—and then you arrived. You're the only reason I stayed."

"The first time we met, you were so military," Zach said. "I thought you really didn't like me because I wasn't."

She smiled and squeezed his hand. "I fell in love the first time I saw you. I knew you felt the same way. I tried my damnedest to not like you. Did I ever tell you I hate this place?"

Zach smirked. "No, it's the first I ever heard of it."

"You're such a dork. A cute dork—but a dork." Azalea chuckled.

"Why do you hate Memnon so much?"

"Mainly because I miss my family, but the Commandant's crazy-ass doctrines don't help either."

"Really? I wouldn't know."

She stopped in her tracks. "Really? Really?"

"Do you mean stuff such as?" His voice lowered an octave. "*I love the white man and the yellow man and the brown man. Some are my dearest friends, but the Illuminati experiment of multiculturalism has proven to be an utter failure.*"

"Damn, you sound just like him." Azalea grinned, shook her head, and turned somber. "Imagine how that makes me feel? My multicultural family is an utter failure."

Zach nodded. "Do the things you hate include?" His voice lowered again. "*The different races and classes of our nation have proven in the past to unite under a common cause, but have shown time and again that we cannot live together in the same communities?"*

Azalea chortled. "Your imitation of Liddell is spot-on."

"Our great nation is falling apart under an oppressive one-world government that pits the classes and races against each other for their own ends." Zach paused. "Does that sound about right?"

"Enough, enough. I think I'm going to be sick." She put a hand up to her mouth and laughed.

"If you hate it so much, why didn't you leave earlier?" Zach asked.

"Because the promise of being abduction-free was so alluring. Isn't that why you came?"

Zach's body tensed, and they walked silently. She knew Zach was holding something back.

"Come on, tell me," she asked.

"That's one reason. I'd rather not say the other reasons."

"I need honesty in a relationship."

He stopped, faced Azalea, and placed a hand on each of her shoulders. "It's complicated. I'll tell you one day." His gaze intensified. "You know I'm telling the truth."

Azalea nodded. "Don't keep a girl waiting too long. Promise me."

Zach leaned in and kissed Azalea. "I promise."

She grabbed both of Zach's hands and locked on his gaze. "Let's leave Memnon together."

"I can't."

"Why?" Her mouth agape.

Zach pursed his lips. "It's complicated. I need to stay."

"Damn it, Zach." She sighed. "I don't want to be here, and I know you feel the same way. As much as I hate being abducted, I hate this place even more." She sensed his discomfort. "What are you keeping from me?"

"I believe Memnon protecting us from abductions is a lie. We're still being taken by the Dumal and being experimented on."

"How do you know this?"

"I'd rather not say, but it's happening."

She nodded. "I believe you. Remember, I'm the human lie detector."

"One more thing. Promise you won't tell anyone else."

"I promise," she said and paused, sensing Zach's internal struggle and observing his furrowed brow. "Is there something else?"

Zach compressed his lips before speaking. "Only three other people know what I'm about to tell you. No matter the outcome, promise you won't tell anyone."

"I promise... unless you're confessing to murder." She laughed but stopped when Zach looked downward. She cupped his chin and lifted Zach's face. "I'm sorry for not taking you seriously. You can tell me anything."

"You may not like it."

"Try me."

"Just so you know, I love women."

She guffawed. "That's your big secret?"

Zach hesitated, then spit it out. "I'm attracted to men, too."

Azalea gazed at Zach and grinned. "So, you're bi. I'm fine with it—unless there's some hot dude I need to worry about."

"Are you kidding? I'm head over heels for you."

"Your secret's safe with me," she said and sealed her promise with a kiss.

∞

TWO WEEKS LATER

Memnon Preparatory College
Sumter County Alabama
Tuesday, May 31, 2016

Zach tossed and turned, knowing at 0800, the private jet would depart for Xiuhcoatl, and everything would change. The snoring from several barrack mates didn't help either. He finally nodded off a little after two in the morning.

A violent shake and flashlights jarred Zach from slumber. "Sergeant Davidson. The Executive Committee required your immediate presence."

In a daze, Zach rubbed his eyes, sat up, and yawned. "What's going on? A little going away prank?"

"This is official business, Sergeant Davidson," Landry said.

He glanced at his watch. "It's 0323. What's going on, Marcus?"

"That's Sergeant Landry to you." Landry glowered at Zach. "We have orders to bring you to the executive offices immediately — even if we have to drag you there."

"Oh, come on. You don't have to make threats. This is stupid."

Another MP tried to hand Zach a robe and slippers.

Zach refused the clothing. "Oh, you've got to be kidding me? I can't get dressed?"

Laundry grabbed the robe and slippers from the private and tossed them at Zach. "That's our orders, Sergeant. Immediately means now."

∞

Zach sat in the lobby of the executive offices. Two stern-faced guards blocked the conference room door, and another pair guarded the lobby exit. A junior officer at the reception desk kept busy at his computer. Zach was pretty sure that he was playing solitaire.

He'd look up occasionally and say, "I'm sure it won't be much longer, Sergeant Davidson."

Zach struggled to keep his eyes open when the conference

room door opened. He instinctively stood at attention to Commandant Liddle in combat fatigues and Azalea in a pink bathrobe and slippers.

She stared at the floor as Liddle walked her out with a fatherly arm around her slouched shoulders.

"There's no dishonor in admitting the truth," Liddle said. "Memnon isn't for everyone. It will be for the best."

Azalea gave a slight nod. "Thank you, sir."

She lifted her head to meet Zach's gaze. Tears welled, and she mouthed, *I'm sorry.*

Zach's heart sank. *What did she do?*

Liddle addressed the guards at the lobby door. "Gentlemen, please escort Ms. LaBatier to her quarters."

"Come in, Sergeant Davidson," Liddle said.

Zach's heart raced after entering, seeing six bigwigs too busy reviewing notes to lift their heads to acknowledge his entrance. Liddle deposited him at a body length removed from the large conference table. He felt practically naked, standing in a bathrobe to face his inquisitors.

Liddell took a seat on the opposite side of the table between the head of base security, Major Johnston, and Mrs. Williams, Memnon's primary benefactor. Next to Williams sat the school's headteacher, Dr. Blake, and next to Johnston sat Zach's father. At the head of the table, Dennis kept busy on his laptop. Opposite Dennis sat an out-of-place Caucasian man Zach didn't know.

Liddell looked up from his notes. "At ease, Sergeant Davidson. Do you know why you are here?"

A cool breeze entered his robe as Zach took a wide stance and crossed his hands behind his back. "No, sir."

"There have been accusations you aren't loyal to Memnon's mission," Liddell said. "Do you understand the significance if such is true?"

"Yes, sir, I do."

"Please elaborate."

"Because every individual's commitment is paramount to the success of the mission."

"Exactly," Liddell said. "You have also taken an oath to defend and uphold Memnon's mission. Is this not so?"

"Yes, sir."

"Have you ever violated your oath?"

He shook his head. "No, sir."

"Do you want to remain part of Memnon's mission?" Major Davidson asked.

"Yes, sir."

Major Davidson looked at his notes. "Did you tell Ms. LaBatier that you wanted to leave Memnon?"

Zach paused as his heart split in two. "No, sir."

"On your honor, you've never told Ms. LaBatier that you wanted to leave Memnon?" Davidson asked.

Zach's stomach burned. "No. Never, sir."

He observed the adults look at Johnston for confirmation. Their actions confirmed the rumor to Zach that the head of campus security was empathic.

Mrs. Williams removed her horn-rimmed glasses and gazed upon him. "May I call you Zach?"

"Yes, ma'am."

"Zach, why do you want to be part of the Memnon Society?"

He looked up and to the right. "I had a strong desire to stop being abducted and to learn how to use my Eagle Eye abilities. I also love my country, and I want to defend her. If aliens are coming, we need to meet the threat on our own terms."

Liddle's head shook lightly. "However, we've learned that you don't believe that cultural segregation is a means for strengthening our nation. Is that true?"

How do they know this? Zach thought, then said, "Yes, sir.

That is true."

"Please elaborate."

Zach released the deep breath he'd been holding. "My family and closest friends are of different races. We get along as well as anyone. I really don't see the need to divide ourselves by race."

Liddle nodded. "I used to feel the same way, and my situation was like yours." He paused in thought as a grin overcame his face. "My dear late wife, the love of my life, was white."

He stared blankly and smiled. "My mother is part Cherokee. I consider Commandants Maldonado and Dupre brothers. Yet, we come from such different backgrounds. Alejandro Maldonado left Mexico with only the clothes on his back, and Winston Dupre came from the New England aristocracy."

He gave a somber nod. "Our friendship was forged in Vietnam as we saved each other's lives and watched our comrades fall." Liddle rubbed his chin. "Over time, we concluded most of humanity struggles with race, class, and ethnic differences. Most people aren't comfortable mixing with different socio-economic and ethnic-racial circles. Do you understand, Zach?"

"I understand the concept but respectfully disagree."

"Zach, you and I are unique in our experiences. Few human beings can love those who are different. Most fear differences. Fear leads to distrust, hatred, and injustice."

Zach nodded.

Liddle continued. "From our own history, and the histories of other worlds have shown, homogeneous societies have less strife, violent crime, and class-related issues than multicultural societies."

"Permission to speak freely, sir?"

Liddle nodded.

Zach cleared his throat. "Respectfully, sir, can't an

individual be 100% committed to fulfilling the mission but not always agree with the rationale behind every aspect of the mission? Can't one love their country, obey their orders, and not always agree with the reasons for those orders?"

"Yes. Thank you for your candor, Sergeant." Liddell smiled and gave a nod.

Zach smiled in return.

"I want you to refer to your loyalty oath," Major Johnston said. "In conversations with Ms. LaBatier, did you mock the discourses of Commandant Liddell?"

Zach's stomach churned. "Yes, sir. To my regret, I did."

"If you're committed to the aims of Memnon and loyal to its leadership as you claim…" Johnston's eyes narrowed. "Why would you deride the Commandant?"

"I was trying to impress a girl. Sometimes young men say and do stupid things to get girls to like them."

Liddell nodded.

Zach looked directly at Liddle. "I'm sorry, Sir. I didn't mean to mock you. It was stupid."

"No need to apologize. I was once a foolish young man myself," Liddell said. "With more experience, there's hope for you to accept the importance of our country being segregated, but equal, too. However, that isn't important right now. Your commitment to Memnon's mission is most important. Are you committed to the cause of Memnon?"

"Yes, sir."

"Have you stated that you have knowledge that alien abductions are continuing at Memnon?" Johnston asked.

"Yes, sir."

Johnson tilted his head. "Who told you this?"

"I'm not alone in my beliefs. I have friends that believe it's still happening, too."

"On what facts do you base your allegations? Who told

your friends?"

"No one, sir. We've had dreams of new abduction experiences since arriving at Memnon and Aryana."

Johnston's face contorted. "You base your conclusions on dreams?"

"Yes, sir. My dreams about being abducted have been fairly reliable memories of the past, and I've experienced new abduction dreams since my arrival at Memnon."

Johnson continued. "Why didn't you tell Ms. LaBatier about your dreams instead of leaving her with the impression that you possess privileged information?"

"I don't understand, sir."

"Didn't you say to Ms. LaBatier on one occasion that, and I quote, *we're still being taken by the Dumal and being experimented on*? Couldn't you just mention your dreams?"

"Because she might think I was weird. Like I said before, I was trying to impress her."

"Why did you tell Ms. LaBatier that you hate me so badly?" Davidson frowned. "Do you really consider me just a sperm donor?"

Zach grimaced. "Don't you think this is something for a private conversation?"

Johnston chimed in. "We have nothing to hide and need to confirm your loyalty and commitment to your superior officers."

"Permission to speak frankly, sir."

"Permission granted," Davidson said.

"Again, I was trying to impress a girl. Show her how tough I am and that I rose through the ranks on my own merit — which I did.

"I don't hate you, but let's be honest." His eyes riveted on his father. "I don't really know you. You abandoned us when I was six. You visited me once when I was nine for only an hour. We had brief telephone calls on a few of my birthdays and a couple of Christmases until I was fourteen. I never heard or saw from you again until I arrived at Memnon. Do I hate you? No. Do I have a relationship with you? Not really. You are my superior officer. I've sworn an oath to follow your orders — that's the extent of our relationship. I keep my oaths and commitments. With respect, sir, that's all that matters."

Davidson's voice cracked. "I'm sorry, son. You really don't want to give us a try?"

Zach remained stern-faced. "Sorry, sir. No, sir."

"Are you still committed to Memnon and becoming an officer?" Liddell asked.

"Yes, sir. I am."

"Good man." Liddell slapped the table. "Major Johnston needs to meet privately with you in my office before you're dismissed."

∞

The white man at the end of the table now led the meeting. "What did you conclude from your interview, Major Johnston? Was the boy lying?"

"No. Overall, he was telling the truth," Johnston said.

Deputy Director Smith scrunched his face. "*Overall*, doesn't sound reassuring."

"I relate his recalcitrance to issues with his father and not the mission. He was telling a white lie about not wanting a relationship with Ezekiel."

Davidson's eyes opened wide. "Really? He wants a relationship with me?"

"Yes and no," Johnston said. "He fantasizes about having his father in his life, but fears of being hurt again."

Smith tapped a finger on the table. "Is that all he was lying about?"

"Yes. There was no deception in him. The Sergeant was telling the truth."

Smith crossed his arms and sat back. "I still don't trust him or his friends, either."

Mrs. Williams placed both hands on the table. "If he's a security risk, then let's send young Mr. Davidson home."

Smith's jaw clenched as he stared at Williams. "Cerculus was adamant that the Wilkerson boy and O'Reilly girl were crucial to the success of Phase One and all subsequent phases. Sending the Davidson boy home could jeopardize our standing with his friends. We can't risk them switching over to the Illuminati."

"They're that powerful, eh?" Williams said.

Smith gave a deferential nod.

She clapped her hands. "Well, we can't allow this to happen—so I take it we're all in agreement that young Mr. Davidson must stay for the sake of his friends at Aryana and the success of Phase One."

∞

Exhausted in body and spirit, Zach had barely sat down on his bed when he heard whispering voices from a dark corner of the barracks. He turned toward the approaching flashlights as Marcus Landry moved in front of Zach, and two others positioned themselves behind him.

"Sergeant Davidson, your orders are for you to be ready for transport to Xiuhcoatl Rancho ASAP," Marcus said.

"My flight isn't until 0800. I still have four hours."

"Your flight now leaves at zero-five-hundred," Marcus said.

"That's only fifty-five minutes. Why the change of plans?"

"Don't know. Don't care. But you better get cracking," Marcus said. "We'll lay out your dress uniform while you shower." He shone the light on the footlocker at the head of the bed. "Is this your duffle bag? Where's your suit bag?"

"Why are you being all official in the barracks, Marcus? Give it a rest."

"I fully expect you to be an officer next time I see you. At that point, I will have to call you Lieutenant Davidson, sir!"

"Thanks, Marcus. I didn't know you could get so sentimental."

"However, today, I still outrank you and still consider you a lerpy little shit." Marcus yelled, "Get him, boys!"

The two behind walloped Zach with pillows. He grabbed his pillow to retaliate. Marcus hit Zach from behind. He spun and nearly knocked Marcus over. The laughter and screaming woke the others. Soon, the lights turned on and the entire barracks joined the melee of linen and goose down.

The lights flickered. "Attention!"

They all stood upright in place, pillows in hand.

Liddle and his aide, Dennis O'Bannon, stood near the doorway.

"At ease, gentlemen." Liddle smiled. "I see you're having a little send-off for Sergeant Davidson."

"Yes, sir, sorry, sir," Landry said.

"Relax, Sergeant. I get it. I just came to congratulate the Sergeant for his admittance to Officer Candidate School. Make us proud, son." He nodded at Dennis. "Corporal."

"Three cheers for Zach," Dennis said. "Hip, hip!"

"Hooray! Hip, hip, hooray! Hip, hip, hooray!"

∞

From inside the Gulfstream G550, Zach viewed the dimly lit tarmac. The entire platoon turned out to say goodbye, except for Azalea.

His mind meandered:

Did she share our conversations with a friend?

Was she a mole?

Did she feel guilty about being disloyal to Memnon and decided to come clean?

Why did she have to bring me into it?

His heart ached. Zach hoped one day he'd find a soulmate that he could trust with all his heart. He had been sure Azalea was the one and fought with his might not to cry.

PART 11-COMMENCEMENT

"The world is a dangerous place to live, not because of the people who are evil, but because of the people who don't do anything about it."
-Albert Einstein

SIX WEEKS LATER

Rancho Xiuhcoatl
Luna County, New Mexico
Thursday, July 14, 2016

Liza and Wilkie found the hall's layout eerily similar to the gymnasium at Aryana. Ushers directed Wilkie to the VIP section in the front. Liza's continence fell, discovering her nametag in the middle of the third row.

On stage, executive officers from Xiuhcoatl, Aryana, and Memnon conversed with Dumal officers clothed only in a ceremonial sash. The mostly naked Dumal stood four hands above the tallest human counterpart and seemed to communicate fine without a translator.

On the wall behind the stage, Commandant Maldonado's prominent portrait had a quote below. Directly below Maldonado hung four portraits. Che Guevara. Alexander Hamilton. Antonio López de Santa Anna. Patrick Henry.

The quote under Che Guevara caught Wilkie's eye:

The revolution is not an apple that falls when it is ripe.
You have to make it fall.

The comparison of the two gyms made Wilkie confident that when he arrived at Memnon next week, a portrait of Liddell and four revolutionaries with accompanying quotes would be on the front wall of a nearly identical gym, too.

Commandant Maldonado reached the dais, nodded at the conductor, and leaned into the microphone. "All arise."

A chamber orchestra played *Pomp and Circumstance* as candidates marched from the front door past Wilkie to the back row and made a U-turn up the other aisle before being seated in the rows behind Liza.

Wilkie had to adjust expectations, seeing the officer candidates intermingled in identical uniforms and not segregated by race or species. Until now, he didn't know the Dumal sent officer candidates to Xiuhcoatl and wore the same dress uniforms as the humans. It was the first time he saw any Dumal wear clothes.

His heart leaped as the last of the candidates entered the gym.

Zach made eye contact as he passed, and they both grinned.

∞

Commencement Address Excerpts
Alejandro Tomas Maldonado
Commandant of Rancho Xiuhcoatl

With a wireless microphone in his hand, Wilkie stood next to Commandant Maldonado at the dais.

"Officer Candidates, please remain standing," Maldonado said. "The audience may be seated."

Clicks and trills came from Wilkie's mouth.

Maldonado smiled at the scene. Lithe Dumal officer candidates towering above their brown, black, and white cohorts standing united in purpose. His heart swelled with pride.

"Raise your right hand, and repeat after me your oath of office." He allowed time for Wilkie to translate.

"I, say your full name." He paused again. "…having been appointed an officer in the military of the Federated American States, as indicated above in the grade of Second Lieutenant,"

Seventy-five male and female voices reverberated throughout the room.

Wilkie translated. Twenty-five hermaphroditic voices replied in Dumal.

"… do solemnly swear (or affirm) that I will support and defend the Constitution of the Federated American States against all enemies, foreign and domestic, that I will bear true faith and allegiance to the same…"

∞

Commencement Address Excerpts
Winston Douglas Dupre
Commandant of Aryana Ranch

"… war with the Intergalactic Council's proxies, the Kingdom of the Mai and the Zionist Occupation Government is coming soon… you shall lead FAS troops to victory over our enemies…"

"… Zionist Occupation Government, a cabal of evil Jewish financiers, secretly rule Western governments through their enforcers, the Illuminati…

"… ZOG's aspirations are to create a utopia called Zion out of the ashes of global conflict…"

"… Winston Churchill said *history is written by the victors*…"

"… World War II history that's taught in school is false. The Illuminati created the official history to besmirch the reputation of the National Socialists and Adolf Hitler for being allied with the Dumal Federation..."

Wilkie felt bile rise in his throat. He pulled a water bottle from the side of the podium and took a sip before translating.

"... The Illuminati have propagated the biggest fraud in world history, the so-called Holocaust..."

"... the National Socialists detained criminals and Bolshevik traitors in prison, as any civil society would, but they didn't specifically target European Jews. It just so happened that many Bolsheviks were Jews..."

"... National Socialists didn't exterminate six million Jews. It would be logistically impossible..."

Wilkie nearly retched. His throat tightened, and his desire to translate was nullified. He'd heard firsthand accounts from his Great Grandmother Pascale, the only member of her family to survive Auschwitz-Birkenau.

Liza's voice entered his mind: *I've got you, little brother. Be calm, big fella.*

Wilkie exhaled. His face returned to a golden tan, and the tightness across his chest ceased. His translation flowed smoothly.

∞

FIVE HOURS LATER

Rancho Xiuhcoatl
Luna County, New Mexico
Thursday, July 14, 2016

The magnificent view from the rocky ridge preempted the anticipation of the reunion. Beyond distant granite peaks, dusk's final pallet of salmons highlighted elongated purple clouds drifting across a fading blue sky. Silhouetted Saguaro cacti peppered the landscape as giant sentries guarding the desert, as a handful of stars emerged from behind cosmic hiding places.

Awestruck by the vibrant horizon, Lisa and Wilkie looked beyond the two-story administration building less than a quarter-mile away. Two miles south, a sudden illumination diverted their attention to the Mexican side of the base. Six clusters of stadium lights created a plasmatic dust column propelled skyward by heavy equipment.

"Don't think about it, Mister," Liza said.

Wilkie held out his hands. "Why can't we go shrouded?"

"We don't have a Navigator."

"Zach should be here soon."

"Even with Zach, Arild wouldn't be too pleased that we did so to satisfy your idle curiosity."

"It isn't idle curiosity! We have to find out what these jerkwads are up to."

Liza pointed below. "There's our boy."

She felt Zach's excitement from a distance. In the dwindling twilight, you could see his exhilaration from the bounce in his step. He jogged from the base of the mesa. At the midpoint, he sprinted the rest of the way. Reaching the top, he bent over, hands to knees. It took a moment to catch his breath before standing upright.

"Holy crap! *What have the aliens done to you*?" Wilkie laughed. "You're freaking tall."

"Aliens, nothing. I've been eating my veggies." Zach grinned. "Dang, I've missed you guys."

Zach rushed to Liza and picked her off the ground in a bear hug. He put her down and bear-hugged Wilkie, too.

"I love you, bro," Wilkie said.

"I love you, too," Zack said. "Where's Jeff?"

Wilkie's deflated body language caught Zach off guard. He put him down. "What? Where's DeBoer?"

"I'm afraid he's playing for the wrong team. He's bought into Dupre's B.S.," Wilkie said.

A somber silence overtook them.

"Are you sure? DeBoer may have his faults—*but being a racist*?" Zach said.

"*You're surprised*? You already knew he's a narcissist," Liza said.

"Yes, he is—but I'm still surprised."

"He's now fourth-in-line for command at Aryana. His rapid advancement is in no doubt because of Heather's influence," Liza said. "I don't know who's more under her spell, Dupre or DeBoer."

Zach stood still, eyes closed, chin tilted down as in prayer.

"I know that it's har…" Wilkie said.

"Shh, please!" Zach interrupted. "I need to concentrate."

Liza felt Zach's troubled heart. "What?"

He raised a palm. "Hold on."

Liza and Wilkie held a long, awkward silence.

In a single motion, Zach's eyes opened, and a finger pointed above the administration building. "Alien ship entering the atmosphere. Coming in fast. Attack mode. It isn't Dumal or IGC."

Moments later, air raid sirens sounded, and spotlights flooded the sky.

Out of nowhere, a softball-sized glowing blue sphere appeared in front of them. The orb expanded until Arild stood in their midst. "Make haste, grab my robe."

∞

"Where are we?" Liza asked.

"Under Mount Mant'ap in North Korea," Zach said.

Liza shook her head. "Arild's full of surprises."

"Where did Arild go… and why are things out of focus?" Zach murmured.

Wilkie started walking. "I don't know why Arild leaves us, but we need to get moving."

"*Huh*?" Zach said.

"We'll explain as we walk. Just keep moving," Wilkie said.

"Arild calls it *The Shroud*," Liza said. "We can see through it. As long as we don't stand in one place for a minute or two, no one can see us."

"They can't hear us either, or vice versa," Wilkie said.

"What's the point?" Zach's lips curled.

"So we can snoop around undetected," Wilkie said.

"I can't see thirty feet in front of us. We're nearsighted spies in the fog." Zach chucked.

"It serves a purpose," Liza said. "I can still use my powers of discernment, and Wilkie can read lips."

Zach thought the empty corridor seemed familiar. He stopped at a secure door at the end of the hall.

"Keep walking. This is the cool part." Wilkie passed through the steel door, and Liza followed. Zach paused, took a leap of faith, and passed through the door.

"If you're wondering how we learned how to shroud," Liza said. "Arild taught us."

"Is this part of the jump team training you'll be doing at Memnon?" Zach said.

"It's related—but being out of phase with normal space is something we keep to ourselves," Wilkie said. "A select few know about this power, and we want to keep it that way."

"You do this all the time?" Zach asked.

"This is our third time," Liza said. "We trained with Arild. The second time, we leaped over to Memnon to keep you out of trouble."

"Really? When?" Zach asked.

"The night they interrogated you. Arild took us to you," Wilkie said. "Liza manipulated your feelings to make them believe you."

"That Major Johnston's abilities are off the charts," she

said. "It took a lot of effort on my part to make him think you were telling the truth."

"But I was pretty much truthful—as trained," Zach said.

"He might have sensed your motives weren't pure," Liza said. "Who's this girl that's got you all tied up in knots?"

"I'd rather not talk about her, thanks—and for saving my bacon."

"Any time, little brother. Thanks for not telling any bald-faced lies. It made my job easier." Liza made eye contact with Zach. "Speaking of Major Johnston, he's a nasty piece of work. Be careful around him."

The group turned the corner and stopped. Zach understood why this place seemed familiar. Holding cells with Plexiglas walls lined the hall. Each contained a single captive.

"We need to keep moving," Wilkie said.

"No!" Zach exclaimed. "We need to help them escape."

Liza sighed. "Believe me, I want to, but I don't think Arild sent us here for that purpose."

They passed several halls filled with detainees and entered a new hall to the screams of tortured souls in the treatment rooms.

"Zach's right. We need to do something," Wilkie said.

Arild's voice entered their minds. *Keep searching. Find the exit. Ride the trains.*

∞

Zach, Liza, and Wilkie passed through an exit door to the summit of a freestanding seven-story metal staircase attached to the wall. Objects over two landings away remained out of focus. They surveyed the blurry white cavern below, unsure if others were on the floor. Workers dressed in white would blend in perfectly.

Liza felt the area was clear. Her intuition had yet to be wrong—but she knew firsthand a skilled empath could mask another's presence or emotions, so her intuition always required visual verification.

After descending, they recognized a polished concrete floor, warehouse racks, pallet jacks, and several forklifts—all a matching high-gloss white.

"This place could use a little color," Liza said.

They found dozens of round metal casks on steel freight pallets. The objects were a head taller than Liza and as wide as a hula-hoop. Painted white, with cooling fins around the circumference and a dozen threaded steel rods anchored to hardened steel lids and to sturdy metal bases. Electromagnetic waves of color encompassed each container.

"I don't know what these contain, but it's beautiful," Liza said.

They neared twenty loading bay doors to the starboard side of the hall. A large rectangular sign hung above the loading bays. Wilkie translated aloud:

"Authorized Personnel Only."

"Always Use Approved Safety Protocols and Procedures."

"Those Violating Rules Will Be Severely Punished."

Zach laughed. "They'd just kick us out of Memnon."

"Let's see what's behind those doors—and get severely punished." Wilkie chuckled.

Arm-in-arm, they leaped to the other side of the doors. No sign of humanity except for tractor-trailers docked at each loading bay and pavement that extended from the loading docks into several concrete tunnels.

Wilkie moved toward a tunnel. "Let's see where these go."

"I don't see an exit or trains," Liza said. "Arild sent us for a specific purpose, and this isn't it."

"How will we know if we don't try?" Wilkie murmured.

Zach paused, eyes closed, head bowed. "These tunnels lead to a harbor in Harbin, China. The path to the trains is back inside."

They leaped back inside the warehouse. Zach took a direct

route to six heavy-freight elevators, with doors tall enough for a double-decker bus to clear.

His finger passed through the elevator call button. "What the crap?"

"A TK could push the button, but we don't have one," Wilkie said.

"A TK?"

"A Telekinetic. TK's can interact with matter through *The Shroud*," Wilkie said.

"Can't we just walk through the door?" Zach asked.

"Even if we did, who will push the button to go down?" Liza asked.

"Point taken," Zach said. "Why don't we just leap?"

"Why don't we just find the exit door? Arild said, *find the exit — and the trains*. We might miss something if we don't," Liza said.

"Fair enough," Zach said.

∞

They found an exit at the far corner. Wilkie translated the script on the door:

"*Danger–Radioactive Material.*"

"*Authorized Personnel Only.*"

"*Wear Personal Protective Equipment & Dosimeter at All Times.*"

"*Those Violating Rules Will Be Severely Punished.*"

"You think this Shroud thingy protects us from radiation?" Zach asked.

"It should be safe," Liza said. "Arild lets us know about these types of things."

They passed through the door and stood atop an identical free-standing staircase as before. The room was white like the previous warehouse, teeming with rows of objects emitting rainbow waves.

"Let's check those out," Liza said.

They approached rows of shiny metal cylinders with cables protruding from the top. The devices stood about ten feet tall and three feet in diameter, and each row was about forty feet long. They neared the stainless-steel structures to observe a wavy, full-visible spectrum surrounding the torpedo-shaped cylinders that looked about the same as from the top of the stairs.

Continuing to the far end, they found six more freight elevators — and an exit door.

Descending an identical staircase into another cavernous room, they couldn't feel or hear the voluminous draft released from the industrial blowers in the ceiling or the HEPA filters that topped ten buildings below.

On the ground floor, they found a handful of men and women attired in white coveralls, surgical caps and masks, and disposable shoe covers moving with purpose from building to building.

Wilkie tapped Zach's shoulder. "Watch this dude."

Wilkie blocked the path of a woman preoccupied with the contents of a clipboard.

"Excuse me, ma'am. Can you tell me the way to the trains?"

The woman passed through him.

"For rude! Walk right through me, why don't you."

Zach nearly fell over laughing. "I got to try that."

As a man exited a building, Zach jumped in the way. The man paused where Zach stood, lost in thought, and changed direction.

Zach slapped his knee and laughed. "Holy crap! How'd we do that?"

"We don't occupy the same space. It's like we're superimposed on them," Wilkie said.

Liza's head shook. "Are we done playing, boys? There's a mission to complete. Wilkie, what does the sign over that door say?"

"*Pathology–Bio Safety Level One.*"

They peeked through a picture window into a medical laboratory. The technicians took notes as they worked at tables with specimens, tabletop machines, and microscopes. The other buildings had windows revealing similar laboratories; except for the four largest buildings being windowless. Wilkie kept reading signs aloud as they passed each laboratory.

Microbiology–Biosafety Level One. Biochemistry–Bio Safety Level One. Genetics–Bio Safety Level One. Exobiology–Bio Safety Level Two.

"*Exobiology*, what the crap is that?" Zach asked.

"The study of extraterrestrial life," Liza said.

The last and most massive buildings were at the far end.

Specimen Repository–Biosafety Level One. Molecular Biology–Biosafety Level Two. Infectious Diseases – Biosafety Level Three.

Wilkie read the sign at the last building. "Biological Agents–Biosafety Level Four."

"That one scares the bejeezus out of me," Liza said. "Pay attention, boys. I think it's important."

"Should we go inside?" Wilkie asked.

"Oh, *heck no*!" Zach said.

"I concur with the tall one," Liza said. "Let's move on."

Nearby, they found six loading bay doors and a single exit door. Wilkie translated the sign, *Arrivals – Exit only.*

∞

Under Mount Mant'ap
North Korea
Thursday, July 14, 2016

Liza, Zach, and Wilkie reached the ground floor of the most massive cavern of the day and empty train platforms protruding from twenty-seven tunnels.

Large overhead signs written in Korean, Japanese, and Chinese stated: *Arrivals*. Wilkie translated the origin cities. Beijing-Shanghai-Hong Kong-Taipei. Seoul-Busan-Pyongyang. Tokyo-Osaka-Yokohama.

With no trains to ride, they linked arms and leaped through a six-story building that split the cavern in half, marked *Departure Hall*.

Before them, football field-length, single-car bullet trains on nine tracks. Over three tunnels read Departures: Chang Tang, Tibet in Chinese. The Japanese sign showed Peak Pobeda, Russia. The North and South Korean trains were going to Orkhon Valley, Mongolia.

Each train had a brushed alloy finish, a single door up front, and was windowless except for the front and rear of the car.

The bullet design of the locomotive engines brought fond memories of travels with Mom for Wilkie. She insisted they get away from the comfort zone of Americanized base life in Okinawa.

During school breaks, they crisscrossed Japan, looking to expand their cultural horizons — mostly by train. Wilkie grinned while thinking about hiking Mount Fuji, visiting Samurai castles, and the ski slopes, hot springs, and the old town of Nozawa Onsen. He remained fascinated by trains ever since and felt an urge to leap back home to look through Mom's scrapbooks of their adventures.

"Everything okay, little brother?" Liza asked.

"I'm thinking about my Mom. Trains remind me of her," Wilkie said.

Liza wrapped her arms around Wilkie's waist and pulled him close. "I'm so sorry, sweetie."

Wilkie walked to the nearest train. "Is this what I think it is?"

"Is what?" Zach said.

Zach joined Wilkie on his knees to inspect the undercarriage. They paid particular attention to dozens of metal plates covered with coiled wire positioned around the undercarriage that levitated a couple of inches above the tracks and no wheels.

From under the train, they grinned and said in unison: "Maglev."

"Boys, look over there." Liza motioned toward another train.

They followed a man and a woman wearing white lab coats, unloading rectangular cases from the back of an electric cart into the front of a train. Conspicuously missing in the cab was an engineer's seat and controls. A technician locked the last case into a metal frame with the others.

"What does the writing on these boxes say?" Liza asked.

Wilkie translated. "Handle with Care. Molecular Biology Specimens-Bio Safety Level Two. The other cases say the same thing."

The technicians departed the train, hopped on their cart, and drove away.

Zach noticed the interior lighting dim as the door closed. In the shroud, he didn't feel the ventilation startup, hear the hum of the electro-magnets powering up, or feel the train ease into the tunnel.

"Looks like we found our ride," Zach said. "I'm moving to the back. Germy-creepy-crawlies aren't my thing."

In the front VIP section, Wilkie noticed the roomy high-back bucket seats with four-point harnesses. In a corner, a wet bar with a bartender's bucket seat and two lavatories opposite. As they reached subsequent partitions, Wilkie observed as rank decreased the chair padding, legroom, and size of the lavatory did, too.

He reached the aft enlisted section with tightly packed

seating and watched out the rear window as the circular metal door descended to seal the tube.

"Buckle up. This is going to be a wild ride," Wilkie said. "If we could buckle up."

Liza noticed the security cameras. "We better keep moving, boys."

Wilkie didn't argue. He wanted to explore.

In each section, digital clocks showed departure and arrival times. The display beneath counted down from 222 days, 23 hours, 22 minutes, and 52 seconds until *Restoration Day.*

In the junior officer's section, Wilkie observed a gauge needle descending toward the 1X10-3 Torr mark. "Hey, Ms. Pre-Engineering Major. Any idea what this gauge is reading?"

"Vacuum. It's a vacuum gauge. *Damn*, it's a pretty high vacuum. *Damn*." Liza said.

"What?" Wilkie asked.

"This tunnel has to be a giant vacuum tube, but passengers need oxygen, so the train cabin has to be pressurized... but why?"

Wilke momentarily looked up and to the right. "I watched a documentary once about a theoretical super-high-speed maglev train that operates in a vacuum."

You could almost see the wheels spinning in Liza's head.

"Penny for your thoughts?" Zach asked.

"You're right, Wilkie. This has to be an ultra-high-speed train. No air means no friction. Magnetic levitation is frictionless, too. This sucker can fly."

"Exactly. In theory, it could go up to speeds over five thousand miles per hour," Wilkie said. "The show I watched said the reason it hasn't been built because it would cost trillions."

Zach did a Dr. Emmett Brown imitation. "Marty, if my calculations are correct, when this baby hits eighty-eight miles per hour, you're gonna see some serious shit!"

Wilkie and Zach chuckled.

Liza rolled her eyes. "More obscure movie quotes?"

"Come on. You've never seen *Back to the Future*?" Wilkie asked.

"Nope," Liza said.

"Put another classic movie on your watch list when this is all over," Zach said. "I can't believe you've never seen *Star Wars* or *Ghost Busters* either."

∞

The car sped up smoothly. In less than two minutes, objects viewed through the front and rear windshields melded into a blur.

"We're going way faster than eighty-eight miles per hour," Zach said. "It's just under fourteen hundred miles from Mount Mant'ap to Orkhon Valley—and the destination clock says twenty-two minutes. This is some serious speed."

"How many miles?" Wilkie asked.

"1377," Zach said.

Wilkie did some calculations on his smartphone. "Average speed is 3744.69 miles-per-hour to be exact."

"See, we hit eighty-eight miles per hour and saw some serious shit," Zach said.

They laughed again.

Liza groaned. "Who has the resources to build a train like this? Not the North Koreans."

"Why not? The beauty of a dictatorship is you can do whatever you want," Wilkie said.

Liza's head shook. "Still doesn't mean they have the hard currency or engineering know-how to build trains like these."

"Get enough mega-wealthy and powerful people from Japan, China, and South Korea with the Dumal technology, and anything is possible," Zach said.

"Don't forget the possibility of corporations, governments—and shadow governments," Wilkie added.

∞

The train decelerated for over ten minutes before exiting the tunnel in a crawl.

Zach proceeded to the front of the train as it entered a spacious arrival hall. Two technicians waited outside next to an electric cart. As the doors opened, Zach bolted through an oblivious technician. Ahead, he saw moving walkways extending into six hallways.

Wilkie came alongside Zach. "The sign says, *Arrivals to New Seoul and New Ryongpong.*"

"What does that sign say?" Liza said.

"Reproductive Center."

She pointed. "Looks like our friends in the lab coats are heading that way. I say we follow them."

∞

The electric cart stopped outside a glass wall. Inside, a gaggle of scientists, in cleanroom garb, engaged in laboratory activities. Outside, the technicians inserted the cases one by one into a trolley covered by a clear acrylic skin. After loading the last case and sealing the door, ultraviolet lights turned on, and the fans on the top whirled. Moments later, a red indicator light turned yellow. The technicians pushed the trolley against an airlock on the glass wall. A green indicator light verified the hermetic seal. The technician pushed a buzzer and gave a thumbs-up to the worker inside. He nodded in acknowledgment.

Liza passed through the glass wall. Wilkie and Zach shrugged and joined her. They paused behind a woman at a computer station with a double helix on the monitor.

"What do you think they're doing?" Zach asked.

"I'm unsure. Some type of DNA testing," Liza said.

"The sign outside said *DNA Sequencing*," Wilkie said.

"Why didn't you tell us sooner?" Liza said.

"You didn't ask."

Liza groaned. "We've got a little work to do on our communication skills, young man. We're a team, remember?"

Zach did his Strother Martin imitation. "What we got here is a failure to communicate."

"I know that. Guns and Roses' *Civil War*," Lisa said.

"No, it's from *Cool Hand Luke*. One of the most famous movie lines ever," Zach said.

"You're both right," Wilkie said.

∞

The team followed a technician into another lab. They observed technicians viewing a monitor tethered to an electron microscope. On-screen, a microscopic needle inserted a double-helix into a white globule.

"It's like Jurassic Park. They're putting Dino-DNA into ostrich eggs," Zach said.

Liza raised an eyebrow at Wilkie.

"The sign says *Cloning Stations*," Wilkie said.

"We're getting a wee bit better in our communication, Mr. Wilkerson," Liza said. "Let's see if you can beat me asking next time."

∞

The team exited the clean room and entered a vestibule with three additional doors.

Wilkie's extended hand moved from left to right. "Behind door number one is the *Staging Hall*. Door number two, *Waste Disposal*. Door three says, *Clone Wombs*. Was that fast enough for you?"

"Perfectly executed, Mr. Wilkerson," Liza said.

"I don't need to be empathic to know which door you want to go through," Wilkie continued.

Liza moved toward *Waste Disposal*. She reached the door and paused.

"Yeah, right," Wilkie said.

She laughed. Wilkie shook his head and walked through the door labeled *Clone Wombs.*

The dimly lit hall had rows of horizontally laid coffin-like objects atop metal trolleys. Tubes and cables protruding from the ceiling into the black boxes. Some appeared to carry blood, and others had a Day-Glo yellow fluid.

Wilkie stuck his face through the lid of one. A dim light revealed a silvery Mylar-like bag suspended in a clear liquid with cables and tubes connected.

Liza's and Zach's faces appeared on each side.

Wilkie smiled. "We've got to stop meeting like this."

Zach grinned. "You think it's a clone or a clown—or cloned clowns?" Zach yelped and jumped back. *"Holy crap! It freaking moved!"*

Liza and Wilkie stood up.

"It isn't alive. We're the only living things in this room," Liza said.

"It moved, I tell you. It moved," Zach said.

"Probably dyskinesia," Liza said.

"Huh?" Zach said.

"Involuntary muscle movement," Liza said.

∞

The team passed through a door labeled *Staging Hall.*

Inside, thousands of men and women were housed upright in glass sarcophaguses in what seemed to be a peaceful slumber. The enclosures racked in perfectly aligned columns and rows extending from the floor to a high-rise ceiling.

The team approached a lean, fit, blemish-free man with thick black hair. An LED display plate with multiple readouts stretched across the middle.

"Private Lee Suk Lin. Gives his serial number, unit, hometown," Wilkie said. "The other stuff is vital signs. Heart rate, blood pressure, respiration, body temperature."

"That's weird. They aren't alive," Liza said.

"The monitors say otherwise," Wilkie said.

"These bodies are empty shells. There's no brain activity in them."

"Empty shells? You sure?" Wilkie asked.

"Positive."

∞

Wilkie translated while walking through sections segregated by rank and social status. Generals with generals, privates with privates. There were areas for scientists, medical professionals, engineers, scholars, and several titans of industry. A large section was reserved for South Korean politicians, operatives, bureaucrats, and their families.

In the North Korean political section, two oversized sarcophaguses gave them pause. In one stood a towering Korean man with ripped tree trunk thighs, gargantuan pecs, grapefruit-size biceps, and six-pack abs you could bounce an anvil off. A giant of African descent stood next to the biggest. Every other clone in the warehouse was dwarfed in comparison.

Zach sang, *"Two of these things are not like the others; two of these things just doesn't belong."*

"More movie references?" Liza asked.

"Sesame Street. You never watched Sesame Street?" Zach said.

"I knew that. Of course, I watched Sesame Street," Liza said.

"Who are these dudes? The Korean dude has to be over six-ten," Zach said.

The name display made Wilkie guffaw. "It's the leader of North Korea."

"The dude's been seriously hitting the 'roids and H-G-H," Zach said, "...and Weight Watchers."

The trio roared.

"Talk about a Napoleon Complex," Liza said. "They didn't skimp on his manhood, either."

They lost it again.

Regaining composure, Zach asked, "Who's the black dude?"

Wilkie read the display aloud. "It's Dennis Rodman."

Zach's eyes went wide, and he moved closer. "Yeah, it's him, alright."

"Where's his tats and piercings—and orange hair?" Wilkie said.

"And wedding dress?" Liza said.

They laughed again.

Zach turned to Liza. "You know NBA players—but you don't know Obi-Wan Kenobi?"

"My dad and I had season tickets to the Warriors. I know my NBA players, and this is *The Worm*."

"*The Worm*?" Zach asked.

"I can't believe you know obscure movie quotes and Sesame Street, but don't know Dennis Rodman's nickname. When this is all over, we've got to brush you up on former NBA players—and you call yourself a basketball player," Lisa said.

"All right, all right. I don't follow pro ball. You know my history with my dad. It turned me off the NBA."

∞

A series of warehouse roller conveyors filled the room and passed under vinyl strips dangling over openings in the opposing wall.

"Transference Center," Wilkie said. "The sign says, *Transference Center*. Did you get that?"

"I got it," Liza said.

Farther along the wall, they found a door. "Transit Lounge. The sign says *Transit Lounge*. Did you get that?"

"Got it, smartass," Liza said.

Passing through the door, they found ten orderly rows

of hospital gurneys, an empty I.V. pole on each, and a monitor trolley opposite. Every fixture was draped with clear vinyl covers. Stocked medicine cabinets with windowed doors lined the walls.

"I've been in a few airport transit lounges, but this looks like an emergency room," Wilkie said.

"Reminds me of donating plasma," Liza said.

Arild's voice entered their minds. *Leave this place. Find your trains and find yourselves.*

"Any idea what he's talking about?" Wilkie asked.

"I believe I do. Lock arms, boys," Liza said. "Zach?"

∞

New Aryana Republic
Northwest Territories, Canada
Thursday, July 14, 2016

Liza, Zach, and Wilkie landed in a train terminal nearly identical to the one in Mongolia.

"Where are we?" Liza asked.

"Underground." Zach grinned. "—Yukon Territories, Canada."

Wilkie pointed at the sign in English. "Hey, Liza. The sign says the train came from *Aryana*."

Liza sighed. "Got it, Bruce."

"That sign says *Arrival Hall*," Wilkie said.

"You really are the stupid little brothers I never had. It's a good thing I love you little turds."

Liza's instincts led to pedestrian tunnels with Zach and Wilkie in tow. She stepped on the movable walkway, expecting to move forward—except she didn't. Wilkie and Zach collided with Liza and sent her flailing to the ground.

Wilkie scrambled to lift her up. "Oh, crap. I'm sorry. I thought you'd move."

"No problem. I thought I'd move too."

They walked nearly a kilometer to enter an arrival hall with roped-off aisles leading to booths with a sign overhead that read *Immigration and Customs.*

They cleared customs without trouble to reach light rail trains ready at tunnels labeled *Trains to New Aryana.*

"Do we wait for a train?" Wilkie asked.

"I say we leap," Zach said.

∞

They stood, eyes wide at clear blue skies, and a noonday sun shone upon immaculate lawns and gardens with gleaming pedestrian boulevards between rows of new four-story townhomes.

The sight of miniature palm trees, flowering hibiscus, and fruited orange and lemon trees on rooftop gardens looked inviting.

A warm breeze carried the aroma of jasmine from a nearby park, none of which the team could feel or smell. They passed racks of bicycles that lined the sidewalk.

"It looks like we're outdoors, but we're still underground," Zach said.

"The sky doesn't look quite right," Wilkie said.

"Dumal technology, I'm sure. There's the transit lounge," Liza said.

The team passed through a waiting area with the vinyl covered medical equipment and into the *Staging Area.*

∞

The team arrived at rows of cloned politicians and administration officials. They shuddered with the realization that the Dumal infiltration into America's democratic republic seemed as complete as North Korea's totalitarian dictatorship.

"I can't believe it," Liza said. "This can't be real."

"Well, we know who we can't trust now," Wilkie said. "Let's see if Representative Callahan's clone is here."

Liza grabbed his arm. "You don't trust him? He's kind of

our boss."

"You trust him?" Wilkie asked.

"I do. I've yet to detect any deceit in him," Liza said.

"But why Callahan? He's one of your dad's most trusted friends," Zach said.

"Arild said to trust no one." Wilkie shrugged. "I've been thinking maybe his recent promotion to Speaker of the House might not be a coincidence — but if you say he's okay, I say he's okay then."

"Do you trust us?" Liza said.

"As if my life depended on it," Wilkie said.

They scanned the political section further and paused at several talking heads seen bloviating on CSPAN and being interviewed on the news.

"No sign of Speaker Callahan," Liza said. "Are you satisfied?"

"I feel much better," Wilkie said.

They moved to the government officials and bureaucrat sections.

"Misters Smith, Black, and the Joneses," Wilkie said. "No surprises there."

∞

The boys diverted their eyes at a petite redhead inside the case.

Liza stepped up to the glass. It was as if she faced her reflection in a magic, clothes-removing funhouse mirror.

Liza shook her head. "What's *wrong* with you two? There's nothing to be ashamed of about the human body. It's a thing of beauty?"

"You're like a sister to us," Wilkie said. "No dude wants to see his sister naked."

"At least they could have made me taller?"

"Napoleon Complex?" Zach grinned.

"If fat, little dictators can get tall and athletic clones, why not me?"

"Because you aren't a dictator. It's good to be the king," Zach said.

"History of the World Part III," Liza said.

"What the crap are you talking about?" Zack said

Liza laughed. "You quoted a movie and didn't know it? When this is all over, we've got to work on your Mel Brooks movies."

Zach moved toward Wilkie's body double. "Look at you. Not a freckle to be found."

Wilkie examined his clone. "No moles. That's good."

"Moley, moley, moley. I'm gonna cut it off, chop it up, and make guacamole," Zach said.

The boys laughed. Liza shook her head.

"Austin Powers, Gold Member," Zach said.

"I know. I saw it," Liza said.

Wilkie viewed his clone's feet. "Hey, they got rid of my bunions, too. I'll miss them."

"Looks like Wilkie's got the same penis designer as *Dear Leader*," Liza said.

Wilkie turned five shades of red and drifted toward the exit. "I'm going to check out the town."

Liza and Zach busted a gut.

∞

New Memnon Republic
Mont Forel, Greenland
Thursday, July 14, 2016

"No! No! No! Oh, *hell* no! This can't be right!" Zach exclaimed.

Wilkie put his hand on his shoulder. "Unless there's two Zachariah Davidsons at Memnon, this is your clone."

Inside the glass sarcophagus stood a short and stocky young man with dark skin and hair. His freckles, red hair, enormous feet, and correlating height were all missing.

"I see a bit of a resemblance," Liza said.

"The crapheads took all of my Mom out of me." Zach seethed. "I guess I'm black enough for the freakin' stupid crapheads now!"

"You Mormon boys need to grow a pair when you curse — and really curse," Liza said.

Zach calmed down. "Two things, Ms. Politically Correct College Girl. First, it's Latter-day Saint, and second, the not cussing part is the way I was raised. It's a cultural thing."

"Sorry, I forgot about the whole Mormon-Latter-Day Saint name thing," Liza said. "And on your second point, you don't seem to censor your movie quotes."

"Exactly! I'm quoting someone else."

"You seem to use certain swear words and not others," Liza said.

"My grandfather is the wisest man I know, and he used salt-of-the-earth swear words to keep his cows in line," Zach replied. "He swore that cows only understood swear words — but never any GDs, F-bombs, or Mofos. I learned it from him."

"Choose one way — or the other. Either use the real swears or don't use them at all."

"You have a right to your own damn opinion." Zach grinned. " — *now shut the hell up!*"

Zach and Liza busted up laughing.

Wilkie remained too preoccupied with Zach's clone to notice. "Sorry, Bro. Looks like they removed your father's height genes, too."

Zach's countenance fouled again. "And kept my Nana's genes. That abomination takes after that side of the family — short and stocky."

"Where's your dad?" Liza said.

"You mean the sperm donor? Over with the other craphead

senior officers, I'm sure," Zach said. "And I mean craphead."

∞

The team scanned Ezekiel Davidson's clone. The resemblance to Zach's clone was uncanny.

"The damn crapheads must think height is a white thing. Effin dipsticks!" Zach punched at Davidson's sarcophagus. His fist passed through the glass and into the clone's head. "I wish I were a TK. I'd punch the damn crapheads in their freaking clone faces!"

"Now, now. Watch your language," Liza said.

Zach shook his head and grinned. "You watch your own damn language, sister."

Arild suddenly appeared. "I hope you learned much."

"Kind of," Wilkie said. "What's the reason for all this?"

"You don't need me to explain what you've seen. I trust the three of you can piece things together. Have faith in yourselves."

"Can't you tell us more?" Liza asked.

"Keep your eyes open," Arild said, " — and be careful."

PART 12-MANAGEMENT CHANGES

"We are only falsehood, duplicity, contradiction;
we both conceal and disguise ourselves from ourselves"
- Blaise Pascal

Rancho Xiuhcoatl
Luna County, New Mexico
Thursday, July 14, 2016

Liza, Zach, and Wilkie instantaneously returned to the ridge of the mesa from the underground city. In twilight's last flicker, the dark-brown Bliss sandstone at their feet was barely visible when the campus lights dimmed. Oscillating searchlights suddenly filled the sky and air raid sirens wailed.

The stereo clangor of steel hatches buffeting sandstone amplified their confusion. From the voids, clinking chain drives lifted cannon gantries from the far corners of the mesa. Turrets traced marks and released an incessant volley. Liza, Zach, and Wilkie's heads moved as if attending the world's fastest tennis match — with exploding balls.

Wilkie imagined multiple ships attacking or a single craft flying in a zig-zag pattern because of the relentless back-and-forth motion. The shelling stopped as spotlights zeroed in on a minibus-sized craft that slid to a halt about a meter above the administration building.

"It's an old Libran piece of crap," Zach said.

"What's that thing hanging below it?" Wilkie asked.

∞

"Hold steady. Steady. Just a moment."

The man held a lighter (purchased at 7-11) and observed the spark descend a green waterproof fuse (obtained from the model rocket section of a hobby store) toward six M-88 firecrackers (bought at a roadside firework stand) inside a five-hundred-gallon fuel storage tank (found on Craigslist), packed with a slurry of diesel fuel and ammonium nitrate fertilizer (stolen from a farm).

"Almost. Get ready." The spark nearly reached the drum. "Ready, set." He pulled the lever. "Go! Go! Go!"

As the craft cleared the building, the detonation hurled it topsy-turvy toward the bluff. At the exact moment of righting the ship, exploding flak contacted the stern. The ship careened toward the mesa with flames trailing. The ship's stern clipped the crest of the bluff, deflecting it upward.

Wilkie instinctively pulled Liza and tackled Zach to the ground in one motion. They felt the heat's caress as the ship passed too close for comfort.

The pilot tried to gain altitude before the craft stalled and went into a nosedive. It exploded on impact about a furlong away.

Liza screamed at the violent percussion felt through the sandstone.

Wilkie paused before getting up and sprinting toward the craft.

Liza and Zach stood up on wobbly legs and gawked at the administration building. The top floor was missing, and the bottom level was in ruins.

Wilkie leaped back. "Come quick! I found a survivor!"

∞

Liza couldn't believe what she saw. Mai and Libran corpses inside the craft. Wilkie had pulled a wounded and conscious Dumal from the mangled wreckage. She believed the Mujar rebellion included Mai, human abductees, and other alien races—but not the Dumal.

The Dumal traitor's gangly legs were displaced in two directions, an arm crushed, and chartreuse blood seeped from abrasions.

Liza felt an intense terror emanating from the Dumal—and an equally powerful hatred. "Don't be frightened. We're here to help."

"You're Cerculus's lap dogs. Traitors to your own people. You should have died with him."

Liza kneeled and placed a hand on the alien's head.

His face relaxed and his eyes softened. "I misjudged you. You are good and noble."

"What's your name?" Liza asked.

"My codename's Jed." He looked at his dead comrades and panicked. "Where Gray Leader? You must find Gray Leader!"

Liza stayed with Jed. Wilkie and Jeff went searching.

"Please find my comrade. He's human," Jed yelled.

"My friends will find him," Liza said.

Jeb seemed to relax as Liza stroked his head.

Wilkie yelled, "We found him! He's alive!"

Jeb stared at Liza. *Help me pass. I'm dying, anyway,* entered her mind. *Help Gray Leader, too.*

Liza held Jeb and whispered in his ear. He exhaled as intercostal muscles relaxed.

∞

The injured man glared at Wilkie.

"You must be Gray Leader," Wilkie said. "Everything will be alright."

Gray Leader turned toward Zach. "What the hell are you

doing with this traitor?"

The man's battered face was unrecognizable—but the voice was familiar.

"Marcus? Is that you?"

"You lerpy little shit. I look that bad, eh?"

"It's a definite improvement," Zach said.

Marcus's laughter quickly turned to coughs. "Don't make me laugh. It hurts like hell."

"Sorry, dude."

"Again, why are you associating with a Dumal collaborator?"

"He's my friend—and isn't a collaborator.".

Marcus pointed at Wilkie. "He's Cerculus's right-hand man. All collaborators must die."

"And you appeared to be a loyal Memnon warrior," Zach said, "but that doesn't seem to be the case."

"Touché. Are you sure about him?"

"I trust him with my life."

Marcus raised one hand and stealthily put the other hand in a pants pocket. "I'll see. Let me touch his head."

Wilkie kneeled beside him.

Marcus' eyes focused on Wilkie's neck as he laid a hand on his forehead. Hidden in his other hand, a dagger was primed to slash Wilkie's carotid artery. Something made him hesitate—then Marcus relaxed. "So, you're one of the good guys. We had you all wrong."

"God-family-country is what I fight for. No one else—Dumal included," Wilkie said.

Marcus tried to sit up but failed with a moan. "We had you so wrong. The Mujar has a standing kill order on you and the redhead."

"Why?" Wilkie said.

"The Dumal are friends to no one. They'll destroy this

planet like all the others. Collaborators are worse than the Dumal."

"When did you join the Mujar?" Zack asked.

"They recruited me at Memnon — before you arrived."

A distant flicker of flashlights and the timbre of security personnel and bloodhounds ascended the bluff.

"We don't have time for this. You need to kill me." Marcus revealed the dagger and offered Zach the hilt.

"*What*? You can't be serious?" Zach said.

"I'm deadly serious."

"I can't."

"Don't let them take me alive. I know too much."

Liza approached. "Jeb's gone." She felt the fear in both Marcus and Zach.

"You're an empath, right? Help me die," Marcus said.

"You're not dying. We can save you."

"Many will die, and the Mujar will fail if they know what I know," Marcus said. "You can't let them take me alive!"

Liza paused. "I don't know if I can."

"Can or won't? Please send me to God now!"

Liza kneeled down beside Marcus. "I can't help someone who isn't already dying."

"They've not trained you in the *Animamotus*?" Marcus asked.

Liza's head tilted. "What's that?"

"The ability for empaths to kill. I'd train you, but we don't have time."

"I can try."

"I'll help you. Two empaths can do anything together."

Liza nodded.

"Before you do so —" Marcus said. "Zach, you're a good dude. This is important. Find Big Dennis and make sure *he's alright*."

"I will."

"Promise me. Tell him that I wanted to know if *he's alright*."

Zach nodded. "Of course, anything."

"Tell him that you and your friends are *alright*, too," Marcus said. "You must tell him. I'm counting on you."

"I will."

"Are you ready?" Liza asked.

Marcus nodded. "Follow my lead."

"All right," Liza said.

"Death to the Dumal Federation and Intergalactic Council! Long live the peoples of Earth!" Marcus shouted and plunged the dagger with both hands into his heart.

∞

Across the surgery, voices screamed in agony.

From the observation gallery above, Deputy Director Smith, Major Johnston, Major Reyes, Major Konig, and Zamu, a Dumal distinguished by a light gray four-point natal star over his left eye, directed interrogations below. Sixteen gurneys with two attending Grays each, robotic arms, and leads and wires connected the interviewees from head to toe. The interrogatees were from Xiuhcoatl—except for Liza and Wilkie.

The FAS executive leadership's gaze was adverted by a Dumal with a charcoal four-point natal star over his left eye that suddenly entered the surgery level. He reached the observation window and glared at Smith.

"*Enough!* Who gave you the authority to interrogate my emissaries? This is an act of war!" Cerculus screamed.

"We thought you died with the commandants. How did you survive?" Smith asked.

"The Crown Prince summoned me to the Ergonea. The Conference of Sovereigns called an emergency session, which was quite fortuitous for me but not so for the Commandants, I presume."

"There were no survivors. We believed you perished with them," Smith said.

"Why would you risk eighty years of cooperation by violating Dumal sovereignty in such an egregious manner?" Cerculus asked.

Zamu bowed his head. "I allowed the interrogation, Father. I believed you dead and assumed the mantle of Cerculus."

"My son, you have much to learn. You mustn't assume my mantel until the Sovereigns have authorized such. However, you believed it was an emergency, so you were within your rights."

"In Zamu's defense, we found your emissaries rendering first aid to the rebels," Smith said, "and they were also among the select few that knew about the Commandants' meeting," Smith said.

Cerculus groaned. "And what has your interrogation of my emissaries found?"

Smith hesitated. "Well, nothing—so far."

"Ambassadors Wilkerson and O'Reilly informed me they would meet with their friend, Lieutenant Davidson, on the Mesa. It wasn't a secret to me," Cerculus said. "How would they know the rebel ship would crash near them?"

Cerculus looked directly at Johnston. "Did you interrogate your charge, Lieutenant Davidson?"

Johnston nodded. "Yes. Admiral."

"And what did you discover?"

"Lieutenant Davidson claimed to be hanging out—uh, spending time with friends and that they were at the wrong place at the wrong time."

"Did you find his account truthful?"

"I found no deceit in the Lieutenant."

"I must report your rash actions to the Sovereigns," Cerculus said. "The unlawful interrogation of Dumal envoys may lead to the end of our alliance. They are victims of Serendipity—

nothing less, nothing more. This ends here!"

Cerculus waved a hand. Robotic arms retracted, electrodes dropped off, and the gray aliens attending to Liza and Wilkie fell dead to the floor. "Rise, my friends."

Liza and Wilkie sat up.

Wilkie scanned the room, toward the observers above and back to Cerculus. "You promised no more abductions. No more experiments. *We're through!*"

Wilkie grabbed Liza's wrist, and they both disappeared.

Cerculus glared at Smith and yelled, "You *fool*! Look what you've *done*!"

PART 13-DIFFICULT CHOICES

"Faust complained about having two souls in his breast, but I harbor a whole crowd of them, and they quarrel. It is like being in a republic." — Otto von Bismarck

THREE DAYS LATER

ABQ International Sunport
Albuquerque, New Mexico
Sunday, July 17, 2016

Waiting near his flight's departure gate, Lieutenant Zach Davidson grinned and squirmed in his chair, thinking about hugging his mom for the first time in nearly fourteen months. The flight to Salt Lake City couldn't happen fast enough. He tolerated the scheduled one-hour airport layover fairly well, but an additional two-hour delay for a mechanical issue was excruciating.

He kept his mind busy pondering the insanity of last Thursday and trying to drown out the incessant earworm playing over and over in his head. The chorus line's verbiage made him struggle on two fronts.

The Clash song was one of Mom's favorites, which made him miss her more;

Liza and Wilkie, quitting their missions, gave him something to consider.

Should I stay or should I go now?
Should I stay or should I go now?
If I go, there will be trouble
And if I stay, it will be double

Zach grimaced. *Wilkie quit, why can't I?*

Should I stay or should I go now?

Four hours earlier, Zach and the other recently commissioned FAS Second Lieutenants waited in Rancho Xiuhcoatl's aircraft hangar. Dressed in civilian clothes, they gazed at the ground crews preparing a fleet of private jets to take them to connecting flights home.

He figured the other graduates were also trying to process the Commencement Day Massacre and their orders not to discuss the terrorist event with anyone. He was sure they were also debating if they should resign their commissions and stay home.

Zach also knew the others had less on their minds than he did.

What the heck was with those underground cities? He thought. *Why did they make that freaky clone of me? I still can't believe Marcus was a Mujar terrorist.*

He worried how Wilkie's abrupt resignation from the Dumal might affect their greeting him at the airport or hanging out together during his ten-day leave.

Should I stay or should I go now?

They had much to discuss.

∞

Zach's heart raced when passengers with special needs and young children had finished boarding the aircraft, and the call came for Zone 4 ticket holders to board.

Finally, I'm going home, he thought.

He worked his way back to the rear bulkhead window seat, placed a pillow against the interior wall, laid his head against it, and quickly nodded off.

A few minutes later, the intercom system blared, jolting Zach awake.

"Good morning. This is your captain speaking."

Zach expected the standard pre-flight safety instructions as the seats looked full, and only the flight attendants stood.

"We ask that you stay seated while we help a passenger disembark. We'll be on our way to Salt Lake City soon afterward."

Zach shuddered as a flight attendant locked eyes on him as she took long strides toward the back of the plane.

"Mr. Davidson?"

Zach nodded.

"You need to bring your carry-on items and return to the gate."

His heart sank. "But why?"

"They didn't say."

Zach grabbed his duffle bag from under his seat and climbed over the passenger next to him. As he walked up the aisle, many passengers turned back and glared at him as if he had caused the flight's two-hour delay.

A flight attendant near the forward exit door smiled and said, "Thank you for flying with us."

Zach glared at him. "I didn't."

Hot air blasted Zach's face as he entered the non-air-conditioned jetway. He jogged up the ramp toward the terminal gate to avoid being roasted in the stifling July heat.

A gate agent stood at the terminal door and pointed toward two men dressed in black business suits. "Mr. Davidson, those gentlemen need to speak with you."

Zach froze with the shock that MJ-12 might be on to him

before he moved toward them.

"Mr. Davidson." The man pulled an ID card from his suit pocket. "I'm Special Agent Wheeler with the Federal Bureau of Investigation. This is my colleague, Special Agent Marsden. We're here to escort you back to Rancho Xiuhcoatl."

FBI. Okay, not men in black. "Why? I haven't seen my family in fourteen months."

"We need to take your witness statement about the terrorist attack."

The FBI's involved? Zach thought.

"Can't I answer your questions in Salt Lake?"

"It's best if you show us what you witnessed onsite," Wheeler said. "We'll get you home as soon as we can."

"Okay. Fine."

∞

A basement classroom became Rancho Xiuhcoatl's temporary executive boardroom while investigators continued sifting through the rubble for human remains and collecting evidence from the former boardroom.

The Federated American States' leadership committee, including Acting Commandants Johnston (Memnon), Reyes (Xiuhcoatl), and König (Aryana), Dumal Fleet Admiral Cerculus, and Deputy Director Smith (DOJ) neared the end of their two-day strategic planning meetings.

All eyes in the room were on Johnston standing in a corner.

"Thank you, Agent Wheeler. We'll see you soon." Johnston hung up and put his mobile in his pocket. "Lieutenant Davidson will arrive in twenty minutes."

Cerculus's head nearly touched the ceiling as he stood. "It's imperative you get the Lieutenant's cooperation in training the Memnon's jump teams. You cannot let him follow Mr. Wilkerson and Ms. O'Reilly. He's our only hope for convincing them to rejoin us."

∞

As the full-size SUV reached Xiuhcoatl's main campus, Zach locked eyes on the smoldering and blackened rubble from the former administrative building.

The vehicle stopped in front of a four-story tall classroom building next door with many windows blown out.

Wheeler exited first. "Right this way, Mr. Davidson."

He entered the building, headed down a stairway to the basement level, and opened a classroom door. "Please find a seat, Mr. Davidson. We'll be with you shortly."

The two feds stood guard outside the door.

Zach scanned the room and figured the windowless basement classroom with one exit door doubled as a holding cell. At the front of the room, two young women in Xiuhcoatl uniforms stood from their chairs and turned toward him.

Zach spoke as he neared. "Is the FBI doing group interviews?"

"The FBI?" Gina Hernandez said. "I was told this was an emergency meeting with Major Reyes."

"So, the game's afoot." Zach grinned and extended a hand. "I'm Zach Davidson."

"Sergeant Hernandez." She shook Zack's hand. "And this is Corporal Zapata."

Zapata shook hands. "Are you a Memnon Cadet, Zach?"

Zach nodded. "Lieutenant Davidson."

"Why are you in civies, Lieutenant?" Zapata asked

"I was heading home when the FBI made me return as a witness to the terrorist attack."

Hernandez tilted her head before speaking. "FBI on campus? Senior leadership wouldn't get them involved."

"Their IDs said FBI."

Hernandez shrugged. "Whatever."

They turned toward the squeak of the door as two

executive officers dressed in battle fatigues entered.

Zach, Hernandez, and Zapata stood at attention.

Acting Commandants Reyes and Johnston headed toward the seats behind the teacher's desk and faced their charges.

"At ease. Please take a seat," Reyes said and sighed. "To say that the events of the last few days were a disruption would be an understatement."

Johnston gazed at Zach. "I'm sorry we interrupted your leave, but we're stuck between a rock and a hard place and wouldn't have done so if we didn't urgently need your help."

"What can I do to help?"

"We need you to start your jump team instructor training tomorrow."

Zach's mouth opened wide. "What about my leave?"

"I wish we didn't have to ask this of you, but everything changed on Thursday. Your friends are no longer part of our cause, so they won't be training you as planned. It's all a personnel and timing issue."

"What about those fake FBI agents?" Zach leaned toward Johnston. "Respectfully, sir. Why did they lie to me?"

"They are real FBI agents and need to interview you."

Zach pressed his tongue through compressed lips before gently shaking his head. "You can't expect me to believe we invited the Feds to investigate alien-rebel terrorist conspiracy?"

A grin formed on Johnston's face. "Normally, that would be the case, but we have allies within the D.O.J. who are conducting an off-the-books investigation."

Zach tilted his head. "So, why the urgency?"

Reyes nodded at Zach and glanced at his charges. "Corporal Zapata and Sergeant Hernandez recently certified as jump team instructors.

"In two weeks, they will conduct a ten-day basic jump team training course, which gives time for them to provide you with an expedited instructor training, starting tomorrow. Afterward, you will assist them with instructing the Camp-X jump teams."

"We're running out of time, Zach," Johnston said. "War with the IGC proxies is months away. We can't afford to delay your training, and, ultimately, delay the training of Memnon jump team personnel by you."

"I understand, sir."

"Can we count on you?"

"Of course." Zach felt bile rise in his throat and thought, *Why in the hell am I doing this?*

"Good soldier." Johnston nodded at Zach. "I knew we could count on you."

∞

TWO DAYS LATER

Wilkerson Home
Abundance Township, Tooele Co., Utah
Tuesday, July 19, 2016

From his living room loveseat, Bruce Wilkerson, Sr. sipped his orange juice and enjoyed the dawn-accented yellow and peach roses at the edge of the picture window.

I'm glad he's done with all that alien nonsense. He sighed at the thought of Wilkie's homecoming, then grimaced. *Zach should be here, too.*

As Bruce pulled the sports section from his Salt Lake Tribune and scanned the headlines, the nose of a black SUV pulled into view. He rose to the window, looked around the corner, and counted two more vehicles.

Bruce opened a nearby credenza drawer, placed his index finger on the lockbox's bio-metric sensor, and retrieved a silvery semi-automatic before holstering it behind his back.

Ding-dong!

"I got it," Bruce yelled while heading toward the front door.

With one hand behind his back, he partially opened the door.

Two earpiece-wearing men in dark suits filled the doorway. Other similarly dressed agents stood around the perimeter. "Mr. Wilkerson, someone's here to speak with you."

They stood aside, revealing a familiar face at the base of the steps.

James Callahan made eye contact with Bruce and grinned. "Sergeant Wilkerson, please tell me you've upgraded to a standard-issue Beretta or Glock and are not holding your grandfather's antique .45 behind your back?"

Bruce holstered and removed his hand from the Colt 1911. "Why would I change now?"

Callahan chuckled, then noticed as his security detail reached inside their jackets. He bound up the steps and turned. "Stand down! He's not a threat. If Sergeant Wilkerson wanted to shoot me, he could have done so years ago. Secure the perimeter while I meet with the Sergeant... alone."

Bruce stood aside and extended a hand toward the living room. "Welcome, Congressman."

Two agents followed their charge, but Callahan stopped them before they crossed the threshold. "Captain Wilson, when I said alone, I meant alone."

"Sorry, Sir, but protocol requires that two members of the security detail be with you at all times."

"It'll be alright, Brad." He put a hand on the agent's shoulder. "There's no one I trust more with my life than with Bruce Wilkerson. He's saved my ass more times than I can count."

Callahan closed the door behind him.

∞

Livermore Municipal Airport

Livermore, California
Tuesday, July 19, 2016

James Callahan and Bruce Wilkerson, Sr. headed down the Learjet's airstair toward an adjacent Cadillac Escalade.

Bruce "Wilkie" Wilkerson, Jr., stood at the jet's doorway, appreciating the light ocean breeze laced with the mint-like fragrance of Blue Gum Eucalyptus, and put on his sunglasses. He descended on the tarmac as the driver held open the rear door. Wilkie beamed, seeing Liza O'Reilly seated in the middle.

"Where's Zach?" Liza asked.

Wilkie paused before entering, and his face dimmed. "He's not coming. He's staying for jump instructor training."

"With who?"

"April Zapata and Gina Hernandez."

"I guess we're not needed anymore."

∞

In a conference room at Lawrence Livermore National Laboratory, Wilkie, Bruce, and Liza faced James Callahan and four others in white lab coats for nearly an hour.

"Is there any way we can talk you out of this?" Callahan looked intently at Wilkie. "Your infiltration into the Dumal is irreplaceable."

Wilkie glanced briefly at his dad, shook his head lightly, and looked back at Callahan. "If it means the Dumal still experimenting on us, then it's a hard no."

Callahan gazed at Liza and raised an eyebrow.

"No, for me, too," Liza said.

"GEICE still has need of you." Callahan leaned in. "If we remove your toe chips, would you consider a lesser role?"

Wilkie's head bobbed. "Probably not."

"Same," Liza said.

"Liza, Wilkie, your skills could be helpful in keeping

the Dumal in check in a less direct role, but we'll respect your wishes."

Biting his lip, Callahan turned toward the doctors in lab coats. "This is Doctor Sharma and Doctor Novak. They'll go over the toe implant removal procedure."

"Liza," Karen Sharma said, "I'll be leading the surgical team, removing the Dumal data chip from your hallux, while Doctor Novak's team works on Wilkie. We do the procedure under general anesthesia…"

"Why not a local?" Liza asked.

"For reasons unknown, local anesthesia does not fully anesthetize the area, and removal of alien technology causes neurogenic shock in less than 11% of the cases. Shocky patients respond better to treatment while in an induced coma that anesthesia provides."

Liza nodded.

Sharma continued. "The anesthesia and recovery are the longest part of the surgery. It takes less than three minutes to make the incision and extract the chip. The total time on the operating table is less than thirty minutes. Post-op recovery is 45 minutes to two hours."

"Removing our implants will stop the Dumal from experimenting on us?" Wilkie rubbed his chin. "You're certain of it?"

All heads turned toward Callahan.

"Intergalactic Council rules are pretty clear. Once a test subject's data collection implant has been removed, further testing can only resume with the express permission of the test subject."

"I thought the Dumal wasn't part of the IGC?" Liza asked.

"Although the Dumal Federation is not a member of the IGC, they rarely run afoul of IGC pre-colonization rules for fear of direct military engagement."

"There are risks with general anesthesia and any surgical procedure," Sharma said. "Of the over 900 extraterrestrial hallux chip removal procedures Dr. Novak and I have performed, two patients experienced permanent brain damage from neurogenic shock, and one patient died from a reaction to anesthesia. All three cases happened in the early stages of developing our chip extraction procedures. Literally, our 9th, 11th, and 27th patients."

Sharma put her palms on the table and smiled. "We've got the procedure down pat."

∞

A surgical team surrounded Wilkie on the operating table while Bruce Wilkerson, Sr., and James R. Callahan watched from the observation gallery.

"Out, intubated, and ready," the anesthesiologist said.

Dr. Novak looked at the digital x-ray of Wilkie's toes on an overhead monitor and nodded at the ultrasound technician.

She applied gel on a thumb-sized linear transducer and moved the wand on the big toe's exposed skin not covered by sterile drapes.

"Got it," Novak said.

The technician wiped away the gel. A nurse swirled a disinfectant swab around the surgical site.

Novak marked Wilkie's left great toe's largest bone with a black sharpie and dropped it on a tray.

"Number 22 scalpel."

Novak made a 9mm elliptical incision around the dot. "Nate, let's see this bad boy."

"Allis forceps," Dr. Nate Cavanaugh said and held his palm open. He clamped down on one edge of the incision and gently folded back the tissue.

Novak leaned in and pointed his headlamp at the opening. "Irrigation."

A nurse placed a 3mm hollow-tipped suction & irrigation

cannula in the incision. She pressed a button, irrigating the wound with sterile water. A second button cleared the operation field of fluids and loose tissue with suction.

Through 4x magnification loupes mounted at the base of his glasses, Novak observed the black lentil-looking device flush on the proximal phalange.

"There's my bad boy," he whispered and held out his hand. "Blunt-nosed forceps."

Novak placed the tweezer tips on the foreign object and pulled. He thought his mind was playing tricks as if the chip tugged back.

"This one's really attached." Novak dropped the tweezers in the pan and held out his hand. "Crocodile forceps."

He opened the scissor-handled forceps and clamped down on the chip, locking it in place.

"Let's try this again." Novak pulled and twisted. The chip lifted a few microns, revealing tendrils attaching it to the bone before it pulled back again. "Did you see that, Nate?"

Cavanaugh nodded. "The roots look more active than usual."

"Curved micro Metzenbaum." Novak held out his hand.

He tilted the forceps and slightly raised one side of the chip, cutting the roots as quickly as possible. Tilting the forceps opposite and cutting the roots on the other side, he pulled in vain, as the previously cut roots had already reattached.

"Nate, take over the Croc. Slant the chip to one side, and I'll cut the tendrils, then I'll slip the Metz underneath the chip to get to the others. Yank as soon as you see me make the last cut."

Cavanaugh placed his fingers in the forceps' rings. "Ready."

"On the count of three. 1... 2... 3."

Novak opened the scissors wide and clipped the roots. He slid the cutters deep across the other side and snipped.

Cavanaugh yanked the device away, then dropped the forceps and the chip onto a tray.

"Great job, team." Novak beamed. "Irrigate the site and close it up, Nate."

A rush of loud beeps ended the revelry.

"He's tachycardiac. BP's dropping," the anesthesiologist said.

All heads turned toward the anesthetist. "Going into V-FIB."

".5 mg intravenous epi, stat!" Novak said. "We're losing him."

∞

"Losing, who?" Wilkie sat up on the surgical table and scanned the practitioners surrounding him.

"Hello? Losing, who?" He waved his hand at a doctor, who didn't react. "Right here?"

"Nate, initiate CPR."

Cavanaugh moved forward and leaned in. "Starting CPR."

Wilkie turned around for a look as he ascended off the table and hovered above the scene. Below, he faced his pallid reflection on the operating table with a tracheal tube in his mouth while Cavanaugh made compressions on his chest.

In his surreal moment, Wilkie heard Liza's voice enter his mind. *So, this answers the great mystery.*

Liza, where are you? Wilkie observed Liza pass through the surgery's wall and float toward him. *What mystery?*

The mystery of…

The voice of Arild of the Chájehit interrupted. *Liza, Wilkie. Come see.*

Wilkie stood at the edge of a giant crater, with Arild at his right and Liza to his left. Dust and rubble surrounded them in all directions.

A large black object at the bottom of the basin caught

Wilkie's attention. The rounded item had columns below and spaces for tall windows above. It appeared to be iron with its edges melted away, as he estimated only a third of the original design remained.

Liza scanned the crater. "What are we looking at?"

"Where an edifice to democracy once stood," Arild said.

Wilkie tried to envision a complete structure of the object, as it seemed somewhat familiar.

Arild put a hand on Wilkie's shoulder. "Imagine it painted white and set atop a magnificent palace."

Wilkie was working on it for a few minutes when he realized. "Holy crap! Is that the US Capital dome?"

Arild nodded and turned around. "Stand witness."

Wilkie and Liza turned away from the crater and scanned the National Mall. It looked like the wind had toppled the Washington Memorial over. Dirt filled the reflecting pools. Lincoln Memorial was gone except for its historic steps.

They looked to the right where the Whitehouse once stood, and only a portion of the south portico remained standing.

"What happened, Arild?" Liza asked.

"Come, see."

∞

Arild, Liza, and Wilkie appeared on a vista overlooking an endless sea on their right and a bay on their left. The skyline view was crystal clear, but dust and ash in the stratosphere dimmed the mid-afternoon sky.

After scanning the barren landscape, Liza shook and sobbed.

"What?" Wilkie asked.

She struggled to raise a hand to point before plopping down on the bare earth, wailing uncontrollably.

Directly below, Wilkie looked at a towering steel structure rising from near the shore, with a few rusty cables dangling from the top. Its orange girders stood out against the bay's blue waters and the earthy terrain for miles around. Across the bay, he saw the ruins of a metropolitan area to the south.

Looking east, he gasped at an unscathed island landmark — recognizing Alcatraz Prison. He now realized the destroyed city and tower were San Francisco and a fragment of the Golden Gate Bridge.

Liza picked herself off the ground. "Arild, take me home. Please take me home now."

∞

San Anselmo
Marin County, California
Unknown Date

Arild, Liza, and Wilkie arrived in a quaint Northern California town twenty miles north of San Francisco. The main street held a dust-covered mix of Spanish mission, old west, and art déco architecture and abandoned cars lining the street. The absence of people, barren landscape, and skeletal remains of mature pine, oaks, and elm trees stood testament to the desolation.

"It can't be?" Liza cried and took off running.

Arild put a hand on Wilkie's shoulder. "Leave her be."

They observed Liza reach the nearest intersection and turn left.

"Give her a few minutes."

∞

Liza jogged uphill for what seemed an eternity before stopping in front of a Craftsman-style home on a hillside. Dirt replaced the front lawn. Formerly green bushes and trees around the yard were barren.

She shuddered and crept toward the porch. Finding the door locked, she punched in her four-digit security code, but the backlighting of the keypad didn't light up, nor did the deadbolt's tumblers whirl.

Liza bounded toward the other side of the two-car garage, opened the vinyl gate, and headed toward the backyard patio. Reaching under the gas barbeque grill, she removed the magnetized spare key holder.

After working the key, she entered through the mudroom door and flipped the light switch off and on without a reaction.

"Dad! I'm home!" Her heart raced as she rushed toward the great room. A layer of dust covered the kitchen counters, appliances, and living room furnishings, and cobwebs gathered in the corners.

"Dad! Where are you?" She rushed up the stairs and straight to the master bedroom and stood at the threshold. "Daddy?"

Liza felt a sense of relief as she reached Dad's side of the queen-size bed and saw a familiar tuff of auburn hair sticking out of the covers on the pillow. "Daddy?"

She inched the covers back.

"Daddy! No!" she shrieked, collapsed on the bed, and wailed uncontrollably on top of her father's quilt-covered remains, only his skull exposed on the pillow.

After crying gallons, she ran out of tears and stood. *Maybe it's not him.*

She pulled back the covers and shivered, seeing her father's Bulova Devil Diver watch around his wrist bones and his favorite silk pajama shorts covering his pelvis and femurs. "Daddy. Daddy. What happened?"

Liza dragged the quilt over her dad's remains and left for her bedroom down the hall.

She felt nothing at the sight of the petite skeleton dressed in flannel pajamas with long red hair on her bed and mumbled, "I should have known."

Liza didn't remember heading down the stairs, going

outside, and leaving the front door wide open as she stood on the porch and looked off into space as numbness coursed through her veins.

"Liza?" Wilkie said.

She slowly turned her head toward Arild and Wilkie on the sidewalk, revealing an ashen face streaked with tears on her cheeks. Her red and puffy eyes seemed to look past her companions.

Wilkie walked up to her. "What's wrong?"

She gave a distant stare. "Everyone's dead."

"Who's dead?"

"My dad's dead. I'm dead. Everyone's dead."

Wilkie turned toward Arild. "Is my family dead?"

"In this outcome, you perished with your loved ones."

"No. No. No. No. No," Wilkie mumbled as his shoulders slumped, lips quivered, and tears welled in his eyes.

His mourning paused as he tilted his head for a moment, then stood upright and held a hand to his chest. "This outcome?"

"You've seen a small part of what the Dumal *will do*."

Wilkie's eyes narrowed. "Will do?"

"It hasn't happened yet."

"Is this why the FAS built those underground cities? To keep them alive?"

"I knew you'd figure it out."

Wilkie extended his hand toward the landscape. "Why are you showing us?"

"Every choice we make has a consequence. Your and Liza's recent choices will lead to this outcome."

"You mean we have to go back to the Dumal to stop this from happening?"

"No, my friend." Arild smiled. "You've learned all you can from the Dumal and their allies."

"So, how do we stop this from happening?"

"Continue with GIECE, and I will send an experienced guide to train and prepare you. If you stay on course, you will know what to do when the time is at hand to save your species."

Liza's eyes brightened as she raised her head, and a slight smile came to her face. "We can change this?"

∞

Lawrence Livermore National Laboratory
Livermore, California
Tuesday, July 19, 2016

Medical personnel worked feverishly on Wilkie.

"He's been coding for twenty-seven minutes," the anesthesiologist said. "Asystole for five."

"Shock him one more time," Dr. Novak said, "before I call it."

"Less than a 1% chance." Dr. Nate Cavanaugh raised an eyebrow at the lead surgeon.

"We've got nothing to lose."

Cavanaugh turned toward a nurse. "300 joules. Clear."

He placed the paddles on Wilkie's chest and pushed the button. *Buzz. Humph.*

"Still flatline," the anesthesiologist said.

Novak waved off a nurse holding the Ambu breathing bag.

Novak held Wilkie's wrist and scanned the identification band. "Patient is Bruce C. Wilkerson, Junior. Date of birth: August 30th, 1996."

A nurse looked at the ID band. "Confirming, patient name: Bruce C. Wilkerson, Junior. D.O.B.: 30th of August 1996."

Novak rubbed his knuckles on the patient's sternum, but the corpse didn't respond.

He used a penlight and checked both eyes. "Pupils fixated and dilated."

Novak placed two fingers over the carotid artery on the side of Wilkie's neck for over a minute. No pulse. He positioned his stethoscope on different sides of Wilkie's chest. No respiration or heartbeat.

"Too damn young." Tears blurred his sight as he glanced at the wall clock. "Patient time of death. 12:04."

∞

A distraught father, his face haggard, eyes red and puffy with grief, entered the operating room with James Callahan at his side and waited near the double doors.

It's all bullshit, Bruce Wilkerson, Sr. thought. *One out of 900, my ass.*

Bruce dreaded telling Mary and his in-laws, who had already lost a mother and daughter, that they had lost their only brother and grandson, too. His heart ached for Mike O'Reilly losing his only child.

The elder Wilkerson gazed upon his son while the nursing staff removed the endotracheal tube, IVs, and EKG electrodes from his corpse. All but one nurse left the surgery.

The lone nurse lovingly pushed some hairs back in place and, with a washcloth, gently washed Wilkie's face, neck, and arms. She left his side and walked straightaway toward Bruce, put a hand on his shoulder, and with tears in her eyes, said, "I'm so sorry for your loss."

Bruce collapsed on her shoulder, and they both cried for a minute or two.

He finally gained some composure. "Thank you."

"I'll leave you with your son," the nurse said and exited the operating room.

Initially, Bruce's feet refused to budge before he took baby steps toward his son.

Arriving at the body, Bruce fell, arms and face first, onto his son's chest.

"My boy. My boy," he wailed then yowled non-stop.

Callahan did his best. An arm around Bruce's shoulders. A hand patting or rubbing Bruce's back. His five-minute-long effort failed to reduce his friend's anguish.

Unable to speak, Bruce privately adjured the heavens. *Please, God. Please.*

A wordless impression entered his mind as an accompanying peace flooded Bruce's body.

Callahan stood back as Bruce stopped wailing, stood upright, and wiped away tears with his sleeve. His brow furrowed, and he tilted his head, watching Bruce search through the surgical trays, retrieve some forceps, and stared at the tiny chip in its jaws.

Bruce moved to Wilkie's toe and placed the tip of the forceps inside the incision. It felt like something pulled the chip from inside, so he released the clamp.

Both Bruce and Callahan observed the wound pull together from the inside out.

They turned as they heard Wilkie gasp and watched his chest rise and fall, rise and fall, and the blue hue of his face turn ruddy.

Wilkie opened his eyes, jolted upright, and screamed, **"We have to stop the Dumal!"**

END OF VOLUME I

D.B. Gibb is an international business professional and debut author of the science fiction novel, The Heroes of February 22nd, Volume I. He studied international relations and Chinese in college, and later completed graduate work in international trade. Enriched by his extensive travels and fascination with history, politics, culture, and the human condition, D.B. Gibb weaves compelling narratives that transport readers to diverse worlds.

Born in Salt Lake City, he spent his formative years in Southern California before eventually returning to his Utah roots. Throughout his adult life, D.B. has called Hong Kong, Taiwan, Texas, and Virginia home, yet he consistently finds himself drawn back to the scenic landscapes of Utah. He lives in Northern Utah with his wife and loves to spend time with his family. He also enjoys reading, music, barbeque, and sports and outdoor activities, and is a loyal Utah State Aggie and Utah Jazz fan.

Please check out the author's website at www.dbgibb.com

www.ingramcontent.com/pod-product-compliance
Lightning Source LLC
Chambersburg PA
CBHW050724180626
46814CB00002B/592